True to the Code

True to the Code

Stories of the American Character

PETER DEVINE

authorHOUSE®

AuthorHouse™
1663 Liberty Drive
Bloomington, IN 47403
www.authorhouse.com
Phone: 1-800-839-8640

Published by AuthorHouse   11/26/2012

ISBN: 978-1-4685-8826-2 (sc)

For my wife Maria and the strength of character which, as a new American citizen, she represents.

CONTENTS

FOREWORD

"I could tell you a lot,
but you've got to be true to your code . . ."

W e can't get through this life without submitting to codes. We are, after all, taxed by codes (Tax Codes), tracked by codes (Zip Codes), routed by codes (Airport Codes), garbed by codes (Dress Codes), and even have our behavior regulated by codes (Codes of Ethics.)

But this book is about a different sort of code. The most vital code in our lives is the one by which we live. The one we devise for ourselves. The one that establishes our make-up, defines our boundaries, and empowers us in our quest through life.

In this we have inherited much from our forbearers. The early settlers on this continant, having left behind a world of well-ordered boundaries, settled societies, and rigidly enforced laws and statues, had to rely upon methods of their own devising to survive, flourish, and eventually prosper in their adopted homeland. In the absence of established laws and regulated behaviors, they had to devise for themselves codes to live by, sets of expectations that enabled them to meet the challenges of frontier living. We thus inherited what has come to be known as "The American Way."

The code by which a person lives is not written, and cannot always be clearly identified, even by its author. It is more than merely a collection of habits, although certain habits result from it. It does not come about as a result of making deals with ourselves, although such deals are quite inevitable along the way. Adherence to a personal code is not an essential component of popularity (which is fleeting), celebrity (which is fickle), or even legend (which is fragile), but those who live by strong, positive, and well-defined codes usually produce an alchemy which is more durable that steel and more valuable than a precious metal.

Partly the result of your DNA, partly the result of environment, and wholly the result of your own internal "processing of life," the code by which you live is not always a case of knowing the "right" thing to do, or of turning every situation to your advantage. More than anything, it is a case of knowing yourself, and knowing yourself means knowing your place in the universe and how to find it.

This is a book of stories about people who lived by powerful personal codes. People who seemed to have some sort of internal guidance system by which they operated. They seemed never to adjust to the norm, but through sheer force of will bent the norm to serve their purposes. Convention held no appeal for them. They were single-mindedly fixated on some goal or destiny or way of being that separated them, often by wide margin, from the slow fixed tread of humanity.

They are, with two exceptions, native-born Americans. Affected with the restless, inquisitive, questing spirit of a great continent, they are known for their grand exploits and their sometimes tragic endings. Viewed through the prism of their lives, the American character is brought more clearly into focus: willingness to assume risk; perseverance in the face of rejection or indifference; unwavering personal courage in the face of danger; a relentless, and occasionally fatal, degree of optimism; and a talent for placing oneself in opportune situations and not faltering. Their stories are told here by people who knew them, or had encounters with them, encounters which revealed something about the way they were built, or the forces that built them. While a certain amount of the author's creative imagination has been used to set the scenes in which the principal characters act and react, the historical details—time, place, and surrounding events—are all faithful reproductions of actual fact.

"On the Road with the Admiral" is the first story, and one of only two that features a European. Both Europeans have been chosen for the roles they played in the development of this young nation. The stories themselves came about from the reading of exhaustive biographies and in some cases, proximity to the scenes where our heroes and heroines played out their finest moments. A visit made to Rouen, France, led to "This Man's Army." Spending time in Santa Fe prompted "Armor of Light," and a tour of the NASA Space Center in Houston yielded "The Wingman." Traveling the old Chef Menteur Highway across the Rigolets east of New Orleans, as I have done so many times, was a natural breeding ground for "No Need to Push It." "The Navy Job" is not about a person, but an ocean liner, one which was built and sailed during an era of romance and tragedy, grandeur and desperation, and as such it came to embody the code of an entire nation.

If you are American, through these stories you'll discover something about yourself, your place in the universe, and the code which enables you to make your journey there.

Peter Devine
Houston, Texas, May 2012

ON THE ROAD WITH THE ADMIRAL

In August of that year, I traveled with the Admiral from Sevilla down to the mouth of the Guadalquivir River, a distance of about one hundred kilometers. There is no proper road following the river through that dry and desolate region. In some cases three *burros* can scarcely pass abreast. There are few travelers' inns for lodging, and one's victuals must be bought or bartered directly from the small farmers or landowners along the way, as proper restaurants or *casas de comestibles* are, after one passes south of the southern barrios of Sevilla, simply nonexistent. These hardships were not of great moment to me, I had lived in the province of Sevilla all my 23 years. And I can assure you they didn't trouble the Admiral greatly either. Just ninety days earlier he had received his commission from Their Royal Highnesses, the Kings of Leon and Castille, Ferdinand and Isabella. He was, in essence, *un hombre ya echo*—a made man. What, to such a man, was a little road dust, a reluctant burro, or a meal of *chorizo* wrapped in greasy paper?

The purpose of our journey was to enable the Admiral to investigate first-hand the channel of the Guadalquivir below Sevilla, and the anchorage at Palos de le Frontera, the port from which he would be launching his ambitious voyage to the so-called "New World." That was the Admiral's purpose, in any event. Mine was merely to accompany him, on behalf of The Crown, and to expedite his mission. There were those who would later claim that I was actually a spy of sorts, which is far from accurate. However, I will not be disingenuous and deny the fact that the Queen wanted me to observe this Genoese navigator and assure her that he was a serious man, not some kind of picaresque parody who would bring dishonor on Spain or the Holy Mother Church. In this there is nothing untoward, and I am certain that if the Admiral himself had studied on the matter at all, he would have understood the nature of my mission. But in getting to know him the way I did, I seriously doubt whether this kind of trivial consideration would have entered his waking thoughts.

On our first night out we found lodging in a small livestock shed behind a large *finca*. The owner of the *finca* was absent and the main house was occupied by a caretaker and his wife. The dwelling would have easily had rooms to spare for a couple of weary travelers, but the caretaker was an exceedingly cautious man without a compassionate bone in his body. Though we were dusty and perhaps looked a bit worse for the road wear, we scarcely appeared as vagabonds. Nonetheless, the best he could do, he assured us, was the livestock shed. "Sir, I am in the employ of the Crown. This gentleman is the Admiral of the Ocean Sea, and I must advise you, this will simply not do," I protested. In fact the Admiral had a letter bearing the seal of the sovereigns directing one and all to aid and abet him in his mission. As I spoke I flashed him a glance, but he was not interested in producing the letter. "Let it go," he counseled. Later on, as we tethered our burros and shook the dust from our cloaks, he explained. "I rather doubt that the Catholic Sovereigns are truly much loved in these parts." We slept soundly nonetheless, and were up and away before sunrise without seeing the caretaker again.

I wish I had been a more learned fellow, I might have been able to engage the Italian's active intelligence more suitably as the kilometers rolled by. Others had told me that he was well-read, and admirably outfitted to discourse on a variety of topics, including astronomy, philosophy, history, religion, political matters, and of course, his great love, navigation. As the dry and dusty kilometers passed underfoot, however, he seemed lost in his own thoughts and kept largely to himself. I did make an effort to engage him from time to time on the particulars of his venture. He had calculated rather precisely, he informed me, the distance from Spain to the shore of Cathay: 2,300 leagues, or thereabouts, as I recall. "Of course, those fellows of excellent learning who cluster about the Court with their endearing ways do not agree with my calculations," he pointed out sardonically. "They purr like cats into the ear of the Sovereigns here as in Portugal, as in Italy. Let them go to Hell. They are not men, but are more a species of kept women, there to pleasure their masters at all costs." Here he used a crude sexual analogy which I thought revealed more than a hint of bitterness, but his features remained impassive as he said it, walking beside his burro. In point of fact, the Admiral was a large, long-legged fellow, and the burro was not, and I think they both preferred to travel in that fashion.

During the heat of the day, we slaked our thirst by tipping the *bota* back in our throats. We had bread and *jamon Serrano*, but as the heat rose, our appetites diminished, and we moved along under the pitiless Iberian sun towards the Southern coast. He had three vessels back in Sevilla being readied for the voyage, he told me. "I have no concerns for the seaworthiness of the vessels. Properly caulked and provisioned, they will be up to the task. The crew, on the other hand . . ."

"What about the crew?" I wanted to know.

The Admiral did not answer right away. He was a tall man, a good head taller than what one would consider the mean height of the *Andaluz* or the Moor, and his posture, perhaps to account for this discrepancy, was not one of proud, full bearing. Rather, he stooped as though bearing a weight on his shoulders. When struck by a thought he had a way of shaking his head as though to clear it before he yielded to the spoken word. "Given the proper motivation, a man will perform a duty admirably under most circumstances. Faith in Christ, loyalty to his Sovereigns, the love of a good woman—these are the common motivations that keep most men on the path of good works. Sad to say, they are notably lacking in the hearts of the type of men who make their living at sea. Sloth, avarice, and a desire to cling overly long to their meager lives, this is what we have today. They are of a purely mercenary nature, and hence not to be trusted beyond the confines of their undeveloped consciences."

I looked at the Admiral as he spoke these words, and wondered whether it was hard-gotten wisdom that prompted his opinion, or simply a further expression of the well of bitterness that seemed to spring from his soul. As events unfolded over the course of the coming years, I often hearkened back to his cynical sentiment, and at how unerringly accurate it had proven to be. Whether at the time it was acquired wisdom or a sort of prophecy I could not distinguish.

As the sun worked its way towards the horizon the path which we trod was running quite close to the river on our left side and ahead of us we spied a Gypsy encampment. These nomadic types, known as much for their glad hospitality as for the arts of thievery and calumny which they practiced, were not common this far to the east, but I would venture to say that both the Admiral and myself welcomed the sight of their patchwork tents, their gaunt horses, and their wild-maned children there under the chestnut trees that bordered the sluggish Guadalquivir. As we drew near it became clear that they welcomed the sight of us equally, dispatching a couple of the older members of their ragamuffin brigade to flag us down and invite us to share their hospitality as the day drew to its dusty close.

"Have an eye for your purse, sire," I cautioned the Admiral as we directed our burros down the sloping embankment. "No less of an eye for our livestock," he rejoined.

As we entered the Gypsy encampment, it became obvious that it was not as casual an affair as we had at first surmised. Under the trees in a cleared area were placed half a dozen small tables, each accompanied by a variety of mismatched stools. As we were ushered in, one of the older lads offered to tether our burros while another made an elaborate show of readying a table for us, knocking the stools about and using his sleeves to give the surface of the table a good wiping.

"Care to eat something, gents?" he asked us in that wheedling manner that this craven class of people had perfected over the years. "Or maybe a bottle to take the dust from your throats first?"

"Send your mother over here, son," the Admiral told him. "What we want is a woman's touch."

"As you like, *jefe*," replied the youth, with the Gypsy's customary lack of recognition of his proper station. "It'll be my sister, if that's all right."

"Even better."

The place was pleasant enough, and although the river itself was not visible owing to high grasses, we could sense its quieting presence. The close-set chestnut trees provided a natural canopy that gave the little encampment a cloistered effect. It was clear that the Gypsies had set themselves up in this propitious location specifically to cater to the passing riverbank trade. We were grateful to find them there; to encounter this mongrel race here in a godforsaken site was less onerous than running afoul of them back in the city, where their coarse language, their ragged garments and their innate lawlessness were in stark contrast to the code of more civil behavior which we proper Spaniards sought to cultivate in our towns and villages.

My reflections were interrupted by the sudden appearance of the sister. Even in these races of mixed blood one is occasionally exposed to the touch of the Master's hand at work, and the girl was indeed lovely to behold. She could not have been much beyond 12 years of age was my guess, right on the cusp of her womanhood. Because of their rugged lifestyle, their footloose morals and their lack of proper medical attention, Gypsies typically aged rather quickly. Gypsy females usually bore their first offspring as soon as they entered their female cycles, and by the time they reached their twentieth year they frequently had the look of crones, with sagging breasts, decaying teeth and sallow skin. But this lass was exceedingly comely, bright of eye with clear skin and an untroubled countenance. She was experiencing the first flowering of womanhood, a simple girl as yet unspoiled by the ravages of premature romances or heavy labor. In her hand she bore a bottle of red wine and two cups, which she placed without ceremony on the table before us. "Here to serve you, gentlemen."

The Admiral eyed her. Perhaps he was like me, pondering the glory of her unsullied youth. "What's your name, girl?" he asked, not unkindly.

"They call me Jimena, sire," she replied, somewhat taken aback that a man of means should inquire. Unlike most Gypsy men, she knew her station, and had known it from her earliest years.

"Then so shall we," replied the Admiral. "If it suits you, Jimena, we would enjoy a plate with sliced tomatoes and some Manchego cheese. Is there bread?"

"I believe that some may be procured if the gentlemen so desire," she replied, but did not dance away on her errand at once, lingering there instead as though awaiting some further dispensation from this lanky, soft-spoken figure who had sailed into her world.

"We would ask you to fetch it straightaway," I prompted, taking on the role of the cranky one, *el abusivo*.

Off she went and lower sank the setting sun. The shadows lengthened, a breeze stirred. The chairs felt comfortable after a day spent walking or riding on the burros, and the wine loosed the tongue, even though conversation did not always follow. Soon we would have to see to our night's lodging, a fact which I mentioned to the Genoan.

"We are but a few leagues from the terminus of our expedition," the Admiral said. "There's little likelihood we'll find so much as a livestock shed from here on. Best make our arrangements with these folk."

"There might be some risk in that proposition," I cautioned.

"As with all that is included in this whole affair," the Admiral replied.

In time Jimena returned and set before us a large platter of sliced tomatoes, as ruby-red and succulent as if they had been raised in a plot nearby. Beside the tomatoes there was a generous brick of the Manchego cheese. "Oil and vinegar—shall I bring?" she asked the Admiral with a fetching glance.

"And don't forget the bread," I reminded her. "Do your job."

In short order she returned with two pieces of oven-baked flatbread of the type favored by the Moors who had only so recently been sent packing from our fair continent by the Catholic Sovereigns. In two small glass containers she carried the olive oil and vinegar, which she placed beside the platter before coming near to stand at the Admiral's side. "Is there any other way which I can serve you?" she asked, with a playful smile.

"You can inquire of your family on our behalf for an evening's lodging," I put in. "The night is now upon us, and we would be happy to pass it in this area."

"Don't mind him. He is a businessman," the Admiral said to the girl softly with a chuckle. She leaned upon his arm and peered at the Admiral with such familiarity that I involuntarily glanced around to see if we were being observed.

"Nonetheless," I persisted.

The Admiral gave her an affectionate cuff on her posterior and she danced off on her mission.

"She's very forward, don't you think?"

"She's the same age as my Diego," the Admiral responded, leaning forward to douse the tomatoes liberally with the oil and vinegar. "Affection is sadly lacking in the lives of these children."

With that, we ate uninterrupted and with good appetites. The bottle of wine was empty as we consumed the last of the cheese with the scraps of flatbread which remained to us. Then, out of the gathering dusk, one of the men of the encampment approached us. Dressed in the usual slovenly but serviceable garments of his people, he had a disconcerting air of straightforwardness about him. "A word, fellows."

"Fellows, not at all," I corrected him. "Gentlemen of Sevilla to you, sir."

"Whatever," said the man. "Titles or not, you've got the same appetites as all of us. Which of you is it that wants to be with the girl?"

At this point I stood. "I beg your pardon, friend. You are speaking to the Admiral of the Ocean Sea, and you will by God keep a civil tongue in your head!"

The Gypsy eyed the Admiral. "Admiral of the whoremongers, is that it?" He laughed slyly. "No offense, fellows. Both of you, if you like . . ."

"*Asi es,*" confirmed the Admiral, who had been regarding the obstreperous cretin with an unchanged demeanor. "I am the Admiral of the whoremongers, if you like, and I am quite taken with the young woman. Name your price."

"Now you're talking," the fellow responded. He paused with a touch of drama, as though he were about to enter a most secret negotiation. "She's completely a virgin, you realize."

"In that I will have to take your word, sir," the Admiral rejoined. Though I had to assume at this point that he was being ironic, there was no sense of mockery in his tone.

"As well you may," the Gypsy assured. "Now to the particulars. You want to be with her for just a tumble, or will you be looking to hold her to you through the night?"

"Oh, much more than that," the Admiral assured him. "Tonight and every night henceforth." As they carried on, I spied Jimena herself visible at a distance between the trees. Her gaze was leveled in our direction, and I wondered whether she was a willing partner in this negotiation.

"Perhaps the great Admiral has not understood the question: the girl's virtue can be had for a price. What's it to be: a quickie, just to tickle the fancy, or a full night of wild abandon?"

"Call for the girl," the Admiral instructed. "Bring her forth." There was a bit of iron now in the Admiral's tone, and the Gypsy quickly determined that producing the goods might work to his advantage. He turned and beckoned towards the girl. "*Ven pa' 'ca!*" he shouted impatiently, lest the moment escape him.

Jimena approached but not with the girlish abandon as before. Whether her newfound sense of restraint was a result of her elder's imperious tone, or of her own understanding of the unfolding drama, she now came forward with a more measured tread and a circumspect gaze. The Admiral raised his arm and gestured, and she came obediently to his side, whence he encircled her with that arm.

Together, across the table, they regarded the gypsy, who seemed to feel that his moment of triumph was at hand. *"'Ta buena, no?"* he asked with a knowing leer, referring not to Jimena's comeliness, not to her sweetness of character, but crudely to her potential as a sexual partner.

"I confess to being smitten at first glance," the Admiral confirmed, looking at the girl. "Let's have no more of this pointless buffoonery. I've already asked you once: name your price."

"You'll keep her with you throughout the night, then," the gypsy affirmed. "The price will be forty Maravedis."

"Sixty, no less," said the Admiral. I confess at this point to being completely at a loss at the Admiral's apparent abandonment of Catholic piety no less than for his folly as a negotiator. I frankly did not see how I could, under these circumstances, deliver a favorable report on his character to the Queen when he had been so badly upended by a couple of miserable Gypsies on the riverbank in Andalucia.

"Sixty and done!" exulted the Gypsy after a moment's hesitation.

"Are we both agreed on my terms, then?" the Admiral queried. Jimena, for her part had buried her face in the Admiral's tunic. She might have been crying, but I could not see her face.

"Agreed that the girl will be yours for the night, we are. Paid fully in advance, of course." The gypsy's eyes were already greedily eying the Admiral, hoping momentarily to see his purse forthcoming.

"*Hija*, look at me," the Admiral coaxed the girl. "I want to hear from your lips. You have not been with a man?"

At this juncture, Jimena withdrew her face from the folds of the Admiral's tunic and cast her gaze somewhat beseechingly upon the Admiral. She then turned and looked at her own kin with a less kindly demeanor. "It is as he says," she reported before wrapping her arms around the Admiral's neck and burying her face once again in the curve of his arm.

"Very well," said the Admiral. "Kindly round up all the child's worldly possessions and give her leave to say her goodbyes. We shall be traveling on shortly in order to make our camp."

At this the Gypsy's agile mind began to grasp that the negotiation had somehow gone awry. (And I confess that my own mind awoke from its slumber and began to perceive the thrust of the Admiral's strategy). "There need be no moving on. A night's lodging thrown into the bargain," the Gypsy. "You can take her right here under our lovely trees, hombre."

"The child now being a ward of ours, we shall take her forthwith from this damnable environment to a place more suitable for civilized discourse," the Admiral informed conversationally. He continued, however, to hold the girl close and made no move either to rise or to reach for his purse, waiting perhaps for the Gypsy to catch the full import of his intention.

The Gypsy was not long in recovering his wits. "Manolo," he shouted over his shoulder. "Manolo, *ven 'pa 'ca!*" The Admiral beheld him impassively, but I reached to my belt and loosed the leather binding upon my dagger. "Come down here, man!" the gypsy urged his as-yet-unseen comrade. We have a thief in our midst!"

Manolo appeared around the corner of one of the tents. He was a full head taller than the first gypsy, and bore a long, well-formed staff. But he also had about him a dense scowl that indicated that despite his role as an enforcer, he was likely not quick of wit. The Gypsy, for his part, had stepped back from the table and now stood fully erect to lodge the formal charges.

"This son-of-a-whore has come in here and seized my Jimena, claims he's going to throw her on his burro and ride away with her, pretty as you please . . ."

"Hold your tongue, you worthless liar." The Admiral's voice was pitched low and hard, and had an element of menace to it that was completely at odds with his careworn aspect and his shambling demeanor. He continued to hold Jimena, who had pulled her face clear and was regarding the two Gypsies as her benefactor spoke. "The fact is, we struck a bargain, and now you're having second thoughts. For sixty Maravedis you have sold me your Jimena, and once the money changes hands, she will be coming with me."

"Going with you?" the Gypsy responded with manufactured incredulity. "And what do you take me for, that I should for a price part with my own flesh and blood?"

At his the Admiral actually chuckled. "Why, I have taken you just as you have presented yourself:

as a businessman. Are you telling me that this was not your intention? That you are willing to sell the girl's virtue, but not part with the girl herself?"

"*A ver si me cago en la ostia,*" the gypsy said in a low, ugly growl. "Jimena, come to me!"

"I want to accompany this man," the child said in a small voice, as though she could hardly believe her own words. She remained in the Admiral's loose embrace, her hands grasping his tunic.

"You'll accompany him in hell!" cried the Gypsy, seizing a chair which he wielded over his head. Taking this as his cue, Manolo moved forward and swung his staff, rather carelessly I thought, in the direction of the Admiral's head. For my part, I was entirely too slow to react to this sudden eruption, and instead stood watching it unfold as if in a dream. Shielding the girl, the Admiral rolled to one side while raising an arm to ward off the blow, but such was his strength that he actually managed not only to deflect the staff but to seize it as well and deprive Manolo of any opportunity to follow up his assault. Then, as quick as you please, he stood and brought the staff down sharply across Manolo's shoulders with such force that the big gypsy was deprived of his footing and went to the ground on his knees. By this time I had pulled my dagger from my belt and the two of us stood facing the Gypsies across the table. With a fearful shriek, Jimena scooted away from the lot of us and fled in the direction of the gypsy encampment.

Pitching the staff aside, the Admiral now reached for his purse and tossed several coins onto the table, directing me at the same time to fetch the burros. "I believe this will suffice for the meal," he said to the Gypsy. "As for the girl, I will consider our bargain dissolved. But mind, when I pass here two days from now, I will expect to see her whole and in good spirits. This failing, I will fetch a complement of the King's cavalry back here to put your encampment to the torch and land you and your associates in prison for as long as you shall breathe." He paused for good effect. "Now get out of my sight before my temper grows short and I decide to settle our differences here on the spot."

As it then developed, the Admiral and I departed straightaway, and once our feet were again on the path towards Palos we did not stop until the first faint streaks of dawn came up in the East. During this time, our conversation was limited, even though my mind wrestled with questions which arose from our encounter. They were, however, rapidly subsumed by the busyness of the next two days, during which time we reached the extremities of the Guadalquivir at the place called Palos de la Frontera. There we conducted a survey of the tidal behaviors of that region, and of the possibilities for safe anchorage thereabouts, speaking at length with local fishermen and traders knowledgeable on these subjects. One night the Admiral even managed to recruit two or three young men to his expedition, charging them with making their way to Sevilla at their own expense in the next 72 hours and reporting to a certain party. Before we departed the tavern he entrusted to them these particulars written out on a piece of butcher's paper. (I do not know whether this commitment was ever fulfilled.)

On the following day we departed Palos with our trusty *burros* in tow and made our way north. As the sun passed its meridian we once again neared the place on the river where the unsettling encounter with the Gypsies had so recently taken place. At this juncture, I checked the disposition of my dagger and eyed the Admiral closely to see if he too might register apprehension at the possibility of repercussions resulting from the heated exchange.

There was no need. The encampment was gone. Perhaps in response to the dire warnings issued by the Admiral, or perhaps because of the cyclical nature of their wanderings, save the matted grasses near the trees and some debris left from their shiftless lifestyle, the Gypsies had disappeared entirely.

"Just as well that the lot of them have decamped," I commented as we passed abreast of the now-quiet scene, unable to contain entirely my feelings of relief at not having to pass through the gauntlet of their wrath. "A shame for the poor young lass, however." The Admiral, immersed in thought as he so often was, made no response to my brief editorializing.

"Would you in fact have carried her away?" I could not help but venture the question, as it had been foremost in my mind since our departure.

"That young lass has her destiny to face, as each of us do," replied the Admiral at length.

"But you offered her the opportunity to change that destiny."

"I merely did my part as a subject of the king. Only God can offer her such an opportunity."

"Still, I must know, if it pleases your grace: would you have carried her away as your child, or . . . ?"

"Or as a child-bride?" The Admiral at this point chuckled to himself. "Have you any inkling of the scope of this expedition, dear Luciano? Of the honor that has been conferred upon me by our Catholic sovereigns? If you have followed our business of the last several days with any alacrity at all, the answer to your question should be obvious." I glanced at him and detected there what I interpreted to be a parrying gaze, almost an invitation to register such a guess. It was fleeting, however, and the moment quickly passed. It was not until two days later, as we made our way on the road just south of Sevilla, with scarves across our lower faces to cut the choking dust stirred up by volume of traffick on the dry summer roadway, that he chanced to utter a comment which might have been the key to the mystery. We had conversed earlier on that morn regarding parenthood, with him having asked me of the disposition of my own family.

"Married with two nippers on the hearth, sire," I had informed him. It had been one of the very few times during our brief sojourn that he had evidenced any interest of a personal nature in my life. "Both lasses they are," I added as an afterthought. He absorbed this information without comment, but some time later, likely still pondering the topic, he said, "Any man would be proud to have a daughter such as that Gypsy lass, and I no less than any other."

I last saw the Admiral on the quayside there in Sevilla some thirty days later, on the morning of 5 August as his small fleet made ready to depart for the anchorage at Palos, and from there to the

New World. I had already submitted my report to the court by then, a report in which I commended their royal majesties on the selection of a man and a mariner so admirably suited to the task at hand.

"His natural talents for leadership combined with his good Catholic sense and a commendable measure of restraint in the face of wrath or misunderstandings (both of which are certain to occur in a venture as prolonged and problematical as that which he undertakes in behalf of the Crown) give me great assurance that Spain has done well in entrusting her New World destiny into the hands of the honorable C. Colon . . ." I wrote.

On that August morning our parting was brief and without ceremony. The quay was thronged with humanity, many of whom seemed to have some pressing issue to place before the departing mariner. I marveled at the irony, this rather sudden exaltation of station coming to a man who had for so long traversed alone the roads of the empire as a virtual vagabond, dependent upon the good graces of strangers for his next meal or his night's lodging. Which is not to say that he seemed in any way affected by such; he wore that same distracted and distant, almost contemplative air, as he had during our travels together. Though I was able to exchange with him a firm and heartfelt handshake, I could not say for certain whether, in the moment, he was able to distinguish me from any other who offered the same courtesy. But, in light of his subsequent activities of widespread renown, and the great fame (and infamy) which they conferred upon him, I always felt a calm sense of admiration for the man from Genoa, not only for the lack of adornment that attended his words and his person, but for the unwavering strength of character that lay submerged beneath them. And although it goes against all my upbringing and training, I persist in believing that out there somewhere is a proud and determined Gypsy woman who feels the same.

Luciano Bellido Nieves, Conde de Orgaz
Merida, Spain, 1521

GONE BACK
TO IRELAND

The features editor, Grant Wyndham, and I were not on the best of terms, I'll grant you that. He thought I was too old to be writing features (I was 37), and I thought he was too young to be assigning them (he was 26).

So when he threw me the 25-year anniversary piece, I could tell he didn't expect much to come of it. America had moved on, and moved on in haste. The last quarter of the century had seen sweeping changes, especially in the Western lands. We had places to go and a raw continent to develop, and these backward glances were simply not our style.

Nonetheless, I bent myself to the task. Did some digging around. Had the good fortune to encounter a survivor who was willing to recall and had the memory to do so with some alacrity.

What follows is the story I filed.

Along the Rosebud basin, under the breezes of spring the prairie grasses are singing again. The inhabitants of the region called them the Greasy Grasses. They ripple and bob as they sing the old stories. The stories of the pounding hooves. The stories of the whistling arrows. The stories of the ragged gunfire, the muffled shouts, the harsh war cries and the awful sounds of men dying violently and at close quarters. The stories that have endured and entered the American lexicon forever.

Almost precisely three quarters of the way through the tired and troubled century that we have so recently laid to rest, a two-day running gun battle ensued on these high and lonesome plains nearly a thousand miles north and west of San Francisco, California. It was a battle that was two hundred years or more in the making, and when it was over, so too were the fortunes of a great Indian nation.

Fought twenty five years ago this month, it has already entered into the pantheon of Great Moments in the history of our continent, despite the fact that the engagement was one of the most infamous military setbacks in recent American history. As surely as the one nation died during the engagement, another was being born. The birthing pains had begun in serious a decade or more earlier. Gettysburg. Chicamaugua. Chancellorsville. Shiloh and Antietam. Places where the dead were piled in mounds so high they blocked out the sun, and the stench of death lay heavy on the land for weeks after the battles had concluded.

Once the War Between the States had run its bloody course, enlisted men and volunteers returned to the factory and the farm while many of those in the officer corps went in search of other opportunities to ply their trade. Places where unit leadership, combat experience, and soldierly discipline were in high demand, as they have been periodically since the beginning of recorded time.

Many took commissions in the Regular Army of the United States, and formed the backbone of a fighting force that now turned its attention westward, where the boundaries of the empire were rapidly expanding despite the resistance of the long-time inhabitants of the region. Retired Army scout Avery P. Elwood knew those inhabitants well. *"I lived among the Plains Indians for near 25 year, and they was by and large a peaceable people. Kind of simple-minded. Almost like children in some ways. We talked that they was red-devils, hostiles, bloodthirsty savages an' the like. Well, they no doubt had some customs that run plumb against our grain, but let's consider, they was a free people livin' in a free land, until we come along an' placed our boot on their neck. By the time Sheridan come up with his plan to send in the bluecoats an' gave 'em a free hand to tighten the screws, wasn't nobody listenin' no more. It was hogkillin' time again."*

One would be naturally tempted to call the speaker an "old man" but there is something of a vitality in his features that belies his years. Although he was somewhat coy about his age, anecdotal evidence would lead one to believe that he has seen his sixtieth year come and go, perhaps some time hence. Portly and erudite, with a high-pitched voice and surprisingly delicate mannerisms, he seems more like a retired schoolmaster than a fearless frontiersman. His presence in the raucous and run-down boarding house on Post St. in our fair city's Tenderloin District further serves to enhance his status as an ageless storyteller with a memory as long as that of the prairie grasses themselves.

In 1870, A.P. Elwood had been initially contracted by the Army for services as a Scout. In late 1873 he was assigned to a cavalry outfit headquartered in Ft. Riley, Kansas. The unit, as he recalls, was less impressive than the legend would have us believe. *"You got to remember that the kind of trooper who came west after the war was not always your best citizen. Scalawags, bushwackers, ruffians. Hot-tempered and cold-blooded, with no more regard for the morals of polite society than a rattlesnake. Half of 'em was drunks, three quarters of 'em had never been in combat, (which we used to call seein' the elephant) and near ever' one of 'em was just as inclined to take French leave as to turn out for roll call. It takes quite an officer to shape men like those into any kind of a reliable fighting unit."*

Among those officers who had accepted Army commissions after the War, there were a number of foreign nationals, many of whom had been solicited from overseas by Secretary of State James B. Seward at the outset of the war to bolster the officer corps of Mr. Lincoln's armies. Scots, Dutchmen, Germans and Englishmen all served with distinction in the war which counted 600,000 casualties.

The greatest contingent of foreign-born officers, however, came from Ireland. Political and religious strife, periodic famines, and English tyranny all seem to have been factors in the readiness of so many young Irishmen to seek their fortunes on foreign shores.

It was at the age of 20 that young Myles Keogh left his home in County Carlow in response to an appeal from the Vatican to come to the defense of Papal interests in Italy. There, as a second lieutenant, he saw his first action, which included being a part of an army that was surrounded, forced to capitulate, and briefly imprisoned. It was a pattern that would recur during his career.

In 1862, in response to Secretary Seward's appeal, Keogh left the elite Papal Guard, and along with a number of his mates, made his first Atlantic crossing. Commissioned as a Captain, he joined the Federal Army, was assigned to the staff of Irish-born General James Shields, and plunged into action at the Battle of Shenandoah, where he and his troops nearly effected the capture of veteran Confederate General Stonewall Jackson.

Stories of the young cavalryman's cool-headedness and boldness in battle rapidly circulated, and he was invited to join the staff of General George McClellan, Commander of the Army of the Potomac. After McClellan was removed, Keogh was attached to the staff of General John Buford. In the all-cavalry actions of Stoneman's Raid and Brandy Station the Irishman further distinguished himself. In June of 1863 he was engaged in a skirmish against the vaunted Confederate cavalry leader J.E.B. Stuart.

On June 30, General Buford led his forces into an unremarkable way-station called Gettysburg. During the furious actions of the next week, 8000 troops fell, but Buford held his line. At the end of this momentous conflict, Myles Keogh was recognized for "gallant and meritorious services" and received a brevet promotion to the rank of Major. He was, at that time, 23 years of age.

Following the illness and death of Buford, Keogh joined General George Stoneman on a series of raids behind enemy lines; at Macon, Georgia on July 31, 1864, they found themselves surrounded, had their horses shot from under them, and were captured and imprisoned. During his imprisonment Keogh contracted malaria and struggled with depression, and after three months was freed along with Stoneman himself in a prisoner exchange arranged by General William Tecumseh Sherman.

By war's end, virtually every fighting General on the Union side knew Myles Keogh either by reputation or by having been in combat alongside him. At the age of 25 he had been brevetted to the rank of Lieutenant Colonel. His skills as a leader of cavalryman were by now legendary. He went looking for a new post.

"It wasn't long after that, along about '71 I guess, that I first come in contact with him," A. P. recalls. *"Down at Ft. Riley in Kansas. He was a Company Captain then. I Company, Seventh Cavalry. Myles Keogh stood out from any cavalry officer I ever met. Tall, ramrod straight and fair-minded, he never put on no airs. He was born to wear the uniform, looked like. Had a natural sense of leadership about him. On a horse or on the ground, you just knew that if you was ever in a scrape, this was the one fellow you'd want to be with.*

"Unfortunately for Captain Keogh, the outfit was headed up by a fellow name of Custer. George A. I done my best to stay out of his line of sight, and I wasn't the only one."

George Custer, like Keogh, had gained widespread fame during the war for his battlefield exploits. In many regards their careers paralleled one another. They were only one year apart in age, and each was known for bravery under fire and willingness to engage the enemy. Gettysburg was only one of the major battles in which both participated with distinction. When the Seventh Cavalry was formed in 1866, Custer became its first commanding officer. The regiment consisted of twelve companies including 45 officers and some 700 troopers. Quartered at Ft. Riley, Kansas, the Seventh Cavalry was tasked with patrolling and pacifying the region, keeping it safe for the increasing numbers of settlers that were pouring in from the east as well as for the railroad crews that were laying the track that would eventually link both halves of the continent together.

What set the two men apart, however, was Custer's gift for relentless self-promotion. To this end he curried the favor of Presidents and politicians, business potentates and publishers. He designed his own extravagant uniforms, published accounts of his exploits, and commissioned large portraits of himself. In short, he did all he could to call attention to himself, to stand out from the long blue line. In so doing, he incurred the enmity of many of his fellow officers and a substantial measure of distrust on the part of the men under his command.

This distrust was rooted in another of Custer's well-documented peculiarities. While he was famed for his aggressive, headlong cavalry charges, among the troops it was well-known that the units under Custer's command regularly suffered the highest casualties in any engagement. As a leader he seemed all too willing to sacrifice lives to attain the goal of greater glory for himself. But it all paid off. While Keogh was being celebrated as a 25-year-old Lieutenant Colonel, Custer, at the age of 23, had already been brevetted to the rank of General.

Myles Keogh was seldom in evidence during those first years, spending most of his time on "Constabulary Duty" in the southern states, where the Army had its hands full overlooking the reconstruction of civil society following the devastation wrought by the war. Much of his time was spent with new recruits that were being culled from opportunistic Civil War veterans who flooded the western lands after Appomattox. As with every duty he had ever been assigned, Keogh proved adept at the task of creating a viable fighting force out of the lightly trained and undisciplined raw material at hand.

"Not everybody fell in love with Keogh from the get-go," Elwood remembers. *"These fellows was a rough-and-tumble crowd, and many of 'em made the mistake of assuming that a man who spoke and dressed and handled himself the way Captain Keogh did must be a useless dandy, not fit for the hard life the west had to offer. Once they saw him in hazard situations, they learned different. He won 'em over by hard work and*

solid leadership. Custer wore men out. Myles Keogh built men up. That's about as simple as I can put it."

While skirmishes with war parties of the region were not uncommon, the tribes, primarily Cheyenne, Arapaho, Kiowa and Comanche, protected their women and children by carefully avoiding large-scale engagements with the better-armed, more mobile cavalrymen. Their war parties moved fast, struck quickly, and vanished back into the rugged lands they knew so well. Accustomed to pitched battles against an enemy who thought and fought like they did, Custer and his troops were frustrated by plains warfare. Itching for a "fair fight," the "Boy General" longed to demonstrate the fighting superiority of his regiment, as well as burnish his own credentials as the country's foremost Indian fighter. In November of 1868, he got his chance.

"Wachita? That was quite a set-to, all right, if you've got a stomach for shooting women and children. Black Kettle and his wife was shot in the back, if you want to know the truth. They was a few braves in the encampment, no doubt o' that, and they gave as good as they got. But it was not the Army's finest hour, and the business with Elliott, well, that just about tore it as far as Custer's reputation went with his own men. He'd been known as a petty tyrant all along, but to cut and run leaving his own men to fend for themselves in that situation? Troops don't forget that. And officers remember it even longer."

The encounter in the deep snows near the Washita River in Oklahoma Territory provoked strong reactions throughout the country. Custer and his forces surprised and overran Black Kettle's encampment of some 250 souls. Among the more militant factions, it was hailed as a grand victory over the renegade hordes. Custer himself portrayed it as a clear demonstration of his own glorious leadership as well as the indomitable fighting spirit of the Seventh Cavalry. Though he claimed to have killed as many as 103 Cheyenne warriors with only 21 losses among his men, his own scouts later reported that no body count was ever taken, as the warriors who had fled the village during the initial assault regrouped and launched a counterattack of their own. It was during this stage of the battle that Major Elliott and a small band of troops were cut off and annihilated while Custer withdrew to the safety of his supply train. Reports circulated that Custer's troops had taken "sadistic pleasure" in shooting women and children, and it was said that the bodies of the innocents had outnumbered those of Indian warriors.

Coming only four years after Chivington's massacre of Black Kettle's non-combatants at Sand Creek, the encounter along the Washita was seized upon by those who took a more accommodating stance on the Indian question as another example of the American military run amok, and they soon began to refer to it as the Washita Massacre. After Sand Creek, one enterprising reporter went so far as to discuss cavalry tactics with the legendary frontiersman and Indian fighter Kit Carson, who was blunt in his assessment: *"Jis to think of that dog Chivington and his dirty hounds, up thar at Sand Creek. His men shot down squaws, and blew the brains out of little innocent children. You call sich soldiers Christians, do ye? And Indians savages? What der yer 'spose our*

Heavenly Father, who made both them and us, thinks of these things? I tell you what, I don't like a hostile red skin any more than you do. And when they are hostile, I've fought 'em, hard as any man. But I never yet drew a bead on a squaw or papoose, and I despise the man who would."

Myles Keogh, off in Texas on constabulary duty, was not present at the Washita, but as commander of H Company, Captain Frederick Benteen was. As one of Major Elliott's best friends, he was particularly disturbed with the outcome, and his grief, as we shall see, may have resulted in significant consequences.

In 1873 the Union Pacific Railroad was beginning its westward push. In order to protect railroad workers and maintain the peace, Custer and his Seventh were relocated some 400 miles to the northwest to newly-founded Fort Abraham Lincoln. It was there, in the summer of 1874, on 500 acres of rolling prairieland on the banks of the Missouri River that A.P. Elwood was able to observe the two protagonists of our story in a more intimate setting.

"The General organized a hunting party, and as I was passing through and staying at the fort, I was invited to tag along. It was the kind of a high-falutin' western outing that would've made those eastern swells envious: the wives, dressed all in their Sunday best, accompanied us. The troops had gone ahead and pitched a big shade tent in a grove out there, probably ten mile or so from the fort. There were maybe two dozen of us in the party, and while the men went out to shoot, the wives set up a feast of cold meats and beer. Them hills was teeming with

game, and I'll venture to say that not a man came back with his bag empty.

"The General was quite a showman with his sombrero and his dandy buckskin jackets; he was a natural center of attention, but I'll tell you that Keogh cut a more of a manly figure. He was a good head taller than Custer, dressed all in black with his short-brim hat and a cane that he carried to support an ankle that had been shot up in the war. He dint have no wife nor woman in his life, but not many of them women could go long without givin' him a once-over. Custer usually ran hot and heavy, but Keogh was always cool, collected, and kept to hisself. They got along cordial enough, but my observation was that the General dint have no particular use for an officer that stood taller than he did, and I don't mean just in the physical sense o' the word, either.

"That night, after we got back to the fort, they put on a grand affair in the main dining room o' the fort. Brought in the band, the officers all decked out in parade uniform, the ladies in finery as good as any you'd find in St. Louis or San Francisco. Captain Keogh was there early on, mingling with his officers and givin' the ladies a gracious turn on the floor. He had a large measure of what you might call that Irish charm. The General didn't show until after Keogh had departed, and the affair never had quite the luster after he was gone. If the Seventh had a heart, that man was it."

In 1875, to facilitate their interest in exploiting the natural resources of the Black Hills, the U.S. Government directed General Sheridan to come up with a plan for clearing the area of hostiles once and for all. They were to be rounded up and sent to reservations managed by the various Indian

Agencies designated for that purpose. Frustrated by the slow pace of garrison duty and as always in search of greater glory, the enterprising Custer lobbied hard for the job of leading the expedition tasked with that responsibility. Despite the General's frequent run-ins with politicians due to his unruly nature, Sheridan vouched for him, and eventually Custer secured the appointment, with one important caveat: he was to operate his forces under the direct supervision of Brigadier General Alfred Terry, military commander of the Dakota Territory. The deadline for the completed roundup was January 31, 1876.

That deadline had already been eclipsed when, on May 25, Custer and his senior Company Commander Myles Keogh rode out of Ft. Lincoln at the head of 511 troops, 13 officers, and a pack train of 150 wagons. Anticipating an historic campaign, Custer had invited along several newspaper correspondents, one of whom filed the following report: *"General George A. Custer, dressed in a dashing suit of buckskin, is everywhere. The General is full of perfect readiness for a fray with the hostile red devils, and woe to the body of scalp-lifters that comes within reach of himself and his brave companions-in-arms."*

The plan of action called for a three-pronged approach, with Colonel John Gibbon coming from the west and Brigadier General George Crook coming up from Fort Fetterman to the south. Once in the area of the Yellowstone River, the three columns would converge on the non-treaty hostiles, entrapping them and driving them to the reservation or slaughtering them if they resisted. Custer's route called for an overland march in excess of 300 miles. Averaging 15 to 18 miles per day, it was getting on towards the middle part of June before he and his troops found themselves penetrating the Indian strongholds.

It is worth noting at this juncture that the Seventh Cavalry was operating under a number of assumptions that would prove badly flawed and would ultimately lead to a result none could have envisioned. The first mistaken assumption was the actual number of Indians at large in the territory. Due to conflicting and incomplete reports on the part of the various Indian agencies (whose job it was, after all, to keep track of their charges), it was estimated that there were likely between 800 and 1,000 souls to be reckoned with. The actual number was apparently some three times that, if not more.

Another assumption was that the hit-and-run fighting strategy of the Indian warriors would limit battlefield engagements, and make the task at hand more a case of finding and "rounding up" these loose parties rather than actually meeting and defeating them in strength. Such was the Seventh's thirst for fighting glory that it was never taken into consideration by the unit's chain of command that there might be too many hostiles to handle; the chief concern was there might be not enough to go around.

And finally, there was the one hundred fifty year collective memory of white versus Indian engagements. Indian warriors were shadowy presences, cowardly fighters and devious dealers;

they were more given to thievery and butchery of innocents rather than noble and concerted efforts in honest combat. It was a conviction deeply held not only by George Custer but by virtually every one of his troopers and officers that a single company of the Seventh was a fighting force superior to any number or disposition of Indian warriors. Certainly Custer's own much-ballyhooed experience on the Washita was ample proof of that!

Given these convictions, the strategic caution and necessary reconnoitering that the Seventh might have accorded a force of fighting men of their own race were largely discarded when dealing with the Indians. Indeed, the whole excursion was deemed something of a frontier adventure, and one that would be certain to yield ready acclaim to each participant. The Indians were there for the taking, and the Seventh was in the fortuitous position of being among those who would be in a prime position to take them.

Curiously, among those who did not entirely share this view of ready conquest and certain triumph was Myles Keogh. A man sometimes given to melancholy and soul-searching as well as a veteran of fifteen years of unrelenting combat on two continents, the Irish-born officer approached this expedition with a certain trepidation that caused him to pen a letter to friends in distant New York State, directing for the disposition of his body should he meet an untimely end. For this reason, his final resting place is in fact far from the rolling plains where his presentment of disaster would be uncannily borne out.

On the morning of June 17, the Indians served notice that their old strategies had been revised and yielded to something new and frighteningly different. A force of some 500 warriors boldly attacked Crook's column, which was twice the size of their own. After a heated engagement that went on until mid-afternoon, the hostiles withdrew, leaving Crook to lick his considerable wounds. The Indians moved off to the North, into Crow lands, where they eventually set up a new camp along a winding stream they called Greasy Grass. The Whites called it Little Bighorn.

Unaware of Crook's setback, the Gibbon and Terry/Custer columns converged on June 21 and it was determined that while Gibbon moved up the Yellowstone to block its mouth, Custer would proceed to the Rosebud; the pincer movement would flush the Indians out of their encampments and trap them between the two American forces for annihilation. Still anticipating a bumper crop of hostiles for the killing, Terry's last words to his headstrong subordinate were, "Custer, don't be greedy. Save some for us." Custer assured him that he would do so, and the troops of the Seventh pushed off north and west for their rendezvous with destiny. Just another hunting party, for all of that.

A.P. Elwood, who had joined the column two days earlier, picks up the story: *"Thing you got to recall is at this point, the Indians had been pushed about as far as they could go. Their last sacred stronghold, the Black Hills, had been took over by the white man, and now here he came ready to drive them finally from their hunting grounds and put 'em up in pens like cattle. That's why they lit into Crook the way they did, and that's why, once the word got back to the Agencies, thousands more who had already allowed themselves to be pacified mounted up and come out for the showdown. The Seventh had no more idea of what they was up against than the day they was born.*

"From the time we left Gibbon, we pushed hard to close the trap. Covered seventy mile or so in just three days. Like I done tol' you earlier, Custer's so-called invincibles were nothin' of the sort. Near half of 'em was green troops, had never seen the elephant, as we say, their horses were near about worn out, they was not happy with their hard-ass General Custer, and they was no more disposed for a big fight than they was ready for eternity. The Cavalry business ain't all the romantic life that's been talked up to be. Yer saddle sore, yer wearing those scratchy woolen uniforms, it's hot as blazes, unless you've got some in yer bags you ain't had a drop of whiskey in a near a month, and yer not gettin' much of the coffee you normally require either. The Indian, he knew how to live off the land and was mighty nigh at home doin' it. The cavalryman lived out of his saddlebags, and as a result felt sickly and poorly more often than not, especially after a forced march of a month or more.

"Which is why a good Cavalry officer is worth his weight out there on the plains: because he's got to enforce discipline and create some kind of morale among men for whom neither one comes natural. I looked at that line of troops and knew that Captain Keogh would have his men ready no matter what. About the rest of 'em, I couldn't be sure.

"On that particular mornin' (June 25) it was still and hot, but Hard-Ass had his troops on the move early. We'd

picked up the Indians' trail on the second day. I could see from the number of travois and pony tracks that there was a sizeable number of 'em on the move. I made note of it, but to be honest I didn't make much of an issue about it with the General. At this point I already had a bad feeling about him being in such a hurry, and to point out the large numbers of Indians in the area would have only whet his appetite all the more, which we didn't need.

"Along about midday the Crow scouts got us to the top of a ridge where we was finally in sight of the encampment, maybe five mile away. We looked through the scope, but all you could really see at that distance was kind of a white blur of teepees. At this point the Crow scouts had a pretty good sense of how the Indians was gatherin' up. Curley tells the General, "There's enough warriors down there to fight for many days."

"In that case I guess we'll just have to get through 'em all in just one day," Custer says to 'im. Like I say, his appetite was up. For him it looked mighty like another Washita: push hard, use the element of surprise, ride hard down into the encampment, catch 'em in their teepees, shoot 'em down like ducks in a gallery. By this time it was just past midday, and you could tell he was in an all-fired hurry to get the hogkillin' done before dark set in.

The first order of business was the disposition of his troops, and while this was bein' sorted out, I eased my mount over to where Captain Keogh set on that big bay of his not far from the General and his other officers. "Captain," I says. "I wisht we wasn't in such an all-fired hurry to get down in that valley." I trusted his instincts, and wanted to get his sense of the situation.

"He was sitting tall and straight in the saddle as was his custom, a fearsome sight of a cavalry officer if ever

there was one. He looked at me from under the brim of his campaign hat, gave me a little smile. "We can't have those hostiles skedaddling off into the hills on us, now, can we, lad?" was what he answered. Considerin' the way things turned out, I come to conclude later that he meant the comment as ironic.

"Here's hoping we all get through, Cap'n.," I said to 'im. I hated to part company with 'im, if you want to know the truth. I had a bad feeling about what was coming, but whatever the outcome, Captain Keogh was one man who was indestructible, we all knew that.

"As it turned out, the General divided his troops into three units: he sent Major Reno with three companies to strike the upper end of the encampment while he and Captain Keogh took five companies an' moved off in the direction of the river to strike the encampment near the center. Three companies would be held in reserve and stay on the ridge with Captain Benteen. The last of the twelve companies was accompanying the pack train, and would join up with Benteen shortly.

"As a scout I was released from duty once the military tactics took over ; pretty much free to follow my own line as long as I didn't get in the way of things. So I decided to remain in the area with the Benteen unit, and just see how things developed, and how I might be able to make myself useful.

"We watched from that ridge as the rest of 'em took off. Reno's people was at a hard gallop, to get into position before the Indians were alerted. The General's command, over 200 men in all, moved out to the northwest in a more orderly fashion. With the guidons snapping in the breeze and all the dust in the air from the horses' hooves, it was easy to believe for a moment

*that the Seventh would be finding the glory the General
was looking for.*

*"After they all disappeared from sight, that ridge was
one lonesome damn place, I'll guarantee you o' that."*

While A.P. waited with Benteen's troops on the
ridge, one of the seminal battles of American history
began to unfold along the river in the valley below.
Even 25 years later, the precise chain of events
remains shrouded in mystery, obscured by the
considerable distances involved, the fragmented
nature of the engagement, and the highly subjective
viewpoints of the surviving participants. But even a
casual review reveals a picture that is often at odds
with the history advanced in the popular accounts
of our day.

As ordered, Reno struck first. Just past the
hour of 3:00 PM his troops reined in their horses,
dismounted, set up a skirmish line, and delivered
their first volleys into the Northern extremity of
the village. Within a very short time, there came a
shocking outpouring of mounted warriors crossing
the river to engage them directly, as they had engaged
General Crook the week before. Within minutes
Reno found his command, which numbered some
140 souls, badly outmatched. Hundreds of warriors
galloped down his flanks, intent on cutting him off
and dispatching of his unit entirely. Remounting,
Reno and his men raced for the river, forded it, and
sought refuge on the wooded bluffs on the other
side, where he and his command would spend the
next 24 hours hanging on for their lives and waiting
for support from Custer (which was never going
to arrive). These were Indians who clearly had

no intention of being shot while sleeping in their teepees.

The initial movement of Custer's five companies is less certain. Eager to engage, Custer did not linger to await the outcome of Reno's charge, but moved to bluffs near the river for a closer view of the village. The enormous encampment that he finally saw was shocking enough, but perhaps assuming that the element of surprise was still in his favor and that the warriors were still in their tents, he paused only long enough to scribble his infamous note to Benteen *("Come on . . . Big Village . . . Be quick . . . Bring pacs")* before spurring his mount and leading his forces down towards the river in preparation to assault the village.

It was an assault that never occurred. By now the inhabitants had been well advised of the fact that the bluecoats had arrived intent on carrying out their murderous mission. Instilled with supernatural confidence as a result of Sitting Bull's well-documented visions and no doubt buoyed by the strength of their own numbers, the hostiles came out to meet the challenge. Lakota and Cheyenne warriors on their agile and well rested ponies, many of them carrying repeating Winchester rifles, came streaming out of the village in unending numbers. War clubs, coup sticks, and countless quivers of arrows completed their armament for war. Even a cocky battlefield commander like Custer realized as their numbers rapidly mounted that he had met a force to be reckoned with. A skirmish line against such an enemy was impossible, a frontal assault pure folly. Benteen could not possibly arrive in time. Custer took the only reasonable decision open to him. He and his troops turned and ran for the high ground.

It was not an orderly withdrawal. Pursued by a bloodthirsty horde, Custer's command scrambled pell-mell towards the high ridge near the place where they had earlier reconnoitered the village. As they rode, a rain of arrows and rifle fire unleashed by their pursuers began to take its toll judging from the trail of bodies (both of horses and men) later found at the lower elevation. If Benteen was aware of their plight, there was little he could venture in the way of support. Becoming aware of Reno's dire situation, he had moved quickly to support the entrapped troopers and now those six companies were digging in together to withstand a concerted attack of perhaps as many a thousand warriors.

Now divided into two separate commands neither of which could communicate nor align itself with the other, the Seventh Cavalry's defeat was all but assured. Beset by a well-armed force outnumbering them by as many as twenty to one, the only questions became, how long would it last, and what would be the ultimate cost in lives?

Once he reached the ridge there was another ugly surprise awaiting Custer. Not only was the available space too confining for five companies to adequately set up defensive perimeters and make a fight, but the brushy concentrations that might have shielded the troops from deadly rifle fire were of no defense against arching arrows. (Some troopers' bodies were penetrated with so many arrows that the shafts had to be cut away before the bodies could be laid in their shallow graves).

Following standard cavalry practice, the men dismounted, with every fourth trooper holding the reins as the other three returned fire against the enemy. When horses fell, they were used as breastworks. But under the acute pressure being exerted by the warriors, this battlefield discipline quickly eroded. Soon the horses were being shot or released outright as every man took to firing. The Indians quickly seized the panicked mounts, many of which carried rifles and ammunition. The tide of battle, if it had ever favored the bluecoats, shifted rapidly as they found themselves coming under increasing fire once their own weapons were turned against them. As their casualties mounted, their rate of return fire decreased proportionately. With the outcome of the encounter becoming horrifically clear to the members of Custer's command, what has heretofore never been reported must now be told: as it became apparent that no hostages would be taken, a number of troopers began to turn the muzzles of their sidearms on themselves in a final effort to escape the agony of a prolonged or piecemeal death.

Shortly before 5:00 PM, a final charge by the emboldened warriors swept across the ridge, their horses' hooves pounding straight through Custer's last position. Less than thirty minutes after the hostiles had come out of the village in pursuit, the shooting began to taper off. There were no white men left to kill. There was, however, a tale left to tell.

A.P. Elwood remembers: *"Like I say, the Indians had us all roostered up in the woods near the river until late in the afternoon of the second day. They had come back to try to finish the job early in the morning, but we was well dug-in at this point, and had the ammo to hold out. We didn't know what had gone on the previous afternoon across the river where the General was, but we all knew that the shooting over there had gotten hotter than a whorehouse on nickel night, and then died out entirely. When Custer never showed up at our location, we figured there was a chance he had cut and run on us the way he run out on Elliott at Washita. Benteen never said it, but I know the thought crossed his mind.*

"It wasn't until the morning of the fourth day that the first search parties arrived on the ridge. I wasn't with 'em, since I had been assigned to start back to Ft. Lincoln with Reno's people, but I got the story later from some of Crook's people who was there. An' I ain't hardly forgot what they told me.

"After lying out in that hot sun for the better part of three days, the bodies had all gassed up pretty good and turned black. From a distance they thought there had been a buffalo hunt up there, and that maybe the Indians had got run off before they could field-dress their kills. Of course, they soon discovered different.

"There's no point goin' into the naked details. It weren't pretty. Of course the Indians had made off with all the uniforms, boots, and weapons. They had cut the bodies up pretty good, hacked off limbs an whatnot, but that wasn't out of pure deviltry, like some fools would have you believe. It's part of their death ritual. Never mind all that.

"Custer was laying in a wide-scattered group. Pretty clear that near the end, it was ever' man for hisself. There was no sign of mustering or anything like that, just men getting cut down or killin' themselves where they stood. Complete disintegration of military discipline, you might say. Like as not they died cursing the man who brought them there. "Let us out of here, that damn fool has gone and gotten us all killed."

"But Captain Keogh and his I company was nowhere to be found on that hill.

"It wasn't until later that day, down the hill on the far side of the ridge that they came across the rest of the Seventh. What happened was this: Captain Keogh seen right off that Custer had made a bad decision putting himself an' his people up on top of that ridge. So he made his own command decision. As you'll recall, he'd been surrounded and cut off a time or two in his life, so there was no sense of panic. He mustered I company and broke out of the encirclement, moving fast towards the gulch at the bottom of the hill. Thought maybe he'd have a better chance of savin' the lives of his boys an' holdin' on until reinforcements arrived. A purely strategic decision.

"Well, at this point there was so many hostiles in the fight that they could keep the pressure on Custer and still have plenty warriors to follow I company down the hill, which is what they did. I company never had the chance to reach the gulch. They set up a perimeter as best they could, and made their fight right there. And it probably didn't last very long.

"When they found the Captain, he was lying at the center of a cluster of his men. His sergeants, his guidon bearer, his troops stayed right with him until the end. His horse, which was still alive, wasn't far from his master's *body. They trusted him and his judgment, and if it came to it that they was all dead men anyway, then that's where they wanted to be: with the man who had brought them there.*

"That horse of his, a big bay name o' Comanche, turned out to be the only survivor among the five companies of horses and men that rode with Custer that day. I seen him some time later back at Ft. Lincoln after they had nursed him back to health. Hell, he lived on another 10 years or more as the regimental mascot. Lived in comfort. He'd earned it.

"After all that went on, it was no great shock to me that the Seventh got tore up that way. It was in the cards. But the army and the politicians done beat the devil around the stump tryin' to place the blame, all the way up the line to Sheridan himself. Fact is, they had the wrong man in charge that day, simple as that. Myles Keogh never would of put his people in that situation. But that's the army for you.

"For me, Myles Keogh never died on that battlefield. I don't think of him that way. Too much life in the man.

"I just think of him as gone back to Ireland."

Initially buried along with the 262 fellow troopers who lost their lives that hot summer afternoon, Myles Keogh's body was exhumed the following year and, in accordance with his last request, transported to Auburn, New York, where he was interred with full honors in a proper ceremony. Custer also went back to New York, and was buried with full military honors at his alma mater, West Point Military Academy.

Word of the Seventh's shocking defeat reached Washington on July 3, just as the United States launched its Centennial celebration. The timing was unfortunate for the Sioux Nation, as, ignoring all that had gone before, Americans of all political stripes were inflamed with a passion for revenge. In three hundred years of warfare against the Europeans and then the Americans, the battle along the Little Bighorn represented the largest-ever deployment of Indian warriors, and the largest-ever loss of life on the part of the whites. In its wake, the Black Hills were soon flooded with army detachments, and within 12 months the Sioux Nation had largely capitulated. Crazy Horse, the Oglala war chief whose charge it was that had finally overrun Custer's position, turned himself in and was then shot while incarcerated at Camp Robinson, Nebraska in September of 1877.

Sitting Bull, the Hunkpapa Holy Man, full of disdain for the ways and means of his white enemy, held out somewhat longer, but with their lands occupied and their food supply exhausted, he and his followers turned themselves in five years after the battle. He struggled to adjust to the ways of the conquerors, even joining Buffalo Bill's Wild West Show for a time as a popular attraction. In 1890 he too was shot while a prisoner at Standing Rock Agency in North Dakota.

Two weeks after Sitting Bull was dispatched, the Seventh finished their grisly task near Wounded Knee Creek in South Dakota. There they surrounded a peaceful encampment of some 350 Lakota Sioux, mostly women and children, and on a pretext of resistance rained down fire on the unfortunates with four rapid-fire Hotchkiss guns. When the massacre was over, the frozen bodies were pitched into a large ditch. As one contemporary newspaper account put it, General Miles had "checked the Indian noise" at last, and the Seventh rode home in glory.

Now, twenty-five years after the Seventh's encounter with Sitting Bulls' warriors at the place known as Greasy Grass, the prairie grasses once again bow their heads gently before the summer breezes, and sing their songs. Although most of the bodies have since been transferred to permanent burial sites, markers of stone and wood dot the hillside where the men of the Seventh Cavalry fell. Those who were there that day have scattered and taken their memories with them. But as long as the grasses remain, so will the songs.

And this is but one of them.

I filed the foregoing story with Grant Wyndham on the 20th of June, 1901, ample time for the editorial board to properly vet the piece and place it in the Examiner's feature's section for the weekend that would mark the anniversary.

Two days later I received a handwritten note in a script I did not recognize, but the brief message and the signature soon spelled it out clearly enough:

Mr. Kerr,

> *We are not in the habit of exalting the exploits of foreign nationals at the expense of our American heroes. You might consider doing a piece on the horse instead.*

Hearst

So my story and A.P. Elwood's heartfelt testimony died an untimely death under the heavy hand of the Examiner's new owner, the publishing wunderkind, William Randolph Hearst. With regrets I filed it away, hoping that at some future time, when America was ready to revisit this particular period of her history with a less jaundiced eye, the story might yet see the light of day.

And so it has.

Andrew Kerr
San Francisco, California, 1911

Slim Takes Flight

My old man had a saying. Well, he had a few of 'em, but one in particular. Understand, he was in sales most of his life. He sold door to door, business to business, sold retail and wholesale, seemed like practically his whole life was built around sales calls. And if there was one thing that really cranked him up, it was lousy weather. In rain, sleet, snow, howling wind, with the sky practically sitting on your shoulders, he would bundle up and head out to make sales calls. His philosophy was that the guy who showed up at a prospect's door under those conditions had the sale halfway made before he ever spoke a word. "Bad conditions bring out the best," he used to say, and you'd never find him huddled by the telephone or putting his feet up on a rainy day.

I remember thinking of that saying of his in the pre-dawn hours of May 20, because what we had was "pissy weather" as my mother would have called it. A low, ragged cloud cover, spitting rain, raw blustery air. Stay-in-bed weather for most of us, sales call weather for my old man. Flying weather? Not on your life is what I would have said. But if bad conditions brings out the best, then I guess the best would just as soon go flying.

We were clustered in the small hangar at Curtiss Field where we'd spent the last three days going over the Whirlwind with a fine-tooth comb. This particular J-5A, a nine-cylinder, air-cooled radial engine operating on a four-stroke cycle, had been expressly designed for the occasion. I quote from a manufacturer's brief that was released some months later and breathlessly reprinted virtually throughout the country: *The cylinder featured fins machined on the steel barrel, with only the upper 1.75 inches screwed and shrunk into the aluminum head. The valves were placed at a greater angle to the cylinder axis, inclined at angles of 35 degrees verses the 8.5 degrees of the previous cylinders. The valves were of the tulip type, and were machined from tungsten steel. The hollow exhaust valve stem was partially filled with a sodium/potassium salt mixture to assist in cooling. The combustion chamber was hemispherical, with spark plugs located at the front and rear. These cylinder changes provided much better cooling (particularly of the exhaust valve) and much better breathing, resulting in improved fuel consumption. Rocker arms and push rods were completely enclosed, a first for any air-cooled engine made in the U.S. Casting technology still did not allow the rocker arm chambers to be cast with the head. Rocker arm lubrication was accomplished using grease fittings. The Lindbergh engine had specially built spring-loaded grease reservoirs that allowed around forty hours of continuous running without manual greasing of the fittings. A new three-barrel carburetor solved mixture distribution problems that had plagued earlier models.* Given all this, I think we can be forgiven if we felt a proprietary affection for the Ryan's 500-pound engine. Of all the major components that would go into the Transatlantic effort—airframe, powerplant, and pilot—you can guess which we at Wright thought was the surest bet.

The distance from Curtiss Field to Roosevelt was about two and a half miles, and our little caravan got carefully underway about a quarter to five in the morning. They had lifted up the tail skid of the Ryan and lashed it to the bed of a small delivery truck. I clambered onto the running board of the truck with my collar turned up and the brim of my hat low over my eyes. As the field representative for Wright, I was there to insure that our motor was properly cared for, and my only real contribution that morning was to insist that the J5 Radial be covered with a tarp until it was ready to be started. But the fact is that I never even got the chance to take care of that little bit of business. I had poured myself a cup of coffee and came out of the dispatcher's office to attend to the tarp business only to find a couple of the boys already snugging down the tarp across the Wright. I did a quick double take, and right there behind me was Mr. Lindbergh. I ended up thanking him for his service when it should have been the other way around. He just slapped me lightly on the shoulder and grinned.

"That's what we're here for," he said.

By the time we had bumped up the gravel path to Roosevelt it was after 6:00, and they positioned the Ryan at the western extremity of the runway with its nose pointed east, towards Paris. Colonel Lindbergh, widely and familiarly known to the press as "Slim," must've ridden over in one of the automobiles, because I didn't see him during the transit. (At the age of about 25 with that unspoiled countenance of his he looked a lot more like a Boy Scout that a Colonel, but I could never bring myself to cross the threshold of familiarity with him. Here was a guy who was quietly going to strap himself into a wicker chair and meet an almost certain death over the frigid, trackless Atlantic, while I was going home to St. Louis on the evening train. I could not pretend that we were in any way cut from the same, or even a similar, bolt of cloth. He was always "Mister" to me.) Riding on the running board was actually good for me. The cold drizzle and the raw breeze helped to clear my head. With our flying future uncertain, I had taken the opportunity to go out to Yankee Stadium with a few of the fellows the evening before to get a load of "Murderer's Row"—Gehrig, Ruth, Muesel, Lazzeri—and we got to drinking beer both during and after the contest. Over the course of the evening we were "overserved" as my pal Tommy Cheatum liked to say, and I was still feeling the effects when they woke me up at the Garden City Hotel at about 3:30 AM. "Better turn to, looks like he wants to go," I was told. (The '27 Yankees, incidentally, had no hangover, they went on to win the pennant by nearly 20 games and swept Pittsburgh in the Series.)

Meanwhile, despite the atrocious weather, an impromptu party had broken out at Roosevelt. I don't know where they came from, these New Yorkers, but hundreds of them had begun to congregate in the area, to the extent that a dozen uniformed policemen were hastily trucked in to fend them off and keep them out of the way as the boys began fueling the aircraft and proceeding with the final checklist. Part of it might have been that the press had been covering the whole event pretty carefully, and it was only a question of who would be making a run at Paris on this particular morning, Byrd or Lindberg. Commander Byrd's Fokker was already hangared there at Roosevelt, giving him the inside track, as it were, but, possibly to his eternal regret, he took a pass, later saying that his aircraft needed more testing. We'd already run-in the Whirlwind for one hundred and fifty hours straight, so 36 hours didn't seem quite so intimidating to us. At some point during the fueling, Byrd, never willing to stand outside of the spotlight for too long, did his meager best to upstage our operation by wheeling out his aircraft, taking to the air from our runway, and buzzing around the field for over an hour, as if to say, "You see, I could very well be making this little Paris run today myself, if I so desired." On several occasions I observed Mr. Lindbergh glancing skyward as the Fokker swung by and detected in his countenance no more than a pilot's casual approval at the sight of an aircraft performing in its element. In fact, most of his attention was kept upon the fueling process, which involved a bucket brigade of about eight men passing the five-gallon jerry cans from a truck to the aircraft where one of the Ryan mechanics stood on top of the engine cowl and carefully filtered each can through a piece of chamois until all five of the plane's tanks were full. It was nearly 7:30 in the morning by the time this process was completed, and a lull came over the restive, growing crowd as the next phase, the most dangerous phase, now approached.

There are a few things that need to be understood to properly appreciate the gravity of the moment. Mr. Lindberg, wearing what I guessed to be his typical flying uniform—army breeches and boots and a light gabardine jacket over a long-sleeve shirt, with a diagonally striped tie knotted loosely around his slender neck—stood near his aircraft alternately scanning the sky and patting his pockets, entirely focused. If I had to guess, I'd say he was going through a mental checklist that had been thoroughly reduced and refined over the preceding weeks. Not far from his mind had to be the knowledge that within the last eight months, six aviators had either perished or gone missing in attempting the feat that Mr. Lindbergh and his Ryan were about to undertake. On this morning the two most recent aerial adventurers, the French heroes Nungesser and Coli, were still unaccounted for after crossing the French coast at Etretat just six days earlier. While Mr. Orteig's $25,000 certainly added a bit of spice to the mix since initially being offered some years earlier, that fact is that aviation had reached the point where it was in a mode of full-on attack. Seasoned veterans of flight were ready to launch themselves and their flying machines against the most forbidding challenges which the elements and the natural topography could provide. Death was certainly on people's minds on this morning, but so was conquest, and I would venture to say that this combination made for an atmosphere that was unforgettable.

Another factor to consider was that every attempt which had been made to date had involved either multiple aviators or multiple motors. (Byrd's Fokker, now quietly back on the ground at Roosevelt Field, had three motors.)The Frenchman Fonck, who was actually present in the crowd that milled about inside the police barricade near the Ryan, had lost two crew members in the fiery crash of his three-motor Sikorsky not 500 yards from where we stood. Davis and Wooster from the Navy had perished together in their three-motor Pathfinder down at Langley just one month earlier. In the face of such catastrophic failures, it seemed ludicrous that the Lindbergh team should offer up just one man and a single motor to take on such a challenge. Such a thin margin for error! Such unreasonable demands upon both man and machine! (We had calculated that during the course of 36 hours the Wright would be called upon to produce 1,430, 000 separate explosions on her cylinders without missing a single beat.) With no-one to spell him, the pilot would have to maintain a state of responsible alertness throughout an entire day and a half, well beyond the limits of what one would consider humanly possible. In fact, as I rode on the train the next day and considered the enormity of the task at hand, I came up with a slogan which Wright briefly used in its ad campaigns in the aftermath: *One Man, One*

Motor, One Ocean. It had a ring, I thought. And it told a tale.

There was one more factor to bear in mind, one which was much more prominently on our minds that morning because it was directly under our feet. Generally speaking, Roosevelt Field's runways were among the best to be found—long, wide, and firm. It didn't take any particular expertise in aviation to conclude that this morning such was not the case. The rains had converted the packed earth to the character and appeal of a Kansas farm road: rutted, slippery, and clinging maddeningly to whatever conveyance one might choose to maneuver across its surface. We had 5,000 feet of runway, which ordinarily would be plenty enough for the Ryan. Even with its fuel of 450 gallons (net weight 2,750 pounds) it could be expected, under normal conditions, to become airborne using only 60-70% of that. But with the mud, the heavy air, and the absence of any headwind whatsoever, the copse of trees and those telephone wires at the eastern extremity, though only faintly visible through the gray, moisture-laden air, seemed uncomfortably close. As if to underscore the point, as we were wrapping up the fueling, down the way one could not help but notice that an ambulance had rolled onto the field and now made its way down the runway to the approximate point at which the Ryan could be expected to free itself from the earth, or fail catastrophically in the attempt. When asked whether they expected to see the young aviator undertake a successful beginning this morning, those hundreds of souls who had marshaled themselves behind the police barricade might have demurely answered "Sure hope so." The thoughts they kept to themselves, however, might have been less hopeful in nature. It certainly seemed a morning more fit for a funeral than a celebration of life.

To balance out these thoughts of dire inevitability, one needed to look no further than the young pilot who now stood on the fringes of the men at work finishing up their ministrations to the Ryan. He wasn't hard to spot, being a full head taller than most of those in his vicinity. Even with the softly rounded shoulders and the slight stoop in his posture, he was a figure that immediately drafted one's attention, as he had first drafted mine some six weeks earlier in San Diego. I had gone out on the train in the company of the Whirlwind itself, which was being delivered to a dilapidated hanger at Ryan Aeronautical Company on the outskirts of this rapidly growing Spanish colonial city. Over the course of the ten days I spent there observing the painstaking process whereby the engine was inserted into the airframe and covered with its jeweled cowling, our pilot was not much in evidence. Apparently he spent much of his time poring over charts of the Atlantic, and plotting his precise course. At one point we were properly introduced. As my Christian name was also Charles, this provided an occasion for some brief badinage: "Never Charlie, right?" he asked me. "Not unless you're buying the drinks," I responded in clichéd workingman's parlance, and immediately thought the better of it, as one could see from his general demeanor that he was as unlikely a barfly as one could hope to meet. He graciously allowed my comment to die an orphan's death, and followed up with "Tell me what I need to know most about your motor," putting us nicely on a professional footing where we remained thereafter.

During the course of my stay we spoke on perhaps three or four occasions. He was, first and foremost, a gatherer of knowledge, or perhaps I should say, information. His clear, penetrating gaze, the care at which he catalogued my responses to his thoughtfully placed questions, and the pauses that often followed these questions as he silently processed those responses all led one to be careful, direct, and use unadorned language when conversing with Mr. Lindbergh. It was, I later thought, a great curiosity that the man whose exploit would unleash perhaps the greatest outpouring of sentimental prose and epic poetry since the death of Lincoln should be so lean and sparing in his own nature. But of course, his poetry was in his fingertips as they manipulated the stick of his aircraft, and his epic was written in the minute navigational calculations which carried him across that trackless ocean where no man had gone before. In the way he carried himself he did not breed familiarity, but at the same time he invited a kind of trust that could easily be mistaken for such.

It should be noted that the young Midwesterner was, by a good margin, the least celebrated of the aviators who had caught the "Atlantic fever." When stood up against the likes of Fonck, Byrd, Nungesser—certified adventurers or war heroes all—he was a virtual unknown. In those days, if you were a pilot you had almost certainly been trained by the Army, but Mr. Lindbergh's subsequent career path had been that of a "barnstormer" rather than a military aviator. If there was any career that better suited a man for the kind of challenge that flying blindly across an ocean presented, one cannot imagine it. Resourcefulness, inventiveness, absolute trust in one's equipment and absolute confidence in one's capabilities—tested and proven over every terrain in every clime and weather imaginable—that was what a man got out of barnstorming. He learned to stand on the wing of an inverted aircraft as it barreled earthward with a wide grin on his face not just to impress the earthbound onlookers but simply because he had trained himself to "grin and bear it" when enveloped by dire circumstances. If he survived it long enough, barnstorming would grant a man a measure of nerveless self-containment that was invaluable. Add to that a half dozen crash-landings and two or three parachute jumps from crippled and falling aircraft and you have a more complete picture of the type of "quiet fatalist" who will put up most of his life's personal savings as well as co-sign a $15,000 bank loan to finance an attempt to risk life and limb (at odds that Lloyd's of London was quoting as 10 to 1 *against*) on a venture of such dubious merit. When I point out that Mr. Lindbergh stood a full head taller than other men, it should be regarded not only as a literal observation, but a metaphorical one as well.

Before we move on, let us add to the portrait a large measure of single-mindedness. I'd had occasion to drink a beer with Ryan's chief engineer Donald Hall, just off the Ryan campus in a section of town that might have qualified back in St. Louis as a "skid row" but in underdeveloped San Diego was regarded more as a "scenic wayside." "It's all about the weight," Hall told me. "He's single-minded about keeping the weight down."

"That makes sense," I ventured.

"Makes sense, sure, but you pay a price. You gotta give up something to get something." Like myself (and Lindbergh too, for that matter), Hall was a Midwesterner, given to blunt, no-nonsense conversation that unscrolled best over cold beers.

"Like for example? In this case, I mean."

"Like a radio. Like a parachute. Like a sextant. Like anything much in the way of food and water. Like a flippin' co-pilot, for that matter." He had just named the principal things that any mariner or aviator would have considered essential to bolster the odds for survival in the event of a mishap. "He isn't even gonna have a windshield so he can see where he's goin'. We put in a periscope instead."

"I was watching the sign painter putting the letters on the rudder this afternoon. Ryan NYP. I get the Ryan, but what's the significance of the NYP?"

Hall looked at me with something of a cockeyed grin. A man who loves his work and who loves his beer will sometimes do that. "Yeah, that was Slim's idea. You gotta ask?"

"I'm askin.'"

"New York to Paris, bud. Like I told you, the man is kind of single-minded that way."

Back at Roosevelt Field, it was past 7:30, and though the air remained heavy and the skies leaden, the spitting rain had all but stopped. With the gradual lightening of the atmosphere, visibility down the runway had improved somewhat, but a thin veil of misty fog still obscured the vision past 1000 feet or so. The fuel truck had retired and Mr. Lindbergh's team—his mechanics, several of the Ryan people, Commander Byrd and a handful of other interested parties - now closed about him as the moment of his departure became imminent. Once the Wright was started, my role would officially be concluded, so I remained in the vicinity but did not invite myself to enter the press of people close to the pilot. From behind the barricades onlookers voiced expressions of healthy encouragement ("You can do it, son!" and "Go get 'em Lindy!"), for all the world the kinds of approving sentiments that American parents might bestow on teenage sons getting ready to engage in a game of football on a modest field somewhere deep in the heartland. It was a Friday morning, and for many of those clustered along the police perimeter, it seemed that the week-end had already begun. Instead of reporting to their places of work, one guessed that after Lindbergh's departure they might very well disperse to taverns or restaurants and pass the day toasting the aviator's continued progress. If unimpeded, he would make landfall in the great French capital on Saturday afternoon, New York time, a time of the week when his countrymen would be naturally disposed to celebration. If his progress, on the other hand, were cut short, the celebration might go on, but more with the character of an Irish wake.

As he moved towards the Ryan, he shook a few proffered hands as he went, one of the last of which was that of Commander Byrd himself. He squeezed into his wicker porch chair, and leaning out, gave a brief signal that indicated that the boys should twist the booster magneto while spinning the eight-foot light-weight steel propeller. This they proceeded to do, and our Wright came to life with a short cough and a comforting roar. While all but the essential personnel moved back out of the prop blast, I remained close by, knowing that our pilot would spend a few minutes scanning his instruments and determining the fitness of the engine to perform its upcoming task. After two or three minutes had passed with all of us caught in the grip of this timeless moment, one of the mechanics began making motions which seemed to be directed at me. I did not move forward until I was certain that this was the case. He gestured, indicating that I should approach the door on the right-hand side of the aircraft. Apparently Mr. Lindbergh desired to visit with me. I snatched off my hat and moved toward the Ryan, into the prop blast, up to the still-open door, face-to-face with the pilot, with our eyes at the same level. Reaching out, he directed my gaze to the one place which I might have expected, his tachometer, a round glass gauge set in the black plywood instrument panel which registered the engine's RPM's. Following his extended finger as it drew close to the face of this gauge, I immediately noted the nature of his concern. The quivering needle registered 1,470 RPM's, marginally less than the 1,500 required for flying performance. The heavy air was the culprit, and we both knew it. In fact, just the day prior I had discussed this topic briefly with one of the mechanics, correctly predicting that such an issue might materialize. "What's the solution if it does?" he had wanted to know.

"Run it in for a few minutes before you pull the chocks," I had told him. "Give it time to breathe properly."

"That's all it takes?"

"It might still be low when he starts to taxi, but when he needs his power, it'll be there."

Now, with Lindbergh's eyes on my face, I wondered briefly if our conversation had ever been relayed to him, as I would have hoped. Certainly this was not the time for that conversation. The engine noise precluded that.

Meeting the pilot's gaze, I realized that I needn't have worried. His was not a look of concern or confusion, just a calm assessment of a present reality which he had wanted to share with the one man who might have translated the information as an impediment to the impending take-off. I nodded reassuringly, and with my right hand raised and palm extended, I moved the hand in and out several times: *"Not unusual at all. Give it another moment or two, don't push it right away. It'll be fine."* With an even demeanor, he indicated with a brief thumbs-up gesture that he concurred with this interpretation. His mouth turned slightly at the corners as if he found satisfaction, and even a bit of good-natured humor in our exchange. Without thinking, I reached with my left hand and placed it on his upper shoulder, near the base of his neck, where I gave a brief comradely squeeze, which he acknowledged with an almost imperceptible dipping of his chin.

As I withdrew my hand, he turned and flashed me a glance, and in his eyes I read a story.

It was the summer that I was 11 years of age. We lived off Rangeline Road in Shelby County, and across the roadway from our old frame house, the wooded hills began. It was a boy's paradise. My pals and I would spend the long summer days traipsing about beneath the spreading oaks, elderberry, sumac, and hickory trees, particularly where they bordered our so- called "Indian Creek." It was a marvelous creek, some twenty to thirty feet wide. A succession of swimming holes had formed where the water was routed out of its course by an outcropping of boulders, resulting in pools of clear, cool water five or six feet deep. We knew every one of them within a two mile spread, and we also knew the best places to hang tires so that we could swing out over the bank and catapult ourselves through the air into the water. In our group there was one lad who was a natural leader, Pete Young was his name. He was a pusher of boundaries, a challenger of fate, and the most daring and inventive of all of us. He was the one who was always urging us to hang the tires a little higher, or seek out the uppermost limbs of a tree from which to jump, asking us to push the envelope of our God-given reticence when it came to feats of daring. On one particular occasion, we had come upon an arching hickory of majestic proportions, and with gusto we set out to scale its heights. Before long, however, Pete was the only one inclined to continue upward, while the rest of us settled on limbs consistent with our respective levels of comfort. I was closest to

Pete when he at last reached a limb that suited him, some ten feet above where I stood with one arm crooked around the trunk. "Charlie, come on up. Up here, pal. You got to see this." As convinced as I was that I had reached my own summit, there was something so earnest in his invitation that I found myself carefully negotiating the distance between us, my heart hammering in my chest. When at last I stood beside him on the outstretched limb, the view was one to snatch your breath away, which in my case didn't require much, since I was not in full possession of it at the time. I looked over at Pete, whose gaze was focused on the creek below, and it occurred to me that he was contemplating a leap. From the perspective of an 11-year-old, the sun-flecked waters seemed a hundred feet below. More likely they were half of that, or less, but even so, such a leap was ten or fifteen feet higher than any we had made all summer. "Petey, you're not gonna jump, are ya?"

"Sure," he said, natural as all that. "Why not?"

"It's awful far, pal. Maybe the water ain't deep enough."

"Sure it is. I can see the bottom from here."

"I know. That's what I mean." I thought this was a rather telling point, and for a long moment as we stood there together, me on the inboard side clutching the trunk, and Pete to the outside of me, steadying himself with one hand clutching a smaller limb, I decided that he was coming back to his senses, returning to the world of the known, of the proven, of the trusted. I chanced to look over at him then and saw that I was mistaken. He flashed me a peculiar look which I have never forgotten, wild and triumphant, and yet oddly confessional, a glance which seemed to implicate me in his endeavor in some curiously personal way, as though he was both relying upon me and holding me accountable. He then hurled himself from the limb.

Now, some 15 years later, I had seen that look again.

I retreated from the Ryan out of the prop blast to wait with the others. After another minute or so, we could see Lindbergh pull the safety strap around his waist and buckle it. He stuffed cotton wadding into his ears, pulled his leather, wool-lined helmet over his head, and buckled it under his chin. A moment later his eyes were hidden from us as he tugged down his flying goggles. The two mechanics pressed in close, and then withdrew. One of them closed the door and leaned his shoulder against it while the pilot secured it from the inside. The two men then snatched away the blocks from the wheels. Lindbergh eased the throttle open.

Having lived through the dawn of aviation into the jet age, as a passenger I still find myself suspended in that mystical moment at the beginning of the takeoff roll, when the pilots open the throttles and place themselves and all the rest of us aboard entirely in the hands of the jet engines. When the powerplants begin to shriek, all pretense of control disappears, all restraints are removed and the aircraft is given open license to gather speed—as much speed as will be needed to "break the surly bonds of Earth." At Roosevelt Field on that long-ago morning, however, there was no such instant exhilaration, but rather a sense of holding one's breath, perhaps uttering a silent entreaty. The muck and the mire seemed to have no intention of releasing the Ryan. As the Whirlwind reached a smoother and higher pitch, a number of us surged forward and placed ourselves at the wing struts, perhaps two or three men on either side. We leaned urgently into the load as though trying to free a wayward auto from the grasp of a roadside ditch. It couldn't have been long before the power of the prop wash and the flying gobs of mud, along with the gathering progress of the Ryan, drove us from our task and we stood, winded and helpless, as the silver machine and her lone occupant fishtailed away from us towards the misty horizon.

I have discovered over the years that few people realize that the Ryan was a purpose-built aircraft. She was built not for speed, certainly not for comfort, but to reliably cover great distances, which meant that her wingspan far exceeded the length of the body itself, (the former being 49 feet, the latter just 27.) As she distanced herself from us, I found myself watching those wings, looking for any indication that the load was being shifted from the wheels to their broad and reliable surfaces. The further they traveled, the less realistic the whole venture seemed, as the sound of the Wright became tinny and distant and the aircraft itself became hopelessly merged with the overreaching sky. Still, we watched and waited. At one point the craft seemed to nimbly leave the ground, only to return with a breathless skip. By now he had gone past the point where he could abort the effort, and we watched in suspended animation as the Ryan skipped again. Then it was airborne at last, low and level, lifting all that weight (fuel accounted for slightly more than half of the craft's total take-off weight) up from the earth. In a serendipitous moment, the gloom in the skies seemed to retreat and afford us all a clear view of those broad wings passing above the wires practically a mile away. We seemed to be holding our collective breath as we listened to the rapidly diminishing sound of the Wright, which lingered even after we could no longer discern the form of the airplane itself. In the end, for the many fervent hopes which we all, onlookers and participants, had invested in this man and this moment, I don't think any of us were really ready to let him go. Perhaps we sensed how empty our lives might become in his absence.

Charles P. Broadbent
St. Louis Missouri, 1977

OUT WITH THE DAGO

Let me tell you what. Normally I didn't pal around much with The Dago. I mean, who did? The Daig was the Daig, he came and he went, and if the sun was to shine on you for a while, you enjoyed it for the moment, and when the Daig left the room, he took the sun with him, and there was no doubt it was gone, and it wouldn't be back before he was.

This was '39, understand. We were on our way to three in a row. This is the Daig's fourth year in the bigs and he's already got three World Series rings. New York, right? You think the sun don't rise and set on the Daig, you got another think comin.' Me, I'm not even a starter, I'm a utility infielder, but with a name like Gimignano, as far as the Daig's concerned, I might be okay. After that day in Detroit, he made up his mind.

It's a doubleheader. First part of September. The Tigers are making a run at us, you could always count on the Tigers to make a run. And like with anybody who makes a run, we take it personal. The first game, I don't play. Detroit wins, squeeze bunt, seventh inning. Second game, I start at shortstop for Frankie Crosetti, who's hampered by a knee that he had injured in a collision the week before. Don't think being a utility player means I can't play. If you're with the Yankees, you can play, pal, even if you have to ride the pine for long stretches. So I play. I get a couple hits. Make a couple nice plays at second. Daig hits a solo shot in the second, then triples home a couple runs in the seventh. He's playing Dago baseball, which means that he intends to personally insure that the Tigers are beaten, and no matter how much they love their Tigers, there's not a single person in Briggs Stadium who isn't getting the message.

It comes down to the ninth, and we're up four-three. The Tigers got runners at the corners with two out. Jack Grout hits one in the hole all the way to the grass. I make the stop going to my right. I can see the lead runner breaking for home, but Grout is no speed merchant, and there's no doubt in my mind I'm going to first. Still, I'm deep in the hole and it's no sure thing. I gun the hell out of it, and the ball gets there on a hop. To be honest, the call could go either way. If we get the call, game over. If the Tigers get the call, they tie the game and put the winning run on second.

Well, the way it goes, we get the call. Game over.

The Daig passes me on the way in, head down as always, toes pointing straight ahead. Taking care of business. Back in the clubhouse, the boys are loose, tomorrow we close out our stay in Detroit with a late game back at Briggs. The place clears out pretty quick. We've got lots of friends in Detroit, everybody has someplace to go. For some reason, I take my time. Some of the writers stop by, want to talk. "Whyn't you just go home with it?" they want to know. In other words, give up the infield hit, hold the lead runner, but give the Tigers another at-bat. "I wanted to end it," is all I can think to tell them. Out of the corner of my eye, I catch an expression from the Daig, tells me that he would've said and done the same thing under the circumstances. He's pleased that I think like him.

Anybody knows the Daig knows that he is always the last one out of the clubhouse. Besides him, there are only a couple of us left by the time I'm ready to go. "Hey kid." He calls me from the stool in front of his locker. He's already dressed, dark blue suit, white shirt, tie. Except he hasn't put his suit coat on yet, he's just sitting there smoking, holding his ever-lovin' cuppa java. "Hey kid."

"Hey, Daig."

"Let's go grab a bite, you and me."

"Sure, Daig." Even if I were on the way to my mom's funeral or I had Hedy Lamarr waiting outside in a taxi, the answer would've been the same. When the Dago calls, you answer in the affirmative. Period.

We hit the avenue and take a cab to Ciro's, which is a small Italian joint off Sandusky Avenue. The owner is evidently a good friend of the Daig's, 'cause we never see a menu, we never see a bill, the food and drinks arrive at the table the same way they would if you were sitting in your own house. There's a nice dinner crowd in the place, but we're set up in what I guess you would call an alcove. It isn't like we're hidden or anything, but nobody comes up to the table just out of the blue. I think they look for the high sign from the owner that it'll be all right, and then they come, very polite, quiet like, paying respects. You can see it in their eyes, they're almost all of dago origin, and while the Daig is one of them, he's also beyond them, he moves in a different world. It makes a deep impression on me, much more than say a wild mob pushing and shoving for autographs. They want nothing from the Daig, he's already given them more than they could have wished for. They come to the table almost out of gratitude, like they were going to mass or something. I'll never forget it.

We eat good: wop salad, then pasta dishes with wonderful sauces, and some veal as I recall. And we drink, highballs to start with, red wine with the meal, and more highballs afterwards. Daig don't talk much. A little baseball. Tells me how he views a couple of players on other clubs. He don't say nothing about anybody on our club, that's the Daig's way. He'll never be caught in a run-down between clubhouse cliques. He stands alone, it will always be that way. We talk hitting, and if you spent just a few hours with the Daig, and you could remember what he said, you could probably write the definitive book on hitting. Provided it was okay with the Daig, of course. Otherwise, he'll carry it to the grave with him, and I doubt any living mortal will ever be able to recapture that kind of understanding about the science of hitting a baseball. But mostly, he's not thinking much about baseball, and the more highballs we pour, the more it's obvious the Daig's mind is wandering, and you don't have to be a mind reader to figure out where it's going.

By the time we leave Ciro's it's after eleven, which feels like a lot later in Detroit than it does in New York. We don't need no cab, there's a big black Buick waiting for us on the curb, courtesy of the management, I suppose. We pile in. Understand, when you start the evening with the Daig, you're on his program for as long as it lasts, no questions asked. It ends when the Daig says it ends. "Let's see if we can't find some company," Daig says to nobody in particular, but I guess the driver already has his instructions, and off we go in the direction of Hightower Avenue, which was all private residences at one time, but it's no secret that during Prohibition a number of these residences were converted into private clubs—the kind of places where, if he knows a few people and can be counted on to behave himself in polite company, a man may be pleasurably entertained right through until daylight. Or at least as long as his cash holds up and he don't wear out his welcome with the house staff. I had been to clubs like this on just a few occasions, but since getting married a couple of years earlier, I had cut back on my carousing, so to speak. Still, my wife is long gone now, and so is the Daig, and I see no shame in relating the harmless events of a long ago evening that had such a impact on a young ballplayer. So to relate.

The lady of the house, as it were, meets us at the door, and it's clear that this is another joint where a visit from the Daig is considered somewhat of an honor. Although, unlike some establishments, it's strictly a cash business, honor or no. But the Daig lights up the place, he really does, and as we're ushered into the main salon, it seems like every girl in the joint comes out to greet us. Let me tell you what, the Daig brings out the best in the ladies, even the ones who know he's not likely to date them. I been around enough of the ladies to understand that they're working girls by and large, punching a clock, making bank deposits, catching colds, going to the seashore, taking care of their mothers, and in some cases their children. The blush of innocence, shall we say, has long since worn off. But when the Dago stops in, they become the girlish romantics that men want to believe they are. They flirt, they become coquettish, they turn up their headlights. The lady of the house parks us on a big overstuffed couch and brings us a bottle and a coupla glasses. I'm 22 years old at this time, and Daig is about 25, and we are living the life of kings strictly because of our abilities in hitting and catching the old horsehide. I remember having this thought at the time. I'm not big on nostalgia, and it didn't last long, but it was there.

We're pouring drinks and horsing around. The Daig has evidently given one of the girls the eye, because she comes over and sits on his lap. She's cute as hell. Got a little bob cut, nice lips, real smooth skin, along with a laugh that makes you feel good all over. The two seem awfully familiar right off the bat, and it occurs to me that maybe the Daig has dated her before. "Kid, pick one you like," Daig tells me, and I realize that now he's got his date, the other girls will be getting back to work, and I'd better choose one before I'm stuck with the left-overs. I've been eyeballing a gal that's got a kind of a Carole Lombard look about her, which is pretty popular at that time. So I give her the high sign, she comes over. "Let me buy you a drink," I tell her, and she says "That'll be great." She doesn't plop down on my lap right away or anything like that, I guess I'm not a lap-plopping kind of guy. "Why don't we go someplace quiet?" she says, and as we leave the room, I catch her looking back at the Daig and the girl on his lap. Kind of makes me feel bad for a moment there, but when we get to her room, she makes it up to me pretty good, and that's as far as I go with that part of the story.

It was maybe an hour and a half later, and when she's satisfied that I'm satisfied, she says "Be a sweetie, and leave a girl alone so she can put herself back together, won't ya?" I say "Sure enough, doll," and I get dressed and make my way downstairs and back into the living room, or main salon, whatever you would call it. It's now about two in the morning and the place has quieted down considerably. One or two ladies pass through with gentlemen callers, but they don't pay any attention to me. I go to the sideboard, pour myself a stiff one, sit down to sip it, and I guess I fall asleep right there on the divan. It's something between a catnap and solid slumber, 'cause I don't know anything until I wake up to the sound of a man and a woman together. I mean, *being* together. I look up, and there across from me is the Daig, right back in the chair where he began the evening, and on his lap he's got my Carole

Lombard. Carole's got her dress hiked up and she's facing him, and the Daig is, as the sportswriters used to say, joltin' her real good. His hair is mussed and his tie is missing, but he has his white shirt and dark trousers on, along with his shoes and socks, almost as if he was about to walk out of the door and Carole changed his mind at the last minute. And the Daig has a look on his face, I've never for one minute forgotten it. Don't even ask me to describe it. It's just a look. He's facing Carole, but honest to God, I doubt it made any difference, I don't think he even seen her. His eyes are open all right, but he's seeing something else. Maybe a Bob Feller fastball up in the zone. Understand, the Daig always thought Feller was overrated. He was a darling of the sportswriters, and Daig always went out of his way to get to Feller, rough him up the best he could. Well, my Carole, bless her heart, I never seen her face, but she was gettin' quite a ride out of the Daig, and no complaints. I lay real quiet and just let them have at it, and when he was done, he was done. Carole wanted him to go a little more, but that was all she wrote. He had Carole off him in no time at all, never looked at her again. I often wondered if Daig planned it that way. I mean, to end up with the girl I had dated, and to give her the jolt right in front of me. Of course, it was never mentioned again, but over the years I've come to conclude that that's exactly the way he planned it.

"Hey kid," he says, like he knows I'm awake and watching. "Hey kid, let's catch some coffee at the hotel, whattaya say?" He's pulling on his tie as he speaks.

"Sounds good, Daig," I say, and I'm as good as ready to roll. Once we're out on the front steps, we start walkin', lookin for a cab.

"This afternoon we got Auker," he says to me. Meaning the Detroit rightie Elden Auker, a real Yankee nemisis. "Something tells me we're gonna ring 'im up real good." He pauses to light a cigarette, and squints at me across the match, but I don't say nothin', and we walk some more until the cab comes.

Vincent Gimignano
Cleveland, Ohio, 2002

THE NAVY JOB

For fifty years now, I haven't spoken of this. Except to my wife, who understood it because she had been there at the time. She's gone now. After forty six years of married life together she departed suddenly. An embolism. The doctors had assured us that her frequent headaches were the result of an allergy. (We should've been wary of that diagnosis. Not many people in these so-called Florida "retirement communities" suffer from allergies. They're legally banned. The allergies, I mean.) But with Carolyn gone, I feel the need to tell this story just once before I too join the long parade of souls who have found their rest (or whatever they find) on the far side of that dark river.

I was twelve the summer I first fell in love. The year was 1935. The place was New York City. It wasn't a girl. It was a ship.

Twelve is a typical age to hold a crush, and New York offered plenty of opportunities. But the object of my affections set me apart somewhat from my peers. It wasn't Joe DiMaggio. It wasn't Fiorello

LaGuardia. It wasn't either of those sexy sirens of the silver screen, Lombard or Harlow (who anyway had died suddenly the previous summer and broken innumerable young hearts in the process.)

No, my first love was actually from France. I had heard she was on her way to New York. Who hadn't? They said later that as many as a quarter million New Yorkers turned out for the occasion of her arrival. I know I was one of them. And if you knew anything about me at all, you would know that wasn't unusual in the least.

This first romance of mine occurred on account of my father. He had emigrated from Russia in 1914, and became a longshoreman who spent his entire working life on the docks at the Port of New York. He had, as many before and after, arrived by ship and been processed through that great palace on the water called the Ellis Island Immigrant Inspection Station. (By the time it was closed in 1954, some 12 million persons had passed through its cavernous interiors). Although he would later become as he put it "a regular fellow" on the Hudson River docks from which the great liners of the day came and went, on the day of his arrival he would not be afforded the honor of setting foot on those hallowed grounds. As was the custom, just after passing abreast of the Statue of Liberty, the German liner *President Lincoln* lay to while tenders clustered alongside to receive my father and his fellow 2,100 steerage mates, ferrying them across the water to "Heartbreak Island," where they entered the great maw of American officialdom which would determine their fates. Across the water they could see the gleaming spires of lower

Manhattan heralding promises which they were not yet qualified to embrace. The *President Lincoln* then proceeded up the Hudson to discharge her first and second (or cabin) class passengers at those portals of privilege.

My father bore no malice for this rude arrival. Later, secure in his profession, with his growing family safely ensconced in the upper half of a small brownstone at 34th St. and First Avenue in a patchwork neighborhood that was notoriously known as "Hell's Kitchen," he took great pleasure in being one of the chosen few who welcomed the great liners arriving from the Old World. He and his fellow union members wrestled their mooring lines over the bollards of the wharves and rolled out the covered gangplanks across which the passengers made their way out of the innards of the great ships that had plied their way across 1,800 miles of one of the most unforgiving maritime environments on earth, the North Atlantic Ocean. Because our neighborhood was so rife with opportunities for mischief, and associations with young men for whom mischief was to become a profession, my father wisely directed my attention to the other side of Manhattan, and encouraged me to spend my weekends and free time near the docks where he plied his trade.

I had just turned 12 that spring, and my mother now permitted me to take the cross-town bus on my own. The docks along Manhattan's west side jutted out into the Hudson River, and the ones I liked to patrol extended from 61st street down to about 22nd street, meaning that, unless it was a weekend and I planned to make a long day of it, I had to pick and choose my targets. Forty blocks was quite a hike, after all. But the *Herald* published a complete shipping manifest every Saturday, and I usually knew which "ocean queen" I was looking for, and where to find her. In the case of the marquee ships, those which had captured the popular fancy, there would often be stories accompanying their comings and goings, with particular attention paid to their star-studded passenger lists. They almost never failed to make mention of certain of their on-board luxuries, their astounding speed, or the safety aspects about which the public was always curious. One ship that I never got to see, to my regret, was the *President Lincoln*, that faithful workhorse which had conveyed my father to the New World twenty-one years earlier. She had been confiscated by the United States during the Great War and sunk by German torpedoes off the coast of France in 1918.

My father's selection of a pastime for me had been an inspired choice. Large ships possess a certain sort of mystical power, with their great bulk overwhelming the senses, and their long, regular lines teasing the eye as they extend hundreds of feet out into the river. The fact that they were built to challenge the ocean itself only added to their allure. The briny, hemp-laden smells that came from them teased my nostrils with hints of foreign shores, and I would sit for hours lost in a young man's reverie. After a time I began carrying a sketch pad with me, and later, on my 14th birthday, my parents presented me with a Brownie Box camera. It had a small faux-leather strap and a baked-on black finish, and with it I began keeping photographic records of my sightings. Occasionally my father and I would arrange to meet for a quick workingman's lunch and he would want to know, "Who did you see today?"

"The *Ile de France* is down at Pier 44," I would report. "Right next to her is the *Mauretania*." Spotting the Cunard line's *Mauretania* was always a special treat. The venerable Cunard liner had, after all, held the Blue Ribband, signifying the fastest Atlantic crossing, for an unprecedented 20 years, longer than any other vessel. She was one of the bona fide "superstars" in an era of magnificent ships, and an ideal creation to stir the imagination of a young boy.

"If I'm not mistaken, the *Rex* is also in. Italian Line, you know." My father dipped his large, stout fingers into his beat-up lunchbox and pulled out two plump Gherkins in waxed paper. He handed one over to me.

"I know. Pier 54. I like the *Rex* fine, but I've never really gone out of my way just to see her." The Italian liner, the current holder of the Blue Ribband, was a handsome vessel, among the largest afloat, but she somehow didn't fit my eye quite like the English or German liners. The English ships were identifiable by their upright, classical lines, while the Germans had a sleekness about them that was almost sinister. "I'm really looking forward to seeing *Bremen*. She's due in tomorrow. I didn't get much of a look at her the last time she was in." The German liner, a former Blue Ribband holder herself, was the sleekest of the lot and fit my eye like no other. Besides my sketches and photographs, I developed tactics I would use to try to capture and retain the forms of these great ships in my mind's eye. I would look away from the form of the vessel, and then, quite suddenly, look back, and let the impression fill my eye with a suddenness that was breathtaking. Or I would turn my back to them, bend down, and peer upside down from between my legs, trying to gain an appreciation of the scope and size of them from this perspective. As the newspapers were constantly reminding us, they were "the largest moving objects ever built by man."

My father had explained to me how the transatlantic passenger trade changed after the immigration laws of the Twenties began to restrict the flow of human traffic from Europe to the United States. That, plus the Depression, had altered life on the docks where he worked. The heyday of the great liners was seriously curtailed. Many of the larger ships (the *Imperator*, the *Leviathan*, the *Paris*, the *Homeric*, the *Berengaria*) began losing vast sums of money for their owners, and were either retired or sent on weekend "booze cruises" to Miami or the Bahama islands. With the sharp decline in immigrant trade, steerage class was phased out (safe to say, nobody missed it), and replaced by third class, or "tourist" class. The frequency of sailings was reduced and much of the allure that had attended the comings and goings of the liners was lost, although not to me. The absence of movie stars, heads of state, famed authors or socialites embarking or debarking in no way detracted from the powerful appeal of the New York waterfront docks for me during the early Thirties. If I wanted a reminder of the glory days, I had only to look across the river to Hoboken, where the giant form of the *Leviathan* (launched as the *Vaterland*) jutted out twenty feet past the pier into the river. At the time she was launched in 1914, she had been the largest and finest vessel afloat, and now, after a career marked by odd incidents and a steady loss of revenue, she was, like the golden era she had come to represent, shelved almost as an afterthought. And she was still the largest vessel afloat.

However, as the end of my school term approached in 1935, the woes of the *Leviathan* were scarcely on my mind. From across the seas a steady drumbeat of excited press clippings was heralding the advent of a new and even greater era in the Atlantic maritime trade. Or, if not a greater era, certainly greater ships. With the Italians and the Germans busily gearing up their war machines, it fell to the English and the French to make one more effort to capture the public imagination and corral the remaining passenger trade by launching ships of which the size, speed, and appointments represented new heights of engineering accomplishment. The French Line had actually launched their entry some three years earlier, but in the depths of the Depression, with passenger trade at a thirty-year low, they were in no great hurry to get her fitted out and embarked on a regular sailing schedule. Her name was *Normandie*, and the titillating bits and pieces of information that were floated our way left no doubt that she was going to be a ship to be reckoned with in so many ways. At 1029 feet in length with triple expansion steam turbines geared to four propellers, she was not only the largest vessel ever floated, but with a revolutionary new hull design, her builders assured that she was going to be the fastest as well. Her propellers were 16 feet in diameter and weighed 23 tons apiece. She had 1100 telephones and 32 ovens capable of roasting 768 chickens at a time. On her maiden voyage she would be carrying $29 million in gold as part of the flight from the Franc. She was, we were breathlessly informed, watched by 50,000 spectators as she cleared the harbor in Le Havre on her maiden voyage. On May 31 big news was cabled from the vessel at sea· during her first 24 hours she had completed a run of 744 nautical miles at an average speed of 29.76 knots, setting a new world record. The *Rex* would clearly be yielding up the Blue Ribband soon.

Much ado was also made as to the stupendous luxury of her appointments, but that was a point that did not impress my father in the least. "A great lady she may be, but who can afford to sail in her?" he asked rhetorically. "She'll soon wind up just like that former queen of the seas over there in Hoboken," he darkly predicted, with a nod in the direction of the *Leviathan*. Who could have imagined how soon his dire prediction would be borne out?

"Still, I'm looking forward to seeing her, Pops," I told him. "Things have been pretty quiet around here."

"You'll see her soon enough."

She had sailed from Le Havre on the 27th of May with great fanfare, and after a brief stop in Southampton, pointed her bows westward. The timing couldn't have been better. Our last day of classes at PS 44 was Thursday the 30th. Her scheduled arrival in New York harbor was Monday, June 3rd. I wouldn't even have to cut classes to be there when she arrived. I had petitioned my parents to let me purchase a ticket aboard one of the large Hudson River excursion boats, perhaps the *Bear Mountain* or the *City of Keansburg*, which would be greeting her in the Upper Bay near the Statue of Liberty upon her arrival, but my mother vetoed the idea. "Alex, they'll be full of hooligans and drunkards," she said. "You just get down there early and find yourself a good spot near the pier. And mind your wallet." My father didn't know where he'd be that day (longshoremen always reported to the union hall before dawn and were randomly dispatched to jobs all along the waterfront). As usual, I'd be on my own. The night before *Normandie*'s arrival, such was the throb of anticipation running through my veins that I could scarcely sleep

As it developed, the perfect day I had envisioned was almost ruined. My mother awoke me from a sound slumber to report that the kitchen sink had developed a serious leak, and that I must track down the plumber and bring him to the house "before the floor is a ruin." Cursing under my breath, I visited our plumber's usual haunts before rounding him up and getting him to the house. By then it was after 9:00 AM. At this advanced hour the cross-town buses were already experiencing the backup of a population that was heading west in large numbers to greet the French behemoth. In fact, the traffic was so snarled that I leaped down and raced the last three blocks on foot, arriving under the big Picard Motors sign at half past ten. I made my way through a crowd that was already shoulder-to-shoulder. Looking up, I experienced the very real sensation of my heart catching in my throat, something that I'll venture is not a common occurrence for a sophisticated 12 year old New Yorker.

The *Normandie* had already arrived, or very nearly so. Over the years New York tugboat captains had mastered the art of coaxing extremely large vessels into comparatively narrow slips between piers. To accomplish this, they used the pier as a fulcrum. Positioning the ship against the corner of the pier about halfway down her length (putting her "on the knuckle" they called it) they then applied the force of their tugs against her bow and leveraged the giant into her designated berthing place. It was a careful and deliberate process during which the ship was essentially passive and looming, her mighty engines still. This was the state the French liner was in when I caught my first glimpse of her. Understand, I was no novice to great ships, my sketchbook had pages of them, as did my photo album. I knew the classic lines of the *Aquitania*, the mighty bulk of the *Leviathan*, the elegance of the *Ile de France*, the racy profiles of the sister ships *Bremen* and *Europa*. But *Normandie* was something different. It wasn't just her size, I knew, although as I stood watching her great black hull trimmed in white I couldn't help but recall once more the overworked catchphrase "largest moving object ever built by man." There was something else, something which I could not initially identify. What I did know was that she filled every crevice of my active imagination. When she sounded her horn to signal "finished with engines," the deep, sonorous bellow reverberated deliciously through every cavern of my being. At the age of 12, my mind could not have accommodated any earthly sight more magnificent or more fulfilling than the newly arrived liner as she was eased into place alongside Pier 88, her great flared bow looming above the gathered multitude like some kind of prophecy.

It turned out to be a prophecy, all right. But God knows it wasn't the one we had in mind.

Normandie's turn-around time in New York on her maiden voyage was four days, and the French Line made the most of it. The ship was opened for 40-minute tours, and at 50 cents a pop nearly 10,000 people took the opportunity. There were lavish dinner-dances aboard for the swells on one or two nights, and the New York dailies exhausted every superlative in their lavishly illustrated extra editions dedicated to the great ship. It was reported that over 30,000 souls had crowded into the Battery during her arrival, with as many as 180,000 New Yorkers jostling for a glimpse during her time in port. For my part, I hung back, waiting until we could be alone together. I had lingered to contemplate her majesty and study her appeal for the better part of the day on that Monday, but yielding to the wild acclaim the ship was generating, I was content to let her slip away without another visit from me. Her regular schedule would put her in New York twice a month for the foreseeable future. I would be patient, nurture my passion, and led the tides bring her back to me all in good time.

By reading the popular accounts of the ship and by studying her on her visits, in time I came to understand what set her apart from the many other liners which had preceded her. Her builders had set out to create a ship that would stand clearly apart from her contemporaries, not only in terms of performance, but in terms of science, and of art. They had eliminated the traditional forward mast and installed a revolutionary new breakwater so that her foredeck presented a clean line and a sensuous curve that were pleasing to the eye, even for those unfamiliar with maritime architecture. The shape, angle of incline, and descending heights of her three massive stacks were likewise the product of deliberate calculation, as much *objects d'art* as any of her interior fittings. She was one of the very few liners ever built that included the extremely costly feature of a "split uptake." This meant that rather than being channeled directly upward in a large central shaft, the gases from her boilers were divided in half and routed through smaller uptakes on either side of the vessel, accounting for the peculiar angled base around her stacks. More importantly, by creating these uninterrupted central spaces the builders were able to install some of the largest and grandest rooms that ever went to sea. Her first class dining room alone was a staggering 305 feet long, 46 feet across, and three decks high—practically large enough to contain an entire transatlantic vessel of an earlier era.

In terms of her fire control system, electric turbines, kitchen service, elevators, rudimentary radar, telephones, air conditioning, raked clipper bow and gracefully angled stern, she represented a great leap forward in the technology of transatlantic travel. Appointed throughout by the most glorious art that could by produced by France's sculptors, painters, and artisans, she was not only a revolutionary creation, but was an expression of seagoing mastery that would never be equaled. Looking back, I believe much of her dramatic impact on the public came from the fact that in the midst of the Depression she made it clear that mankind's history of magnificent achievement had not yet run its course. She represented a future that held out more hope than any of us had been feeling up to that time.

Oh, and of course she lifted the Blue Ribband from the *Rex* on that first voyage, making the crossing in four days, eight hours, twenty six minutes at an average speed of 29.76 knots. On her return voyage she broke her own record: four days, three hours, 28 minutes, averaging 30.31 knots. Her triumph in that summer of '35 was as complete as any her proud builders could have imagined.

Our story moves along, gathering pace. My approaching high school career began to absorb more of my attentions as the gathering clouds of war in Europe began to overshadow any sense of peace. In Spain, Civil War broke out, and my parents spent long evenings discussing overseas events with other Russian émigrés. On the surface, the Spanish conflict was between the government and a group of disloyal Army officers. But with Hitler supporting the officers, and Stalin sending aid to the government, the scenario was widely regarding as a "dress rehearsal" for the wider conflict that was certain to follow, and peoples' loyalties were already being tested. Meanwhile, I was a dutiful but uninspired student. Though recognized by my schoolmates as the fellow who was practically an expert on ships, none shared my passion. My affair with *Normandie* was still one of lonely intimacy, just the two of us. There never was that moment of "alone together," since there was never a time when she was not being observed by scores or even hundreds of New Yorkers, either standing at the entrance to Pier 88, or driving by on the newly-completed West Side Drive, an elevated motorway that, if anything, made competition for viewing even more fierce. Like me, many of these other observers might have been deeply enamored of *Normandie*, although I considered that in their cases it was more likely a case of mere infatuation. Soon, however, my heart would be exposed to intimacy of another fashion.

In the autumn of 1938, as a result of their shared interest in a certain butcher ship on 32nd street, my mother made the acquaintance of a certain Mrs. Zull, another Ukranian immigrant. One blustery October day she invited Mrs. Zull home for a chat over a steaming samovar of black tea. The dear lady chanced to spot one of my sketch pads lying about and at my mother's invitation, perused it. What she saw there that prompted her I never found out, but she determined that her eldest daughter, for whom she had such high hopes (and what parent from the Ukraine does not?), should meet my mother's son, "such a serious young man." Thus a family outing was arranged. We picnicked at Stuyvesant Square as I recall, ending at our house for tea and biscuits. Carolyn was the daughter's name, and she was, in the popular parlance of the day, "a raven-haired beauty" with wide-set green eyes, an upturned nose, and wonderfully formed, marvelously expressive lips—quite a ways out of my league, I thought. My sketch pads again became the focus of attention (her mother made sure of that), and before the afternoon was over Mrs. Zull had cajoled me into agreeing to take her daughter along on one of my excursions to the West Side. I couldn't tell whether Carolyn shared her enthusiasm for the idea, and for my own protection, I decided that she did not, and promptly put the suggestion out of my mind.

Carolyn's mother was not so easily deterred, however, and made arrangements with my mother to see that the excursion went off as planned. Once it did, another followed and then another. Wonder of wonders, this magnificent girl seemed to find something of the same comforts in the open spaces, the briny smells, and the sight of the great liners that I did. As we walked she listened attentively to my explanations of the ships and the perils that they faced. On the bus rides to and fro, she inclined herself towards me so that our shoulders snuggled together, delighting our souls with every lurch and roll of those belching buses. It wasn't until our third or fourth excursion together that an opportunity to view *Normandie* was on the schedule. For some reason, I had a certain trepidation at bringing the two of them into one another's presence. I needn't have worried.

"Oh, Alex, she's an absolute marvel."

"A marvel is she? And how do you know such a thing?" I teased.

"I mean, just look at her. She doesn't look all careworn like the others. Nor fussy. Nor serious . . . ." (Here she made her voice low and dramatic, miming the concept.)

"How then? How does she look?"

"She looks . . ." Carolyn started, and then turned to take in the great resting bulk of the French liner. "She looks like she understands the terrible business of the sea but is completely confident of her abilities regardless. She trusts herself."

It was a seminal moment. From that day forward the so-called expert on ships never looked at ships, or at girls, in the same light again.

In November of that same year, the much-heralded British entry into the high-stakes world of superliners arrived on her maiden voyage, and occupied the slip next to the *Normandie*. The *Queen Mary* was very nearly the equal of my *Normandie* in size, and wrested the Blue Riband away from her on her first outing, by a mere half-a-knot, no less. I later discovered that because of the revolutionary design of her hull, *Normandie* managed essentially the same speed as the *Queen Mary* although her engines generated 40,000 HP less than the Cunarder. No matter. With the two ships side-by-side, one could measure their attributes at a glance, and though there were many who came to love the British liner's elegantly conservative lines, there were none who ever suggested that she could supplant the *Normandie* as the undisputed queen of the Atlantic. I quote here from a maritime writer for the *New York Herald* who took the measure of the two vessels after the *Mary's* arrival: *"The Normandie seems racier, more chic — a Parissiene, youthful, confident that no one on the world is clad more smartly than she. The British ship has the smartness of conservatism, the temperament of Bond Street rather than the Boulevards. Between stem and stern the Normandie is of almost frightening sheerness, with long darting lines unbroken by a single ventilator or cargo winch. The Queen Mary, less audacious, derives her beauty from simplicity and proportion."*

My 16-year old sentiments exactly.

And now, early in the New Year, the year in which the world war erupted at last, there occurred one more signal event in my world, and, like my romance with Carolyn, it originated in our own living room. I arrived home from my late shift as a stock boy and order-deliverer for Young's Delicatessen on 32nd Street (a part-time job after class and on weekends) and was by greeted by a formally set table and my parents dressed as smartly as their budget and fashion sense would allow. "A very wonderful guest for dinner, Alex," my father explained. "Go clean up right away."

He wasn't exaggerating. During his shift that day my father had worked at Pier 88, and though the *Normandie* wasn't in port, he chanced to hear some Russian being spoken between two "important-looking fellows" and did not hesitate to introduce himself. (Understand that my father was slow to acknowledge class distinctions, and as a proud longshoreman considered himself the equal of any downtown swells, particularly if they were invading his turf and were his countrymen to boot.) In this case, one of the two men was a certain Vladimir Yourkevitch, who had introduced himself to my father as a "maritime building contractor—actually a designer of ships." This of course occasioned a longer conversation as my father proudly explained his son's self-taught expertise in maritime matters and his fascination with the *Normandie* in particular. Then Mr. Yourkevitch spilled his secret, one which my father would not reveal to me until our guest was on the premises, at which time he might reveal it himself.

"Let me guess: he's planning another Russian revolution and he wants to make you the new President," I joked.

"And your mother would then have her own dacha near St. Petersburg," my father agreed.

Vladimir Ivanov soon made his appearance, and I was intrigued from the moment he stepped into our home. A man of about forty years of age at that time, he had handsome, regular features and a serious mein about him. With his loosely knotted tie, his rumpled tweed coat and the small mustache that accented his upper lip he had the distinguished and disheveled air of a scholar or a scientist. After they greeted one another in the old tongue, Mr. Yourkevitch presented my mother with a fine bottle of Russian brandy and henceforth spoke only in faintly accented English, a transition which my father was pleased to accommodate.

As it developed, Mr. Yourkevitch had managed his own version of a Russian Revolution, but it had very little to do with matters of state.

"My father tells me you are a political man," I ventured somewhat impatiently as we consumed the tender brisket prepared by my mother.

"No more so than any other," he replied, warming to the game of revealing himself one layer at a time.

"Then you are a building contractor, then?" I confess I was growing weary of being treated as a child trying to guess at a forthcoming gift.

"In a sense. I am actually a designer of ships. I understand that you have quite an interest in ships."

"Have you designed any ships that I might have heard of?"

"Perhaps. One of the ships I designed makes frequent visits to your city. Your father, in fact, has assured me that you have seen her. On numerous occasions." He shot a sly glance at my father and in an instant the enormity of his "secret" struck me.

"But I thought that *Normandie* was designed by the French!"

"Only that part which doesn't touch the water," he laughed.

As the dinner progressed, I pried the astounding highlights of Mr. Yourkevitch's life out of him. A graduate of St. Petersburg Polytechnic Institute, as a marine architect Vladimir Ivanov had designed submarines and dreadnoughts for the Czar himself before the country's turning fortunes chased him to Turkey in 1920. There he worked for a time as a stevedore before immigrating to France. Over a period of some five years of testing, he had produced a radical new hull design which he offered to the

English (it would have been applied to the *Queen Mary*) and being rejected, he presented it to the French. It became the template for the *Normandie*. Her bulbous stem, her clipper bow, her whaleback foredeck, the overhanging counter of her stern, and the underwater form of the hull that produced the greatest efficiency of motion ever seen in a ocean-going vessel were all products of the mind of a man who now sat across the table from me in our humble Hell's Kitchen abode. He had found his way to New York only the year before, and now forty-two ships had been built or reconstructed using his hull design.

We talked late into the evening, and the great man was able to finally take his leave only by the direct intervention of my father. But not before vowing that on one of the *Normandie*'s next visits, we would all dine aboard as his guests.

"May I bring my girlfriend?"

"My dear Alex," he said, and at this point I would have to say that his eyes were actually twinkling. "I fear that the experience of dining aboard *Normandie* might well be a futile exercise without her."

Consulting the *Normandie*'s sailing schedule, I had no trouble convincing my parents that the best time to arrange our soiree would during her visit of May 10-13. The fact that my birthday was May 12 made it an easy sell. When I told Carolyn about the plan, her excitement was possibly even greater than mine, and she immediately took her mother in tow on a shopping expedition to find the right dress. It was the middle of March of 1939, six months after the British Prime Minister Neville Chamberlain had returned from lengthy meetings with Adolph Hitler to tell that world that we could expect "peace for our time." Even at my age, I could tell how greatly the world, and especially those of us on the other side of the Atlantic, wanted to believe in his optimistic declaration.

As it developed, "Uncle Vlad" as I took to calling Mr. Yourkevitvch, was called away to France on a mission of some urgency, and the arrangements for our evening aboard *Normandie* were put on hold. So on my birthday, instead of an elegant dinner in the *Normandie*'s Grand Salon, we dined at home along with Carolyn, her mother, and a maiden aunt or two. The next day was Saturday, and I took the bus over to meet my dad for lunch at pier 70 on 35th St. He knew I was disappointed. "Still, I imagine you'll walk up to visit with her after lunch." He was referring not to Carolyn, but to the ship.

I didn't have the heart for that. "Not today, Pops. The next time I'll see her is when we all walk up the gangway together for dinner."

Uncle Vlad didn't return to New York until the middle of July. My dad and I went around to visit him at his office near the end of the month. It was not what I had expected. He worked out of a single room in a somewhat dilapidated older building on West 54th street at Amsterdam Avenue. His room was dimly lit with a single fluorescent light swinging over a large desk. The floor was littered with old drawings, and the walls were papered with cables, tables, and diagrams that could find no better place of residence. He received us with polite gusto, and showed me some of the original drawings of *Normandie*, presenting me with one as a belated birthday gift. "My deepest apologies, Alex, for letting our dining engagement slip away. Give me a couple of weeks to catch up around here, and we'll give it another go, what do you say?"

But we were out of time.

Normandie completed her 109th crossing and arrived in New York on August 27th. Her return voyage was scheduled for the 30th, as were those of the *Bremen* and the *Aquitania*. That day, with war imminent, the Port Director of New York ordered that all three vessels be thoroughly searched for "implements of war." Then came the word from her owners in Paris: with German U-boats prowling the French coast and the approaches to the English Channel, the *Normandie* was not to sail. Her passengers and their luggage were transferred to *Aquitania*, which, along with the *Bremen*, slipped through the narrows and out into the Atlantic on schedule later that evening. The two liners were scarcely out of sight of Sandy Hook when Hitler releaser his Panzers into Poland. The issue was settled at last. War was to be our lot.

Two weeks later, on a Saturday afternoon, I broke my vow to myself and made the trip over to the Hudson River. Bleak and forbidding, the wharves were now heavily patrolled by Navy and Coast guard personnel. What I saw at Pier 88 was jarring to the senses. My *Normandie* seemed very much her usual lovely self, although less well-attended than usual. In the slip next to her the *Queen Mary* represented a different reality. From the tops of her three graceful stacks to her very waterline, the huge vessel (just ten feet shorter than *Normandie*) had been done over in a coat of drab grey, as dire and dreary as a Manhattan midwinter day. A page in our history had been irrevocably turned. If I had any illusions about what lay ahead, the sight of the big gray hull spoke more clearly to me than any news communiqué or blaring headlines ever could. I wondered how long it would be before *Normandie*'s peacetime *joie de vivre* would be similarly effaced by the sobering colors of conflict.

War or no war, time marched on, and my life with it. Through a contact of my father's I took on an after-school job as a stockman in a warehouse of industrial building materials, and began to think in terms of becoming a construction foreman. I hadn't the natural genius of Uncle Vlad to become a ship designer. Being in the building trades, however, promised a degree of satisfaction, plus, in the city of New York, steady employment. While the German Army gobbled up Eastern Europe and France, Carolyn and I measured our future together, and spent every opportunity in one another's company, going to the movies, walking in the parks, or, one of our favorite pastimes, riding the ferry from the Battery out to Staten Island. The ferry's seven-mile crossing took it through the reaches of the Upper Bay, paralleling the route of the transatlantic liners arriving or departing New York. It was easy to imagine ourselves at some future time with our elbows resting on the railing of the *Normandie* as she moved past the Statue of Liberty towards the open sea and the wonders of Europe beyond. In those days young people's relationships, and particularly those from the "Old Countries," were still guided by a sense of cultural restraint and natural piety. Though we had exchanged fervent kisses and tender caresses, the idea of surrendering our virginity to one another provoked no great urgency in either of us. Only very occasionally did we go over to my old haunts on the West Side. The atmosphere was simply too downbeat and lacking in its former vitality and inspiration. My sketch pads were tucked away in a drawer somewhere, my Brownie forgotten. As my father had predicted upon her arrival in New York years earlier, *Normandie* had become a prisoner of inactivity. Her stacks were now covered with protective shields and her once-dazzling white superstructure was dimmed by layers of grime and streaks of rust. While the *Ile de France* and both the *Queens* had been dispatched to sea on what would turn out to be brilliant wartime careers as troopships, *Normandie* lay idle, a "ghost ship." As one reporter who visited her recounted, *"Our first impression was that of a dank, inactive mechanism, gigantic in size, straining to unleash its dormant power. Many of the crew have not heard from their families since the fall of France. These men watch over their sleeping Normandie as though it were some kind of living thing to be awakened at a happier time."* Coast Guardsmen patrolled her lonely decks as the U.S. Government and the French Line debated her status. Meanwhile, she collected grime. Carolyn and I stopped going to view her.

"Alex, even I could not get us aboard her today, with all the military restrictions on the docks," apologized Uncle Vlad during one of our visits to his office. With the success of *Normandie*, he was in great demand to design hulls for American warships, and had little time at his disposal, although the project which had most excited him had been shelved indefinitely: the design and building of a 100,000 ton "superliner" that would make the Atlantic passage in three days carrying six thousand passengers at $50 a head. He had planned to call her *Bretagne*. "A casualty of war," he shrugged.

But a greater casualty was yet to come.

Roosevelt's Day of Infamy occurred on Dec. 7. Many of my recently-graduated high school classmates, in a frenzy of patriotic sentiment, hurried to enlist. My father read the situation differently. "Roosevelt's War" my father called it. Why did one imagine that the President had signed into law Selective Service legislation a year before the attack? In my father's interpretation of events, Pearl Harbor had been an act of duplicity staged to enable the Americans to jump into a fight that the President had vowed all along to avoid. "The Red Army will take care of Hitler. As for the Japanese, they have overreached and cannot hold," were Otto Radek's pronouncements. Moreover, my mother was in no way disposed to sacrifice her only child to a political madness founded on cynical motives. Needless to say, these sentiments were not widely shared among a population so poorly schooled in politics and so easily inflamed by their newspapers, but even at the age of 18 I knew enough, and was cynical enough, to accept my parents' judgment. And I was about to become even more cynical.

Within a week the official seizure papers were in order, and thirteen ships, including the *Normandie*, were taken over by the U.S. Navy. Given her tremendous potential as a troop carrier, the conversion of the *Normandie* was given priority, and almost overnight 300 Navy sailors, 300 Coast Guardsmen, and 2000 civilian workers flooded aboard to begin the staggering task of readying her to take aboard some 14,000 troops and ferry them to an active war zone. Her glorious bronze panels, statuary and paintings were removed. Thousands of feet of carpeting were rolled up and stashed in passageways alongside rolls of linoleum that would take their place. Doors and partitions came down, telephone lines were disconnected and 14,000 new kapok life preservers wrapped by the bale in tarred paper and burlap were delivered to the vessel. Most of them were piled in the Grand Salon until they could be distributed to the cabins below. The hurried, helter-skelter atmosphere that swallowed up the country in the wake of Pearl Harbor was very much reflected aboard the ship itself, where chains of command were sketchy, supervision was slight, and the urgency to move forward overrode all concerns of careful planning, orderly procedure, or operational safety. While the French had maintained the ship, her state-of-the-art fire control system was manned 24 hours a day, making it virtually impossible for the ship to be destroyed by fire. One of the first acts of the U.S Navy was to close down the main fire control station and vacate its premises.

On New Year's eve, 1941, Carolyn and I went to a party at the home of friends of hers on Long Island. As it was a lengthy train ride from midtown Manhattan, several of her chums from the city were invited to spend the night. It was after 2:00 AM before the party broke up, and we drifted off to our assigned sleeping places. I was on a couch in the dayroom near the back of the house. Once the house was quiet, Carolyn came looking for me. She slid under the blanket next to me and opened her bathrobe. What she offered me then I was in no mood to resist. We consummated our relationship as a couple that night. The way the world was going, there seemed to be no reason to save ourselves for one another any longer.

As I write this, fifty years have passed since February 7, 1942. The day and its aftermath have never receded from my memory. I now live outside of Ft. Lauderdale, Florida in a ghetto of aging, orange-colored people with accents of New York. I have been alone since Carolyn's death last year. From the picture window of my 12th floor condominium I have a clear view across the bay where the cruise ships tie up at Port Everglades. They look like floating hotels, with their stacked-up balconies, their glassed-in staterooms, their top-heavy build-outs. They have no character nor charm whatsoever, and look nothing like the sleek ocean queens of my youth.

The welder's name, the newspapers later reported, was Clement Derrick. It didn't matter, really. It could've been any one of a dozen welders clambering around in *Normandie*'s main salon on that frigid mid-winter day. There was ice in the Hudson and a stiff wind blowing east off the river. Once the torch's sparks hit those flammable kapoks, there was little that could be done. The smoke was pulled into the ventilation ducts and elevator shafts. When it reached the engine room, the Navy crew quickly shut down the generators, leaving the ship without power: no lights, no way to close the fire doors, and no water pressure for the hoses. (For that matter, no fire extinguishers could be found, and there were, incredibly, no trained firemen on hand.) In just half an hour, the fire had engulfed the ship. By this time, a vast plume of smoke was being pushed across the lower end of Manhattan. My mother called me at work. "Alex, honey, there's a fire going on, a big one. Are you all right?" Our warehouse was further east, off of Queens Boulevard in Long Island City.

"Turn on the radio, Ma," I told her, and after a few minutes I made my way out onto our loading docks. The dirty gray/yellow smoke was coming in steadily from the west and rolling off to the South of us towards Brooklyn. I went back inside. I was a leaderman by now, and one of the floor supervisors beckoned to me from his office overlooking the main floor. I went up the stairs and into his office. He had the radio on, and I heard the Mayor's voice. Our mayor, Fiorello LaGuardia, was known for several eccentricities. He was an excitable individual, and his hobby was attending fires. Big fires. In those years, New York had its share of them. From the tone of the Mayor's voice, I could tell he was in his element, but he was talking too fast to be completely intelligible. "Where the hell is the fire?" I asked the supervisor.

"I thought you knew. It's over there by your ship. That big one you're always telling us about."

For some reason, my hearing was no longer working properly. I couldn't make out what he was saying. I glanced at the clock behind his desk. It was 3:30 in the afternoon.

I kept to myself and finished my shift. I caught my bus, made my transfer, got home by about 7:30. (With Government contracts rolling in, we were getting plenty of overtime). My father was in his chair in the living room listening to the radio, which he turned off as soon as I came in the door. He looked at me. "It's not good, Alex."

"Of course it's not good, Pop. We're not good at taking care of things."

"I'll go with you over there, if you want."

"I can't right now. Maybe another time."

It was just as well. As the catastrophe at Pier 88 unfolded, the Army and the NYPD had been called out in large numbers to keep the growing crowds at bay. Every firefighting boat on the West Side was pressed into service to blast water into *Normandie*'s smoldering hull. The service personnel and civilian workers had fled from the ship in scenes of panic, and as night fell, she began to take on an ominous list from the weight of the water crowding her upper decks. Uncle Vlad had showed up on site earlier, and when he realized what was happening, he sought out Rear Admiral Adolphus Andrews, Chief of the Third Naval District, the senior Naval Officer to be found on the crowded wharf. Andrews, a 64-year-old native Texan just one year short of retirement, proved to be a formidable obstacle to *Normandie*'s survival. Understanding that his beloved creation could very well capsize, Vladimir Ivanovich had a simple plan: go aboard with a couple of men and open the now-submerged seacocks to enable the massive hull to flood evenly and settle onto the riverbed, which lay only five or six feet beneath the keel. It made perfect sense, it was do-able, and it was urgent. Yourkevitch pressed his case with the most persuasive demeanor that he could summon. It was like a parent being forced to plead with a stiff-necked court bailiff for the life of his child. I asked him later what he had said to the admiral. Ever the gentleman, Uncle Vlad chose not to divulge the particulars of their conversation, but the Admiral's response, overheard by a number of onlookers including a reporter for the *Herald*, became a matter of public record. His face a stony mask, he abruptly cut off the impassioned Russian and dismissed him with a final blunt declaration: "This is a Navy job! If you don't mind, we've got work to do."

Not more than an hour later, sensing what was likely to happen after all, Andrews ordered all photographers off the scene. With over 100,000 tons of water having been pumped aboard, a handful of harbor tugs were straining against the fire-scarred hull in a desperate struggle to keep her upright. As the tide rose, the list grew worse. Shortly after midnight, all remaining Navy personnel were removed from the ship. At 2:30 AM, almost exactly 12 hours after Clement Derrick's torch had ignited the kapoks, man's most glorious maritime creation rolled over on her side and came to rest in the ice-choked and debris-clotted waters of the Hudson, her three stacks barely 24 inches above the river's surface. It was the most sensational death since the fiery demise of the *Hindenburg* five years earlier and less than one hundred miles away. (For all her majesty, the giant German Zeppelin was more than 200 feet shorter than the French liner.) Only this time, because it was a "Navy job," there were no photographs to chronicle the sad event.

Not that it mattered. There were plenty of witnesses to one of the greatest boondoggles in the Navy's history. This is from an article which I clipped from the *New York Journal American* a few days later:

"You ride past the scene on the West Side Highway and your heart misses a beat as you peer down at the crippled giantess embedded in the mud of the Hudson River. Get a little closer—as close as a triple line of police, Army and Navy men will permit—and the chill of desperation that creeps along your spine is almost overwhelming. The finality of death lies like a clammy hand across the prostrate Normandie. Let the experts talk about salvage. Let the masterminds paint a glowing rebirth for the fallen queen of the ocean. Confronted by the bleak façade of the pier and the mottled bulk of the once-mighty Normandie, you just can't believe it. This is the end, you say to yourself."

Cartoons and editorials in the papers tried to put the tragedy in perspective. One, entitled "Behind

Her Back," depicted the Statue of Liberty (another magnificent French creation) in tears as masses of black smoke arise from the burning liner. *The New York Times* was equally succinct: *"The sight of her hurts the human eye and heart."*

I can testify to the truth of the *Times'* assertion. It was too painful for me. One trip to visit the site, about ten days after the fire, was all I could manage. Things I had learned to care passionately about, even though I wasn't certain what they were, had died, and I felt ashamed to view the inert ruin that had replaced them.

The New York dailies, to their credit, were unsparing in their criticism in the loss of this "incomparable wartime asset." *"It is as though the Empire State Building had teetered on its side and fallen into the street"* observed the *New York Sun*. Naval officials tried to gin up some talk of sabotage, but New York District Attorney Frank Hogan dismissed it out of hand: "In this case, carelessness has served the enemy with equal effectiveness." Between them, Cunard's two *Queens* would go on to ferry 1.3 million troops around the globe during the war, and were later credited by Winston Churchill as having shortened the conflict by as much as a year. Given the *Normandie's* size and speed, she might conceivably have lopped off another four to six months all on her own.

Avoiding the West Side Highway was easy enough, but I was ill-prepared for how long the agony of *Normandie's* ordeal would prevail. Uncle Vlad, undeterred, made another approach to Naval Officials, and explained to them his plan for constructing a series of damns in the ship's interior and pumping them out one by one, a process that he estimated might take as long as five months. Commander William Sullivan, the Navy's Supervisor of Salvage, politely rejected the offer and pursued a different course. This course called for cutting away the ship's entire superstructure, down to the main deck. Former Secretary of the Navy Franklin Roosevelt himself signed off on the plan, and in May the work began. It would go on for eighteen months, at a cost of one million dollars a month, until October of 1943, when the hull was finally righted.

As conscientious as I had been in avoiding all this indignity, I was not to be spared the awe of one last encounter. The war had been over for a year. (Working for a company that produced ball-bearings, I had been exempted from the call-up, and spent the war years providing this essential component to the American war effort).

In September of 1946, now a supervisor at Gmelin Industrial Supply, I was driving one of the company pick-up trucks from Manhattan to Bayonne. My spirits were up that day as Carolyn and I had scheduled our wedding for October 22nd. (We had tried to schedule it earlier, but both sets of parents urged us to wait until "this war business is good and finished.") In the truck, I had made my way through the workaday bustle of lower Manhattan and mounted the ramp to the Bayonne Bridge when I became aware of a curious procession taking place on the waters below. A cluster of tugs, as many as six or eight, were shepherding a massive hull under the bridge's span. With the steel plates of the hull blackened and scarred, it was clearly a salvage operation. In large white block letters across those plates, the hull was identified as LIPSETT, and my mind turned briefly at the wonder of it. In the post-war era there was understandably a good deal of salvage work going on as the old was ushered out to make way for the great renewal that was underway. Being in the building trades, nobody understood that better than I did. As I approached the middle of the span and observed the hull sliding beneath, there was something about the graceful bow and finely tapered stern that caused my heart to leap into my throat, again. It was my *Normandie*, having been declared "war surplus," on her way to the breaker's yard. (For a time there had been talk of converting the hull into an aircraft carrier, but with typical government red-tape hold-ups the talk went on too long, and the moment had passed.) I floored the accelerator and raced across the remainder of the span, down the ramp on the other side until I came to a turn-out where I mounted the curb, skidded to a halt, and piled out of the truck. Turning back, I was able to see the procession as it cleared the span and moved downriver. I impulsively placed my hand across my heart and stood for a long time watching her go, bidding her a silent farewell and a part of myself with her.

My father died in 1967 at the age of 70, and my mother, fittingly, passed just a year later. Our time together had become infrequent in later years (Carolyn and I had moved out to embrace the suburban charms of Westport, Connecticut, and the ninety minute train ride into the city proved more daunting, or more avoidable, than we had imagined.) As is not uncommon with us children of Eastern European origins, I was always given to brooding introspection as a boy, and it was a characteristic that followed me into adulthood. ("The largest room in my house is the room for doubt," I explained on one occasion to a friend.) My father, conversely, was able to relish life on a more immediate basis, serving himself heartily and without apparent hesitation from the smorgasbord of daily experiences that came his way. While I never understood quite how such a straightforward philosophy worked, a philosophy that could bypass history, override regret, and steer clear of melancholy, there was a brief conversation between us in which he may have given me the key. It took place some weeks after the fire at Pier 88. It was after I had made my painful pilgrimage to view the *Normandie*'s overturned hulk, and I was trying to put into words what it meant to me. Since his work took him into the vicinity of the disaster rather frequently, he had found a way to come to terms with it. How could he not? As I struggled to describe its impact on my view of the world, he listened patiently for a time, and then raised his broad hand to still me. When he spoke I couldn't tell whether his comment was meant as friendly advice, a dire admonition, or merely a tactic for survival. "Alex," he said, pushing his palm forward through the air in a gesture of finality. "You can forget about all that."

Only now, having at last discharged my duty in recounting this troubled memoir, can I see that he was right.

Alex Radek,
Ft. Lauderdale, Florida, September 1992

PENANCE IN PAR'BO

They say that whiskey will wreck a man. Enough whiskey. Over enough time. (Neither the quantity nor the time required to accomplish the wrecking have ever been established with reliability.)

They say this in many places. I have heard it in Kansas City, Missouri. I have heard it in Chicago, Illinois. (Midwesterners speak with certainty when they speak at all). I have even heard it in San Francisco, the city where I was born, although here it is put forth with less conviction. In New York it not an uncommon sentiment, and in the far-flung cowtowns of Houston and Dallas there are numerous adherents to that dictum.

Once you cross the ocean, however, (any ocean will do), that kind of anti-whiskey talk dies out in a hurry. Lisbon, Madrid, Paris, Rome, Berlin—their citizens all have long-standing and amicable relationships with hard drink, and will not pretend otherwise. On the other hand, looking to your Middle and Far Eastern terminuses, whiskey is roundly condemned and religiously avoided. If a man has a hankering for the hard stuff, he is expected to come to terms with his demons and not inflict his unwary peers with the particulars of his struggles, or the wisdom he feels he has achieved as a result of them.

When you go to the southern latitudes, however, to the sunny, humid climes which we call the tropics, you'll soon detect a different response to "demon rum." It has been my observation that in the tropics, owing to a combination of factors including topographical, latitudinal, denominational, and the always-important disposition of the Beaufort-Scale, not only is grain alcohol regarded as benign presence, by tropical citizens it is openly and fervently embraced as a bearer of glad tidings, a bringer of succor, and a necessary aid to getting a day's worth of work done, even if it takes a week to accomplish that.

Given this kind of permissive atmosphere, readers may wonder: will a life in the tropics be more likely to make a wreck of a man? Smart bettors will take the odds. A certain type of man, in fact, is drawn to this clime perhaps for that very reason. Spend any time in the tropics and you'll come to appreciate the fact that wrecks are a natural part of the landscape, a feature of daily life. So much so that they are frequently considered treasures, and are pointed out with pride and wonder by the more experienced tour guides listed in Frommers. Shipwrecks. Plane wrecks. Wrecks of old schools or churchs. Picture-postcard relics of the Colonial era. Human wrecks. Depending on the circumstances, wreckage of any sort, whether it consists of the bleached skeletal remains of a PBY Catalina on the side of a hill overlooking San Juan harbor or the dimly-seen figure of a man at one end of the long bar in Jimmy's El Dorado in Rum Cay, Belize, tropical wrecks often possess a certain restrained elegance, hinting at stories left untold, dreams left unrealized. Or perhaps just an abundance of carelessness.

Whatever the case, in the summer of 1942, at the advanced age of 29, I was the act of politely becoming one of those wrecks.

I was by no means alone in my endeavors. In 1942 in Surinam the wreckage was piling up. The war of course had contributed to that, but the chronic primitivism of the local economy, one hundred years of heavy-handed colonial rule, the high humidity, the prohibitive interest rates of the Dutch-owned banks, and the sensation that time was mired in an immovable state were also factors. Getting through the day at hand was a full task, requiring, as Mr. Lincoln would say, a man's last full measure of devotion. And once you got through that, there was the night. And night in the tropics is all the reason you need to hope for another day.

After two decades in these climes, I have concluded that what the nay-sayers and reformers fail to take into account is that, while whiskey is performing its insidious chore of wrecking a man, it will also provide him with an interesting education. Not necessarily the kind of education that will entitle him to a top-floor office with his name engraved on a brass plaque on the door, but an education with a number of utilitarian features nonetheless. Sorting out truth from fiction is one of those features. Recognizing true grit when it makes a chance appearance is another. And understanding underlying human motives may be the most utilitarian of all. Most of these lessons will be transmitted in barrooms, of course, for that is where whiskey's graduate studies are conducted, especially in the tropics, where not everybody in a barroom is a drinker, but all the drinkers are in barrooms.

Paramaribo, the capital city of this polyglot nation, was no exception. In the evenings, when the daytime heat had abated, the bars along Waterkant St. were thronged with wartime personnel. You had your American Army officers, they commanded the forces whose job was guarding the Bauxite mines just a short ways up the Marowijne River. There were Army Air Force and British pilots, most of them in transit and glad of it, and your civilian contractors, who had the most money to spend and knew where to spend it. There were the ever-present Red Cross people, of course your local Dutch functionaries, and a smattering of Aussies, who always seem to turn up when a fight is in the offing. Then there were those few sweaty Germans, who had legitimate business interests in the region along with nefarious designs on intercepting Allied shipping lanes in the Caribbean and reducing the flow of Bauxite coming out the Guyanas and reaching American East Coast ports. Later that year, when the Bogart film "Casablanca" was released, one wondered whether the wartime intrigue in an exotic locale couldn't have been more accurately filmed in Paramaribo.

In the many drinking establishments clustered along Waterkant Street, improbable war stories and fabricated personal histories were the currency of choice. True gen, or as the Army boys like to say, solid intel was in short supply. Throughout the Caribbean basin—Puerto La Cruz, Port-of-Spain, Belize City, Port-au-Prince, Montego Bay—the War Shipping Administration had posted agents such as myself in an effort to expedite the Allied shipping efforts. Being sure that our ships were fully bunkered, provisioned, and dispatched in a timely fashion, along with providing their skippers with the benefit of our best local knowledge were our assigned tasks. Any information we could glean on other questions—how many U-boats had the German navy actually mobilized to the region, what was their disposition, and where were the submarine tenders that were dispatched to fuel and sustain them during their operations—was also of value to the WSA. For the price of a bottle of Cuban rum, British gin, or a blended Scotch whiskey, you could get the real story, and with each glass the teller would become more certain of the facts and more assertive in his presentation of them.

As for the success the Germans might truthfully be having, due to wartime censorship and the sprawling, disconnected nature of the Caribbean itself, this was entirely speculative. On successive evenings I had personally witnessed at least two sinkings in the Gulf of Paria from a lovely rooftop verandah in the hills above Port-of-Spain. This turn of events had caused the WSA to pull me from the lights of Trinidad and dispatch me to the comparatively primitive and remote environs of Paramaribo the following week. "A slip of the lip can sink a ship" went the old wartime admonition, and it was deemed that the slip which caused the fiery ends of the two oil tankers in question was likely mine, a judgment which I disputed in vain. Par'bo, as the Americans had familiarly labeled it, was to be my penance. In a way in was a penance for every foreign national in-country, and we all served our time, separately and together.

Several of the bars on Waterkant St. had outdoor decks that overlooked the sluggish waters of the Saramcoca river. After dark, when the overhead fans stirred the thick air and the city lights glimmered on the turgid waters, it became a perfectly natural environment for wrecking oneself. One evening, while applying myself to the task, I chanced to observe a knot of loose and loud American officers in uniform spilling into the establishment. At the center of the cluster I soon glimpsed the reason for their high spirits. She was slender, blonde and wearing white, a beacon of sensuality improbably descended into our collective darkness. Her laughter, throaty and silver, regularly soared above the self-satisfied barking of male approval that surrounded her. I was in the company of Andrew Goldsworthy, an attaché to the British embassy and a man worthy of his gin, as we looked on at the happy scene. "Methinks the lady doth not protest at all," he remarked. Goldsworthy was a Brit, he was entitled to his Shakespeare. We watched the group's carrying on for a time and then returned to our conversation, which may have had something to do with Goldsworthy's assertion that a Dutch associate of his was deliberately sowing misinformation on behalf of the Germans.

The evening passed without further incident, and in the morning was thought about no more. Lovely lady or no, signs, omens and sightings were quite the norm in these far-flung outposts during the war. Drink up and move along, folks, show's over.

Except that it wasn't. It was just beginning.

I was bellied up to the bar several nights later when I felt a tap on my shoulder. It was one of the American lads, a short friendly Lieutenant with whom I had a passing acquaintance. He reintroduced himself and placed a comradely hand on my shoulder. "Skipper, I wonder if I might borrow you for just one moment. I've got someone who would like to meet you."

I glanced over his shoulder. "Not just here," he said. "Down at the other end." I followed him towards the back of the establishment to a cluster of small wicker tables. I saw the blonde sitting by herself. "Ma'am, the Captain is here," he said, stepping aside in a fine gesture of manliness. I parked myself on a chair opposite the woman as he touched my shoulder briefly and departed.

She was tall and sat up straight, her blonde hair tumbling loosely down the sides of her head. She had lively eyes and a well-formed mouth, with something of a girl-scout earnestness about her. She reminded me of well-bred girls I had seen during my brief college days, her fine features infused with the healthy glow of higher education, proper grooming, and a guiding ambition. No wreckage here, by God. She had a tall drink in front of her and a look of bemused anticipation in her eyes. I could tell at once that she was the type of gal who insisted on getting down to business, but I couldn't tell what the business might be.

"Marty Gellhorn." She extended her hand across the table. The name didn't ring any bells right away.

"Andy Cochran."

"Captain Cochran, isn't it?"

"I could make an exception in your case." She seemed like the bantering type, or maybe I was just in the mood.

"I'd much rather you didn't. I'm quite the unexceptional type."

"Sure you are. I believe I caught a glimpse of you the other night in Freddy's with a group of your American officer friends."

She laughed charmingly. "In that case, let me correct any first impressions that you might have had."

"I'd much rather you didn't. I like them the way they are." That made her laugh again, a thing for which I instantly admired myself.

"I'm glad you're in agreement. *Viva la Republica*," she pronounced, lifting her tall drink in my direction. I raised my Dewars in return. Then I caught it. "Wait a minute. You mean you're Martha Gellhorn?"

"I mean it every bit that I'm able." The "Marty" business had thrown me, that and the easy familiarity of her nature. But the unmistakable reference to the recently-concluded Spanish Civil War brought back at once the name that had become a familiar byline in the reporting of that conflict. She had written primarily for *Collier's*, the pre-eminent weekly newsmagazine of the era.

"I'm sorry I missed it the first time around. First impressions stand corrected." I raised my glass in her direction. "You're one hell of a writer."

She peered at me over the rim of her glass. "Well, I never have gotten caught up in all that objectivity shit, at least."

"Your politics are fine with me, sister. I read all your stuff from Spain." The three-year piecemeal death of the Spanish Republic at the hands of the Fascist rebels had been nothing less than a Twentieth-century passion play, and Martha Gellhorn had chronicled the passion of it. And not from the boardrooms, command posts, or parlors where the bleeding hearts gathered, either. From the streets, ditches, and fields mostly. The places where the real bleeding was going on.

"Seems a long time ago, but thanks for your compliment, Dear Reader."

"Think nothing of it. More to the point is, now you're here in Surinam. I must be missing something." What I wasn't missing, I now recalled, was that this was a woman who had been hired personally by President Roosevelt's right-hand man Harry Hopkins to report on the nationwide impact of the depression and had been so angered by the graft and corruption she had witnessed that she had barged into the White House to tell Eleanor about it and was invited to stay for dinner and discuss her findings with Franklin—the beginnings of a lasting friendship. This was a woman who had inspired the country's greatest novelist to produce his greatest war novel, *For Whom the Bell Tolls,* and dedicate it to her. Not only that, she had written two or three novels of her own, and established a reputation as a war correspondent that few men could equal. She had the status of legend, and the legend was sitting across the table from me. A damned goodlooking legend at that.

"Oh, Surinam." Again her gay laugh. "I came for the beaches."

The discharges of the Surinam's sluggish rivers into the sparkling Caribbean produced a fan of flat brown waters that hugged the coastline and extended twenty miles out to sea. "I'm afraid you've been misinformed on that count," I told her, and even as I did, I could see from her eyes that the joke was on me.

"No, I'm actually on assignment again, probably here for the same reason you are."

"I seriously doubt that. I'm here because they ran out of places to put me. Surinam is the last place that I would expect to see a reporter. Especially one like you, who has something to say."

"Well, *Collier's* at least thought it was worth a look. The Germans seem to think so as well. The whole Caribbean has become a pretty intriguing story." 1942 was a year in which the future of the United States was very much in play, and the bold German incursions into the region underscored the fact that the country was in a fight for its life—a fight which might be won or lost in the sea-lanes traversing the Caribbean Basin and skirting the various coasts which bordered it.

"Well, Miss Gellhorn, if I can help you with your assignment, I'll do my damndest."

"First assignment is to knock off that Miss Gellhorn stuff. First of all, as you probably know, I'm an old married gal, and secondly, I am and always have been just plain Marty." She raised her glass again, by now empty except for the remnants of the ice cubes. "And if this conversation is going to go anywhere, a bottle is probably required. May I do the honors?"

"Not in my bar, you may not. Anyway, there's a war on. The Government's buying."

A fifth of Jameson's Irish Whiskey was never so well spent as it was that evening. Marty was a spirited storyteller and loved to laugh. She regaled me with tales of her travels of the past month, which had seen her island-hopping through the Caribbean in small boats. (One, as I recall, a leaking, stinking thirty-foot diesel, was named, without irony, the *Queen Mary*.) Becalmed at sea, practically devoured by ants, marooned twice, tossed about by storms, she found herself bathing on remote beaches, picnicking in the jungle, and hallucinating the presence of German submarines once or twice. From San Juan to Tortola, Anguilla, St. Martin, St. Barts, and Antigua she had made her way with no travel companion save a rescued cat and the native fishermen whose boats she hired. "It was a true horror journey," she said. "Of course, those are the kind you remember best." The previous year, she informed, she had spent three months in China: hours of tedium in the company of inscrutable Chinese Generals, death-defying plane rides through storms over Japanese lines, numerous physical maladies that eventually reduced her to "a rather constant state of whimpering. It was not for the faint of heart, at any rate."

I wondered why a person would voluntarily submit to these kinds of privations.

"I'm a born peripatetic." She had been on the move since the age of 21, she told me, when she dropped out of Bryn Mawr and took off for Paris with a typewriter and $75 bucks.

"Must've been quite an adventure for a girl on her own."

"Huh," she scoffed, eyeing me. "That's male code for 'you probably slept with a lot of fellows.'"

"You understand male code?" I asked, mocking.

"My husband taught me. He said it would come in handy in certain places." She laughed. "And brother, he knew what he was talking about."

By "husband" she was referring of course to the world-renowned novelist Ernest Hemingway, a man who cast a long shadow among men of my generation as a writer, adventurer, two-fisted drinker, hunter, fighter, and bedder of beautiful dames. (Sitting here before me was certainly proof of the latter.) I poured each of us another generous portion of Jameson's and hoped that his shadow was not going to linger over our evening together. "Men," she said, raising her glass. "You're all shits. And I love you to death."

What had gotten her started, she explained, was a fascination with place names. "I look at maps the way some people stand on the sidewalk and read restaurant menus. I want to taste everything, the more exotic the better. Especially the things I've never tasted before."

"Surinam falls into that category?"

"Sounds like a delightful treat. A holiday of the primitive sort, which is my favorite."

"You did mention an assignment."

"Well, there is that." She paused while I lit her cigarette. One of life's pleasures is that of first lighting the cigarette of a woman you would like to burn down. She exhaled through wonderfully pursed lips. "Haven't you heard? You fellows are all the news."

I made a show of scanning the bar behind us. "Must be a damn slow news cycle."

"Captain, don't pretend you don't know what I'm talking about. The wolfpacks are rampaging in the Atlantic, they're shredding our Murmansk convoys, and now they've decided to pick us clean in the Caribbean too. Surinam's bauxite mines, the oil in Venezuela and all that. Isn't that why you're here?"

At this point, despite the Jameson's, I urged upon myself a sense of caution. Alcohol-fueled, rambling conversation with a captivating female had possibly been my undoing in Trinidad. I couldn't afford to repeat that letdown. "The bauxite mines are the army's business, not mine."

Sensing my sudden reserve, she laughed disarmingly. "Oh, don't I know it? And very proud of it they are, too. In fact, tomorrow I'm scheduled to ride up the river in one of their crash boats to take a look. Your business, if my sources are reliable, is more in the shipping department."

"Look, Marty, you're a great lovely gal, but if we're going to be pals, let's change the subject. I've got nothing to say to you about shipping."

She hesitated for a moment, and then reached across the small table and placed her hand on mine, looking me in the eyes. "I'm sorry, Skipper, that came out a bit snide and snippy, and I don't mean it at all. All I mean is, I need a favor, and they assured me that you were the one man in Paramaribo who could accommodate me. I'm not after state secrets, for God's sake. I just need a boat."

I considered this briefly. "A slow boat, no doubt. To China maybe?" We laughed together, and our boozy cordiality was restored.

"Allow me to be precise: Saramcoca." She said the word deliciously, as if it were an aphrodisiac. Under the circumstances, it may as well have been.

"You mean the river?"

"Cochran, it may be just a river to you. It's one of those place names to me. Irresistible."

"Marty, it's slow-moving, it's muddy, and it goes nowhere. Hell, you look at the maps there aren't even any navigational aids. Except for people wearing loin-cloths, nobody's ever traveled it."

"Precisely the appeal, Skipper. But I have no boat. You're the boat-man. How about it?"

The boat-man. That was me, all right. And viewing her through a filter of Jameson's and the stagnation of his own life, the boat-man was drifting close to the shoals of infatuation with the endlessly fascinating female in his company. The fortunes of war. Or the misfortunes. "You're serious about this boat-business?"

"Try me, mister."

"Don't think the thought hasn't occurred to me."

To her great credit Mrs. Hemingway, having demonstrated her formidable skills of persuasion with the opposite gender, gently pulled back. "I hope you won't think me overly bold, dear Captain, but under the circumstances I think I'm entitled to ask: how did you come by your skills as a mariner?"

"Legitimately, I can assure you." Briefly I ran though my bona fides: for one thing, leaving home at the age of 18, I had been in ships for as long as she had been hunched over her typewriter. I had become a Master at the tender age of 26, and I had sailed three times to Murmansk and back before accepting a position with the WSA. I didn't include the tale of my troubles in Trinidad.

"I was in Puerto Rico just a few weeks back talking to some of the shipwrecked lads. We're taking quite a beating out here, aren't we?"

"We're keeping up." I knew damn well that wasn't true in the Caribbean in 1942, but I had an official position to uphold.

"You poor thing." Again she reached for my hand. "And now you've got this absolute shrew of a woman pestering you about the kind of folly that has absolutely nothing to do with our grand war effort." Although I seemed to remember that she had Midwestern origins, she had either legitimately gained or artfully contrived a passably British way of expressing herself. In the international circles in which she moved, I suspected it was a distinct asset. That, and being the wife of Ernest Hemingway.

Around us the bar crowd had thinned and the room was becoming subdued. "Where are you staying?"

"At the lovely Paramaribo Grand, of course."

I glanced at my watch. Past midnight. "They're going to want to close the doors here shortly. Let me walk you back."

Before we departed she excused herself briefly and walked between the small tables to the lady's room. I watched her go. She was wearing a pair of khaki-colored linen shorts and a trim-fitting white blouse, and watching her cross that small room was one of my greatest wartime pleasures.

We left Vandy's and made our way along Waterkant St. under the hanging branches of the trees for a couple of blocks before turning away from the river and going another two blocks, past the stately Dutch-colonial house fronts to the hotel. She was nearly as tall as me and steady on her feet. I walked with my arm at right angles so she could thread her wrist through it. I had the remnants of our Jameson's in the other hand. Across the way we could hear the strains of a scratchy gramophone playing in the lobby of the hotel. "Good God," Marty remarked. "Big-band music at this hour."

"All part of our tropical charm, dear girl."

"I absolutely adore it."

We sat at a small table near one of the hotel's grand columns, just outside the ring of potted palms that was strung around the lobby. A boy in a white coat brought us glasses and asked if we desired ice.

"And a bottle of water," I told him. Another boy followed in his wake discharging small bursts of FLIT from his spray canister into the muggy air to disperse the bold Surinamese mosquitoes.

"Surinam," she pronounced. She lit a cigarette and sat with her back to the column. "It's everything I imagined it might be."

For a man who viewed it as a damnable banishment from the civilized world, I wondered aloud what she might have imagined it to be.

She reflected briefly. "Unformed. Expectant. Welcoming. A place to immerse oneself in the small rituals of daily life and to rely upon the charity of new friends." She took a draw on her cigarette and exhaled in the direction of the lobby. "Perhaps a place to find something of yourself you didn't know you'd lost."

"Not exactly like being in a hotel in Madrid in the summer of '38, then? The one where you were being shelled every day?"

"We were hit quite a few times, but I suspect most of that was incidental. The artillery in Spain was very much a random affair. The lads were not good shooters at all. Or not good aimers, at any rate." She seemed not greatly interested in war stories, at least not her own.

Out near the potted palms, with the faint scratchy music of the gramophone to accompany us, an air of romantic unreality, rather common in wartime, was pressing in upon us, or certainly upon me. I tried to remind myself that that I was in the company not so much of an alluring female, but of a bold, accomplished American war correspondent. I struggled to separate the two, but the Jameson's and the hour were making it difficult. "And when you're not gallivanting around the islands like this, where do you make your home?"

"In Cuba, with my husband."

"He's there now?"

"When he's not out in the Gulf hunting submarines." She did not seem to believe in that particular cause. At least, not so far as her husband was concerned.

"Two writers in the same house," I ventured. "That's got to be something of a challenge."

"Sometimes you need a big house, I can tell you that." She laughed dryly.

"I wonder what it was about Marty Gellhorn from St. Louis that attracted the mighty world-traveler Hemingway." I hoped this would not be interpreted as male code, even though I knew it was.

"Oh God," she said, and crushed her cigarette out in the white porcelain ashtray. "If you must know, it was my backside."

"And Cuba isn't fascinating enough to keep you at home?"

"More male code, dear Captain: isn't your husband able to satisfy you?" Her eyes grew hard across the table, and then relaxed again. "Well, I'm not cut out to be a domestic, I'm afraid. Too many place names on the map." She upended her glass of Jamesons and looked across at me with a smile. "Let's talk about my boat trip, shall we? As I've said, I'm scheduled to go up to the mines for a look-see tomorrow- or today- with the Army boys, but I could be ready to leave after that."

"Hell, I'll have your boat, Marty. And if you like, I'll go along with you just to be sure you get back to Cuba in one lovely piece." It was a promise I was not entitled to make, but I made it anyway. For Mrs. Hemingway.

"I can pay, you know. Well, *Collier's* can pay, at any rate."

A new melody had made its way onto the turntable of the gramophone. After hearing the first few bars, I stood. "We can take care of that right now. It'll cost you a dance." I extended a hand in her direction. She met my eyes briefly and rose without hesitation. I guided her by the elbow towards the center of the lobby, nearer to the music. The tune was "Begin the Beguine" played by Artie Shaw, and if there ever was a better tune for a romantic interlude, I've never heard it. Its haunting melody and Shaw's bittersweet clarinet assured it great popular success in every wartime theater.

We danced. She allowed herself to come against me with familiarity, but not suggestively. And she moved easily in my arms. I had always been a pretty good fox-trot man. The fox-trot was designed for polite wreckage like me, a simple repetitive motion with a hint of elegance to it. Hemingway's wife was in my arms, but I was able to relax and dance with Marty.

Neither of us could find any reason for further conversation. The dance was conversation enough.

When the tune ended, we walked back to the table to collect our belongings. "And I shall see you . . .?"

"Unless you'd rather brave the crowd at Vandy's again, I'll just come by the hotel this evening. The travel arrangements should be in order by then, but if not, they won't be long in coming."

"You're a lovely sport, Captain, and I will be forever in your debt." She came around the table to where I was and leaning into me, kissed me briefly on the mouth. Her lips were warm, dry, and distant.

"Just tell Eleanor that I can't hold off the krauts much longer all by myself." I grinned jauntily and then turned and made my way down the front steps of the hotel and onto the sidewalk. I would liked to have waited and watched her walk back across the lobby to the stairs, but I guessed I'd have another chance before long.

I guessed wrong.

That afternoon I found myself in the company of the District Manager of WSA and one of his associates who'd flown down on the regular Pan-Am flight, which stopped briefly in Paramaribo for refueling on its way to Rio. (That's how Marty had arrived as well). Their visit was unexpected (the movements of military personnel in a war zone were always conducted under a shroud of secrecy) and of course I was expected to perform the yeoman's task of rendering their brief stopover in Paramaribo as delightfully colonial and wonderfully exotic as possible under the circumstances. As my yeoman's chores didn't end until well past midnight, I didn't trouble to return to Marty's hotel until the following evening. The proprietress, Gertie, was in her thirties, an agreeable, matronly Dutch national with the slightly pallid air about her which seemed to cling to the Dutch despite their long years in the region. "Oh yes, Miss Gellhorn, "she nodded. "A lovely girl, but not with us at the moment, I'm afraid."

"Not with you?"

"Well, she's kept her room, but has gone off exploring, or something like that. Upriver, I believe. Didn't give much in the way of detail." She looked up at me worriedly. "Not in any trouble, is she?"

"None that she can't handle, I'm sure," I responded, not troubling to disguise my disappointment. Apparently Marty had gotten a better offer. Or at least, a quicker one. "No word on when she would be returning, then?"

"She's a girl who keeps her business to herself, I'm afraid," said Gertie, commiserating for the both of us.

"I guess we'll just have to read about it in the dispatches, then," I said, and left the hotel feeling suddenly adrift. Wreckage. It seemed to be my lot.

The days passed. Three or four days, maybe more. I plunged back into my work and tried not to think too much about her, where she might be, under what circumstances she might be operating upriver in the Saramcoca. It was inhabited by local tribespeople, and I didn't think she'd find herself in harm's way, but the woman seemed to have a capacity for attracting adventure, for converting the mundane details of life into sound and fury of some sort. In her sudden and unexplained absence, the details of my life certainly seemed mundane.

Before returning to her hotel, I had in fact found a boat for us to use, and contracted with its owner/

operator for a modest day-rate. The boat was large for a river-going panga, sturdy and stable with a five and one-half horsepower outboard that would have enabled us to cover quite a bit of river in just a few days. I had even laid the groundwork for our excursion with the District Manager during my night out by explaining to my visitors that I was planning a Saramcoca excursion to investigate rumors of an upriver settlement of Dutch nationals that might or might not be involved in providing sanctuary to certain shipwreck survivors. "Wouldn't that be the Army's business?" one of them had wanted to know.

"The Army is here to babysit the Bauxite mines," I explained. "When it comes to shipping affairs, we're pretty much on our own." As implausible as it may have sounded, in the end they both thought it was a capital idea, and my head swam with the idea of three or four days on the river with long-legged Miss Gellhorn. I even allowed myself to imagine how she might choose to express her gratitude to me for services rendered. Those kinds of thoughts will make a wreck of a man quicker than whiskey, but they can also make the days more tolerable, and the nights positively enchanting, even in Godforsaken Surinam.

After a full week, when there was no sign of Marty either in the bars or at the hotel, my tender thoughts had hardened, and I began to regard her as an interloper, a tourist, an un-necessary distraction to men focused on the hard and dangerous business of war. Damnable, in a word. And damnably distracting.

I allowed another three days to pass before I went by the hotel again. "Oh, my goodness, you've missed her," Gertie exclaimed. "The poor thing has come and gone."

"Come and gone?" It was a pronouncement I couldn't bring myself to accept.

"The poor wretched thing." Gertie briefly recounted how Marty had suddenly reappeared in her room one morning, a much different person from the outgoing, confident woman who had swept through our lives a week earlier. Her features were puffy and drawn, her skin a welter of burns from the sun and weeping sores from insect bites. Sporting a broken wrist and too weak to walk, she had barely been able to consume the tea which Gertie had brewed for her, and had remained pitifully ensconced in her room for several days, having lost all interest in further exposure to Paramaribo or its charms.

"She explained to me that she had had a terrible attack of allergies and hoped to be feeling better when her fever went down," Gertie said, and shrugged.

"And did it? Did her fever go down?"

"Oh, I can't say, Captain. The next morning she insisted on being helped into a taxi and went off to the airport for her Pan Am." She watched my face apologetically. "The poor wretched thing."

I left the hotel and made my way back to Waterkant St, where I followed the curve around the harbor to Vandy's. I walked to the back of the long narrow room and sat at the table where I had first fallen under the spell of Mrs. Hemingway, and there I drank highballs alone until late in the evening. Then I walked back to my rooms and went to sleep.

Weeks passed as the episode slowly released its grasp on my waking consciousness. Initially I made polite inquiries in an effort to discover who had provided the boat and accompanied the journalist during her Saramcoca adventure. I was able to confirm that the Americans had taken her to the Bauxite mines but had seen no more of her after that. I also learned that the U.S. Army arranged for polite upriver outings for families of its officers, which led to an unexpected revelation from a certain Army Lieutenant whose wife had been part of such an excursion just two or three days after Marty had been to the mines. "My wife commented that she had seen the lady upriver in one of the villages where they stopped to take some photos."

"How'd she know it was her?"

"Let's see. Sexy, long-legged blonde gal traveling by herself. Kind of fits the profile, don't'cha think?"

"Who was she with?"

"Bunch of nigger locals, near as my wife could tell. You could probably find them if you tried. One of 'em apparently owns a boat, at any rate."

For the sake of my own mental health, I made no effort to find the boat owner. I had to let the story go. Thinking back to the anecdotes Marty had recounted to me of her travels in the Caribbean prior to arriving in Paramaribo, her impulsive decision to make the trip up the uncharted river in the company of local men of unknown reputation was completely in character for her. She had an almost male fearlessness about her, trusted her intuition implicitly, and threw herself at the mercy of strangers without hesitation. It was the only way she could have ever gotten to the unmapped or off-limits places she reached to deliver the stories which she did. With my barely-disguised romantic fantasies, and being a countryman of hers to boot, I might have presented an unnecessary complication to her itinerary. Steer clear of local wreckage. That was probably one of her rules of the road. In time, I came to regard her decision to go ahead upriver without me as a wise choice.

I had limited access to current American newsmagazines or newspapers during my stay in Paramaribo, which lasted another 6 months after Marty had come and gone. It wasn't until late in the summer of '44, more than two years after our meeting, that she resurfaced in my life, or at least her byline did. Having determined to reverse the course of my life from shore-bound stagnation and willful self-destruction, I was back at sea and back in command, sailing in Liberties that were part of the large convoys steaming west out of Oakland, San Pedro, and Port Chicago, ferrying fuel and weapons to the Pacific theater as the Allied forces made their big push toward Japan. During a layover in Guam, in the wardroom of one of our escort destroyers I came across a worn and slightly tattered three-week-old copy of the *San Francisco Examiner*. The name leaped out at me. It was Martha Gellhorn's eyewitness account of the D-Day landings at Normandy, and it was typical Marty. As it would later be revealed, she had been denied a press credential to accompany the invading armada (such credentials were routinely denied female correspondents; apparently the American High Command thought that war was just too damn serious, or maybe too damn scary, for girls to be admitted). So while her world-famous war-novelist husband watched it all unfold from the bridge of a warship located comfortably three miles off the beach, Marty, who had stowed away on a hospital ship to cross the channel, bluffed her way into one of the boats heading for Omaha Beach and spent the afternoon on the bloody sand with machine-gun rounds whistling overhead. Knowing what I knew of her, she probably never flinched, and her account of that day was one of the first and most genuine pieces of the flood of reportage that came later.

It came as no surprise either to learn that soon afterward she decided she'd had enough of being Mrs. Hemingway. The much-celebrated couple parted company before the war ended.

As for me, my love life was going in the other direction. I had, after a comparatively brief romance, gotten married in San Francisco to a terrific girl that I met in a record store. Like Marty, she was a Midwestern girl, from Missouri. Like Marty, she had terrific legs and a well-developed sense of humor. Our first child, a daughter, was born in May of '45, while I was at sea. My wife dutifully signed the birth certificate using the name upon which we had already agreed.

We called her Martha.

Andrew Cochran
Puerto Ordaz, Venezuela, 1958

THIS MAN'S ARMY

L et's get one thing straight right from the start. Unlike Patton he had no love for war, and unlike Zhukov he took no delight in ravaging the enemy. But I'm here to tell you, Dwight Eisenhower was a fighting man's general.

The first thing you noticed about him was a commanding presence.

Of course, you'll say. He was a four-star general, in charge of the whole affair, with a staff of some fifteen to twenty officers and all the trappings that customarily attend a field commander of such exalted status. But there was nothing exalted about Ike. Unlike Patton, he didn't strut about with pearl-handled revolvers making certain that everybody knew just how mercurial he was, and unlike Zhukov, he didn't have that blunt, heavy-handed way with men that left no doubt about who was in charge. No, that wasn't Ike's nature. You just got the impression that he was the hardest-working, best-prepared, and least officious man in the room. He did have a look he gave people who tried his patience. That look cut right through you, and made you feel like you deserved to be busted down two grades on the spot. But if you understood the mission as the General understood the mission, and you gave him 100% in support of that mission, then you might occasionally see him flash the grin. That grin. One of those, and you knew you'd walk across France just to fight under his command.

If you were an Allied general staff officer in the summer of '44, France was the place you wanted to be. And Ike was the man you wanted to be associated with. Forget the sireen calls of Marlene Dietrich, Betty Grable, Rita Hayworth. A fling with a movie star would last you just one night. But at the SHAEF headquarters compound outside Deauville two months after D-DAY, there was the inescapable sensation that you were part of an event (General Eisenhower himself later came to refer to it in his memoirs as a "Crusade") that would likely change the course of history, and your life along with it.

That's a pretty good bang for your buck.

But I'm not here to replay the military events of that long-ago summer. You can read your history books if that's what you're after. I'm just here to tell you about Ike. Because if you understood Ike, you understood what the fight was really about. And that's something that even the history books don't always get right.

Understand first that at this point, prior to his appointment as Supreme Commander of the Allied Expeditionary Forces just five months earlier, this particular Army officer had never held any command above a battalion level in his thirty-year military career. (Equally astounding and little-remarked-upon is the fact that when he was elected President of the United States, eight years after that summer, it was his first elective office at any level.) To call Ike a "force of history" as I did in a piece written for the *Atlantic Monthly* in support of his candidacy in 1952, may be overstating the case (Well, the Democrats certainly thought so), but not by much. It was largely through the "twisted genius" (another phrase that I used in that same article, and which, likewise, did not endear me to the Democratic party) of Franklin Roosevelt that this otherwise unremarkable Midwestern careerist came to find himself placed at the nexus of the greatest military endeavor ever undertaken. Were there other officers at the time who grumbled or politely caterwauled at his appointment? Well, George Marshall got his ears pinned back pretty good from what I understand. But the fact is that events were moving too powerfully and too fast to allow much time for that kind of backbiting. FDR brooked none of it, at any rate. If there was ever a President called upon to exercise the role of Commander in Chief in a more critical phase of our nation's history, you tell me who that might be, because his name certainly escapes me. By August of 1944, when the Allied forces' grand scheme was beginning to click into place, you were either on board with FDR's strategy, or you were sitting on the sidelines somewhere, completely overlooked and forgotten. (And in a time of war, I can promise you, this is a position in which no career officer ever wants to find himself.)

But I digress. Back to France we go. Back to a weekend in early August. I was traveling with the Third Armored Division, writing about the war from the perspective of a "grunt" for *Argosy* Magazine when I chanced to learn that a couple of battalion commanders from Division were on their way in a staff car from our advanced position near Rouen over to SHAEF headquarters at Deauville. I had been with elements of the Division since they had made their way ashore on D-Day plus six, and as they were, for the moment, not advancing, I took advantage of my friendship with a certain Colonel to get myself invited aboard that staff car. Deauville was no more than a two hour drive by a secure corridor that the Allied forces had established, and the opportunity to view the war effort from the exalted perspective of the SHAEF mucky-mucks after humping it with the infantry was a respite (and a perspective) that I thought would be well in keeping with my assignment.

For once, the roads were dry and firm (when it rains, it doesn't take long for deuce and a half troop trucks, heavy artillery pieces and M4 Shermans to reduce unpaved road surfaces to muddy quagmires with ruts as deep as gravesites). Having left our encampment at first light, by 9:00 AM we were sweeping up the gravel drive of one of those sprawling Louis XIV estates not more than five klicks from the coast. As we pulled up to the front of the main building, I beheld a scene that impressed me deeply, and not in a good way. The front steps were uncomfortably clustered with uniformed high-ranking officers of several armies. Once I dismounted and moved around the area stretching my legs, I recognized, besides Great Britain and the U.S., armed forces personnel of Poland and France, and involuntarily flinched at the thought of so much rank assembled rather tightly in one place in an area that was still very much a war zone. A summer sun was making its lazy presence felt, and many of the fellows were smoking and chatting as I made my way up the steps with a singular mission. I went unchallenged past a couple of sentries in full battle dress and found myself in a grand foyer. Moving down the way, I popped my head into the first door on the right and ran smack into the typing pool, a dozen men and women in a smoky room pounding away at their Coronas, churning out the kind of workload that kept an army of nearly a million men organized and on the move.

"Command staff?" I inquired. Barely looking up from their labors, several raised fingers and indicated that the personnel I was looking for were on the second floor. Starting back out the door, I literally bumped into an American captain with a strong jaw, head of wavy black hair and a hell-bent look about him. Drawing back and rapidly scanning me, he took in the somewhat disheveled look of my recently-slept-in field uniform, the lack of proper insignia, and the distinct absence of military bearing.

"You're in the wrong Goddamn neighborhood, soldier," he proclaimed, indicating with a brusque jerk of an upraised thumb that it would be in my best interest to absent the premises immediately. Sleeping in a Louis XIV mansion will have that effect on a man. If, on the other hand, you've been sleeping in ditches and sheds, you learn to dispense with certain civilized niceties.

"I'm right where I belong this morning, Captain, thank you. And I'm looking for your Commanding General."

He drew back, briefly reassessing me. Very briefly. "I'm gonna let that comment pass, son." (There was some irony in this, as the Captain was very likely my junior by several years.) "But if you're not on your way PDQ, I'll have my MP's escort you out the door."

At this critical juncture in our exchange, as we stood in the open door of the communications room, out of the passing parade of busy brass moving through the foyer, one detached himself and made his way towards the door we were partially blocking. He was carrying a sheaf of papers, and wore a single gold oak leaf on his lapel. Pausing in front of us, he raising a quizzical eyebrow in the Captain's direction.

"Sorry, sir, this soldier claims that he has a message for the General."

The eyebrow was now raised in my direction. The Major was a man of few words.

"Major, I'm David Quinn, on assignment with *Argosy* Magazine. And it's true, I'd love to spend a few minutes with General Eisenhower. But in the meanwhile, I came into the building to point out that the concentration of top brass conveniently bunched on the front steps of this building would be a German artillery commander's idea of a wet dream, sir, and I think it would be a great step forward for our war effort if somebody told 'em to break it up out there. Sir."

The Major now redirected his attention, eyebrows and all, back to the Captain, who suddenly began to look suspiciously like our favorite comic-book hero, Sad Sack. "Captain, let's accommodate this here civilian gent and see if we can do something about that unfortunate situation, what do you say?"

Well, my fortuitous pointing out of this obvious breach of military security to a building full of people who were too damn busy and too damn important to think of it themselves beguiled the Major so much that he personally escorted me up the lovely curving stairway to the magnificent second floor of the facility, down a hallway, through two doors, and into a small sitting room. "Wait here, son," he said, and disappeared through another door, this one guarded by two British sentries who did not deign to look in my direction. Not more than a minute later, the Major pulled open the door and gestured me inside. And that's how I found myself inside the inner sanctum and in the presence of the Supreme Commander, SHAEF.

The most important man in the greatest military campaign in history was sitting behind a large desk, the surface of which was cluttered with sheaves of paperwork, several decorative tabletop flags, and at least one ashtray already well-stocked with butt-ends of the day's consumption. He had shed his jacket (hanging it over the back of his chair), but his tie was properly knotted and his shirt sharply creased. When I entered the room, he was on the telephone, but he picked me up with his eyes and tracked me carefully as I came to an uncertain halt somewhere between the door and his desk. The room was not magisterial by any means, but it was amply sized for the Commander's desk, a couple of sitting chairs and a small coffee table. The walls were lined with books and a picture window behind the General's head looked out onto a pleasant copse of trees beyond.

The Major touched my elbow, steering me towards the coffee table, and invited me to sit in one of the chairs while I waited. It wasn't long. The General soon clattered the receiver back into its cradle and was on his feet, coming in my direction. He moved on the balls of his feet and had a flat belly, square shoulders, and erect posture. It bespoke, I supposed, a life of military discipline. I rose quickly. The Major, my sponsor, was still at my side. "Here's your civilian safety counselor, General," he chuckled.

Ike sailed into me, taking my outstretched hand with a firm and fair shake. "You'd think for the love of God we'd be able to look out for ourselves around here, young man. We owe you a debt of gratitude for putting us back on track."

"Not at all, General. I've been traveling with Easy Company of the 506th for over a month now. They've schooled me pretty well in looking out for myself."

Eisenhower shot a glance at the Major. "Bud Shrake's outfit?" The Major nodded in the affirmative. "He's where now, Rouen?" Again affirmative. Then he came back to me. "Which side of the estuary are those boys on this morning?"

"On the near side. The East side. At least when I left this morning." I remember being impressed that a man with such a broad scope of responsibility could possibly have such detailed local knowledge.

"You jump in with that outfit, son?"

"Negative, sir. I came in on the beach and hooked up with 'em about three klicks east of St. Mere on D plus six." There was something apologetic in my tone which he quickly countered.

"Hell, I came in on the beach myself, D plus three. Still plenty hairy once we got inland."

"Plenty hairy all the way to Rouen, sir."

The weight of the day and the decisions pressing upon him could be felt pressing in upon our impromptu gathering. The General was a man who carried himself with an economy of movement, used to batting aside interruptions and distractions as one might bat away mosquitoes at a beach. But he wasn't going to bat us away just yet. "What was your name again, son?"

"Quinn, sir, David Quinn. *Argosy* magazine."

"Well, Mr. Quinn, as you can see, we're running a war here, and I can't keep the dogs at bay for very long. Phil, get us a pot of coffee, willya? (That would be Major Phil). Tell you what. You've done me a favor, and although I know for a fact that you have no appointment, and probably no damn business being in the area, I can give you fifteen minutes for your magazine, how'll that be?"

"More than I ever could have hoped for, sir." Add "media-savvy" to his already impressive list of credentials, I thought.

"Tommy, do us a favor and ride herd on my telephone for a few minutes, will you please?" he directed a Lieutenant who occupied a smaller desk on the other side of the room. Indicating that I should park myself back in the chair where I had been seated, he pulled out the other chair, and hesitated. "And see if you can grab us another chair from outside somewhere."

"Right here, General," replied young Tommy, and presented his chair before he slipped out the door to find a replacement. As he did, Major Phil slipped back in bearing a coffee pot on a tray. He placed three cups on the small table around which we would sit.

"If you don't mind, I'm gonna have Major Ulehein sit in with us, he's my official fact-checker and tries to keep me from putting my foot where it doesn't belong." Media-savvy indeed.

The three of us sat, and the Major poured the coffee. Not surprisingly, I noted that General Eisenhower took his without the adornments of either cream or sugar. I myself was a user of both, but in keeping with the Spartan sentiments of my host, I asked for neither. In fact, as we settled in, my mind was well occupied with how best to structure my fifteen minutes with a man who, at this point in time, would easily qualify as the world's most exclusive interview. (In fact, the subsequent records indicated that General Eisenhower did not sit for a single one-on-one interview again until sometime in early June of 1945 in Washington, D.C., a month after the cessation of hostilities in Europe. It turns out I beat the entire journalistic world by nearly a calendar year.) I was more than dimly aware of the extreme nature of my good fortune, and in those moments available to me as the General lit a cigarette and took a slug of coffee, I resolved to take full advantage of the opportunity. The General, I figured, would expect no less. He extended the pack in my direction as an afterthought. Lucky Strikes, what else? Although I was not much of a smoker, I did understand the value of creating empathy with my subject, and I accepted his offering without hesitation. He even leaned across with his Zippo and lit me up. His hand, I noticed, was rock steady. Upon withdrawing his arm, I noticed that he shot a glance at his wristwatch. Time was marching on, and we had better do the same.

I had dropped my shoulder bag on the floor beside my chair and withdrawn one of my notepads. I was never without two or three pens in the pocket of my field jacket. I knew there was not much point in pressing him on tactics and strategy. The situation was entirely too fluid, and *Argosy* readers wouldn't see my copy for a matter of weeks at the earliest. It needed to be more of a profile piece. And besides, he would probably have to stonewall me on any question of a purely military nature. As this thought crossed my mind, Eisenhower confirmed my prognosis. "Before we start, Mr. Quinn, let me promise you that the Major here is not going to let me discuss anything of an operational nature. Other than that, you're free to take your best shot." He wasn't grinning.

"I pretty much had that part figured that out, General. So let's try something along these lines. I figure most of my readers would be really curious to know: what was going through your mind during the early hours of June 6 when the men were in the boats, in the air, and on the beaches?"

For a long moment he said nothing, and for the first time I sensed how impossibly alone his position had rendered him. What most people don't realize is how very expressive his features were. He was a Midwesterner, through and through. He came from a race of people unschooled at hiding things. Their faces will tell you the whole story. His face was a stony mask of private reminiscence. For a moment I think he actually lost sight of me. Then he took a long pull on his Lucky Strike.

As he exhaled, a thin stream of smoke escaped between pursed lips. "Couple of things, I guess. A great sense of relief that we were underway, finally. The nights of June 3rd and 4th were a lot tougher than anything that came later, I can promise you that." I noticed that he pointedly kept his eyes off of the Major. "And the other thing would be that feeling that comes over you when you commit troops to a fight. If ever in his life a man's gonna get religion, that will be the time."

"Is religion something that's part of your makeup, General?"

At this point his features softened. In fact, I would describe his countenance as boyish. I'm dead serious. At the age of fifty-plus, he still looked like an Eagle Scout. (Which at one point, I'm sure he had been.) "Hard to get by in this man's army without it, I can tell you that." He smiled wryly.

"General, you've been going head to head with the German Army for some time now, both in Africa and now in Europe. Can you tell me what your sense is of the Germans as a fighting force?"

"That's a good question, son, and I'm happy to answer it. I don't think too many people can respect the kind of government that's running their country right now. I could use a few choice adjectives, but Phil, I won't." He shot the Major a quick glance. "What I will tell you is that in the field, the German Army is probably one of the most formidable fighting forces that has ever gone to war. Their troops are organized, they're disciplined, they're well-trained and very well equipped. They don't shy away from a fight. I don't know how much of the Nazi ideology actually gets into the ranks, and I don't care. Our job is to defeat them in battle, and you can bet that they are not going away without one hell of a fight. None of what I've said, incidentally, will be news to our boys in the field who have to carry the fight to them every day. Wouldn't you agree with that assessment, Major?"

"D'you even have to ask?" Major Ulehein's role as Ike's aide-de-camp was becoming understandable. His downbeat personality was a quiet, reliable counterpoint to Eisenhower's more hyperactive temperament, and yet it was clear the two men were of one mind.

"How about if I asked you the same question with regard to the Allied troops under your command?"

"That's only fair, and I'm even happier to answer. As you know, we came in late, and our fellows had a lot of catching-up to do. The Germans, the French, the Poles, and the British had nearly three years of combat under their belts before we reached the continent. So that was a disadvantage we had to overcome. And I'll tell you how we did it. It wasn't so much tactics and strategy, or superior equipment, which, God knows, we didn't have, although we are closing that gap. More than anything, as near as I can tell, it was optimism. Our boys came over here with a tremendous sense of belief in their mission, and with full confidence in their battlefield commanders. I don't care how good a fighter you are, if you lose belief and confidence, you're gonna quit when things get rough. We've got some quitting going on now by the Germans, here and there. Meanwhile, our armies are optimistic, and getting more optimistic on a daily basis. Discipline and preparedness are important on the battlefield, I can't overstate that. But I'll take our inbred American optimism any day." Despite the obvious fatigue and the crushing weight of his responsibilities, not to mention the three-pack-a-day habit that I guessed he had, as he spoke his face took on the holy gleam of true passion. I had certainly touched a nerve. Regardless of the conviction of his sentiments, however, I found myself involuntarily thinking of the men of the 506th back in the neighborhood of Rouen. I had seen them on numerous occasions lying in ditches in 12 inches of muddy, fuel-stained water while being pounded by German 88's. Times when optimism was not their foremost emotion.

"Next question, sir: what would it take to make your job over the next few weeks or months easier?"

"You won't get much of a debate there. The answer is fuel, plain and simple. This army runs on diesel fuel, and lots of it. Keeping up with our daily fuel consumption is job one, for today and the foreseeable future."

"That and the weather," the Major put in. "If the roads stay firm things tend to go a lot more smoothly."

"That would be just lovely, but we sure can't count on it," the General added. He shot an undisguised glance at his wristwatch. I felt I was doing a good job under the circumstances, but unless I got lucky and hit on a topic that really wound them up, I knew my time was just about to end. "General, to delve a little bit more into the personal side, it's no secret that you were kind of a dark horse pick for the role of Supreme Commander. With all respect, sir (and I meant those words with all my heart), what qualities or characteristics do you think recommended you for this responsibility?"

At this, Ike actually flashed that grin of his that would become so well-known later on. It was an endearing, disarming, and thoroughly genuine expression of delight that would have been perfectly at home on the face of a 12-year-old. "Son, you're asking me to sit over here and decipher the enigma of the United States Army. I gave up that campaign a long time ago. We all did." He laughed out loud and glanced at the Major, whose job I understood it would be to formally terminate the session when the time came. My own tidy-enough sense of timekeeping told me I had a good two or three minutes left if the gents were going to play fair. Still, as the boys in baseball liked to say, it was time to swing for the fences.

"Fair enough, General. To wrap this up, I'd like to do a little word-association with you. I'm going to run through some names of people or places with which you're familiar, and I'd like to ask you to respond with the first word or two that comes to mind. A first-blush kind of thing. Okay with you, Major?"

"As long as my name's not on the list, go ahead." Ulehein was simply great at keeping things on an even keel.

"Here we go then, General: let's start with an easy one: Normandy Beachheads."

"Bloody. And bloody lucky."

"Sherman Tanks."

"Indispensable."

"General George Marshall." (This was the man who, it had been widely assumed, would be doing the job Eisenhower was doing today.)

"Genius. Plain and simple genius."

"General Charles DeGaulle." (It was reported that the imperious Frenchman had been a thorn in Ike's side throughout the proceedings.)

"French. Very French." Eisenhower was hedging his bets a bit, but he had fallen into the swing of things. Which way should I swing him?

"General Bernard Montgomery." (His rifts with the American command were an open secret.)

"Careful." Perhaps hedging the bet there.

"President Roosevelt."

"Formidable."

"Winston Churchill."

"A fighter."

"Adolf Hitler."

He watched me levelly. "I'll pass on that one."

"ME-109."

"Deadly."

"P-51."

"Deadlier."

"General George Patton." (The commander of the Third Army was making quite a name for himself as a flamboyant leader).

"Georgie?" It was almost a question.

"Joseph Stalin."

"Rough character."

"Abeline, Kansas." (The place where the General had grown up.)

"Freedom."

"The American fighting man."

"Gift of God."

"General Dwight Eisenhower."

"His humble servant." His hand was on the tabletop now, as if in preparation for pushing off.

"The United States of America."

Here, for the first time, he hesitated. Then, with something of a shrug, as though it were obvious: "First love."

"First love. We can't do any better than that," Ulehein put in, slapping his hand lightly on the table. "As good a place to end it as any." He pushed himself to his feet just ahead of the General. I was a little slower, stowing my gear and retrieving my field pack. By the time I stood, Eisenhower had his hand extended in my direction.

"Hope we made it worth your while. You going back to join the 506th?"

"Probably for another week or so, then it's likely on to another assignment. Just out of curiosity General, forgive me for asking, but what's the general timeline for getting to Berlin?" (When I showed up back at the CP of Easy Company and told them I had talked to Eisenhower, that would be the one question they would want to know about. The only one.)

Ike looked at Ulehein, then back at me. "I think I'll let the Major take that one, Mr. Quinn. Frankly, I couldn't really say. Don't let the fancy title and the big office fool you. I just work here." And with a wink and a nod, he turned on his heel and made his way back across toward his desk, and my surprisingly sudden access to the Supreme Allied Commander ended just as suddenly.

Ulehein moved in, steering me lightly but pointedly by the elbow towards the door. "Let me bring you downstairs," he said. Once we were out the door and bound for the staircase I did not hesitate to follow up.

"How about it, Major? If I get back to Easy Company and tell them I didn't get any word on Berlin, they'll kick me in the ass."

"No doubt," Major Phil commiserated. We reached the stairs and began our descent. "I'd rather go back to your other question—the one about how General Eisenhower came to be appointed Supreme Commander." We reached the bottom of the staircase and he paused. "I'll tell you what the reason is: because this man is a master at getting disagreeable people to agree. Near as I can tell, it's a trait he has in common with our President, which is why the President picked him out of the pack. On top of that, he outworks everyone in his command, he stands up to the flak when it comes his way, and he's not interested in the least on pulling rank, which, when you lead by example, you really shouldn't have to. I've been around all the top brass in this man's army, and believe me, those are qualities that become more scarce the closer to the top you get. I can only say, thank God the President put the man where he is." Having said his piece as bluntly and forcefully as it sounds, Major Phil moved out towards the front entrance, keeping me in tow.

"I appreciate the observations, Major." By now we had reached the entrance and he was ready to turn back, but not before stepping outside with me and scanning the area. The knots and clusters of men that had been present when I had arrived half an hour earlier were conspicuously absent. "I appreciate the observations," I said again, "but I'd still like to get your call on Berlin."

The Major, who was a diminutive sort, not more that 5'4", looked up at me, squinting in the watery glare of the French summer morning. "Son, you're a pretty bright fellow. You've seen how the German fights. You probably have some geographical understanding of the distances and the terrain of this part of the continent. So you know that of all the questions you had a chance to put to the General, that was the only one that could be qualified as being just plain damn foolish. There's still a world of hurt between us and that damn Brandenburg Gate. But if you've got to tell 'em anything back at the company level, just tell 'em that however long it takes, it'll happen quicker under this general than any other commander in this man's army. How about that?"

"Not before Christmas, then?" I laughed.

"Why not next Fourth of July?" Major Ulehein laughed back. As it turned out, his toss-off remark, which was probably made to keep me from carrying too rosy a picture back to the trenches (the fact is that ending the war by Christmas was thought by many to be entirely within the realm of possibility) turned out to be remarkably prescient. He only missed the mark by about two months.

Explaining that I would be lingering in the area until I was able to hook up with my ride back to Rouen, I shook the Major's hand in farewell, and he went back into the building to carry on with his duties. As for me, I hung around in the area for another hour or so, but made good use of the time by interviewing both a British Captain and a Polish Major about their take on the Allied partnership. In each case the mention of Eisenhower's name provoked deference and admiration. And when asked for their thoughts about how much longer the Germans could keep fighting, they each predicted that the war in Europe would be wrapped up by the beginning of 1945. If only that optimistic vision had proven to be the case, how many lives would have been spared? As history will attest, 1944 ended with Allied troops bogged down and dying in the snow, and Berlin seemingly further away than ever.

No wonder Ulehein and the General had deferred from jumping on the Christmas bandwagon. Career soldier Eisenhower understood the German will to resist, perhaps better than any of his subordinates.

Fast forward now, fifteen years. I am at a cocktail party in the lovely town of Nassau, Bahama Islands, a guest of a friend of many years who, like me, was a correspondent during the war. Later he'd had a considerable amount of success in Hollywood as a screenwriter, although like many others who entered that profession, he liked to refer to himself as a "glorified hack." Hack or not, he owned his condo in the Bahamas, wore expensive jewelry and seemed to be able to charm the ladies into his bed with ease, so his life couldn't have been too awfully trying. On this particular evening in the early summer of 1960, there were a dozen or so of us in attendance, and as the guests were mingling and the liquor was flowing, Leonard beckoned us off the patio and into an expansive drawing room where a television set flickered in one corner. In response to the Russian shoot-down of an American spy plane, the President was addressing the nation. One can no longer recall his words on that occasion, but it hardly matters. For those assembled in the room that night, Dwight Eisenhower was an object of derision. His befuddled grandfatherly countenance and his halting syntax (a heart attack and a subsequent mini-stroke had taken their toll) were on full display, drawing snide laughter and expressions of refined disgust. By now everybody sensed that the country was about to turn the page on history. (Just two months later in Los Angeles the Democrats would nominate a

43-year-old shave-tail Lieutenant for the office of the Presidency in a move that only a screenwriter could have dreamed). Ike was old, and he was old news. Stooped shoulders and a paunch had replaced his erect military bearing, and he had turned his formidable weapons not into ploughshares, but golf clubs. It wasn't only Democrats (like the crowd I was with in Nassau), but Republicans who were eager to get on with history. The glow of accomplishment that a resounding Allied victory, engineered in no small part by Eisenhower, should have bestowed upon an entire generation, if not two, had been snuffed out all too soon by Truman's concessions at Potsdam and Russia's pilfering of Atomic secrets. Instead of getting to take an eight-year victory lap, Ike was instead relegated to the role of managing one untidy crises after another as emerging nations pushed their way onto the world stage, pummeling the status quo and elbowing the US in the eye as often as possible. The General was simply not the man for the job, that was the consensus. Maybe he never had been, opined many. The old codger should have pushed off when the pushing was good, and kept his legacy intact. It was the dawn of a bright new world, and the old man would have no place in it.

Standing in the back of the room in that tidy condo, I fought back a wave of discouragement. How little the assembled guests seem to remember those days not so many years earlier when the fate of our wonderful world hung in the balance. How little they realize that, as much as any other factor, it was the robust faith, the frank optimism, and the indefatigatible work ethic embodied in the doddering old man on the television screen that had tipped the balance. Instead of Godless totalitarian regimes scrapping over the corpse of Western civilization, what we had was the freedom to enjoy our martinis on a tropical patio while speaking English and practicing professions of our own choosing.

I finished my drink and moved outside, crossed the patio, and walked across the trimly-cut lawn, navigating by the faint glow of a series of landscape lights. I thought back to the uplifting sight of the General on that morning in Deauville. Light on the balls of his feet, shoulders square and bearing erect, coming towards me with a look of keen anticipation and boundless confidence on his broad, open features, he had represented the future we all wanted to believe in, and still did. I didn't want to lose that. I didn't think that, as a people, we could afford to.

David Quinn
Los Angeles, California, 1965

THE ARMOR OF LIGHT

That business about the road was no exaggeration, I can tell you that. Over the years I heard a number of people describe it, and it came to be regarded as something of a badge of honor once you had withstood the two to three hours of choking dust, gut-wrenching switchbacks, and stomach-churning hairpin turns that made the thirty-five miles it covered seem more like a hundred. And to think, I only did it twice. To this day I find myself a little bit in awe of the folks who covered that ground once or twice a week for two or three years. But I've never spoken to a single one who didn't think it was worth it.

Unlike most of them, I didn't really need to make the trip. In fact, when we could not uncover a single chum, companion, or family member to accompany me, the whole venture nearly died on the vine. But a singularly independent streak that had resided in my breast since my earliest days came strongly to the fore, and I somehow convinced my parents that I was indeed mature, self-reliant, and otherwise charmed enough to be able to manage it quite on my own. Dad was hired in March of 1943, which was kind of a critical point in my life. I had graduated high school in May, turned 19 in June, and had already been accepted by Oregon State University where orientation began in the first week of September. My life was on a well-scripted track, with no time for detours. But already our lives had been somewhat disrupted by this new job, which involved him and mom and my little brother packing up and moving to New Mexico. For how long, I wanted to know. I was probably a little bit petulant about it, I now confess. "For the duration," my dad said sardonically. This was a phrase that we'd all gotten used to during the war years, and it had a kind of wry humor to it, at least until it happened to you. It had been arranged that I would live with my aunt and uncle in Corvallis once classes began, which was kind of convenient. What was less convenient was that instead of a pre-college summer spent with dear friends in familiar haunts, I would find myself on a three-day train trip to Santa Fe, New Mexico, a ride up that torturous road to "The Hill," and a week or so spent in some God-forsaken, far-flung "Goat Kingdom" before I would have to retrace my steps and come dragging into Corvallis pooped and disheveled with just ten days or so to get ready for my encounter with Higher Learning. Two precious weeks shot to hell. Something told me the adventure would be worth the investment, but setting out, I was far from certain.

As I recall, after catching my first train right there in Salem, we followed the coast down to San

Francisco, where I caught train number two to Los Angeles, where train number three got me headed east finally, all the way to Kingman, Arizona. From there, train number four got us over to Albuquerque. After that it was just a short hop on train number five up to Santa Fe. I'm being facetious. There were no "short hops" by train in those days. The rail system had been taken over by the Army, and priority routings always went to trains shuttling troops and trains bearing war materials. If you were a mere civilian passenger, you were destined to spend long hours parked on sidings while these priority trains swept through. Hopefully you had some good reading material or interesting companions in your car, because as the hours stretched on, you and your fellow travelers became something of a community on wheels, suspended in time with no fixed place in the world. The country seemed like a much larger place then, and a great deal of patience and good will was required to traverse it, even for modest distances. The final leg of my journey, from Albuquerque to Santa Fe, was less than eighty miles, and we knocked that out in just six and a half hours—which is about the amount of time I had spent in Los Angeles simply changing trains. So when I disembarked at last, about five in the afternoon of August 6, I actually might have had something like a spring in my step. And, even at my tender age, a desire for something stronger than lemonade to knock off my "trail dust."

As any American schoolchild, I was well acquainted with the legend and lore of the "Santa Fe Trail," and to find myself standing at the very terminus of that famous overland passage made the whole adventure seem suddenly worthwhile. It wasn't hard to imagine how it must have been, when one of those heavily-laden wagon trains rolled in. It was greeted by general pandemonium as a crush of people and animals milled about: full-blooded Indians, mixed-bloods, trail-wizened cowboys, sharp-eyed grifters, and women in pueblo garb bearing hand-made turquoise jewelry all pressed in close to the wagons while dusty dogs chased one another about under the horses' hooves. The whole scene was punctuated by the shouts of the trail bosses and the glad cries of children. Except for a dearth of horses, that was very nearly the scene that greeted me when I stepped off the bus that had brought us up from the station. "Claire, are you quite certain that your parents will be meeting you?" The young man who had attached himself to me during the latter stages of my journey (actually, one of several who had done so) was extra solicitous, and I assured him that I would be fine from this point. As my mother so liked to remind me, I was a girl who had always looked "mature beyond her years," and even around Salem I was frequently having to fend off the unsolicited attentions of males, particularly those in the thirty to forty-year-old range. (Fellows my own age were perhaps a little intimidated by my looks and my less-than-helpless bearing). So I gently gave this fellow his walking papers, and made my way over to the center of the Plaza, where I lingered for a time just taking it all in. The soft, rounded corners of the adobe architecture, the pristine quality of the air at twilight time, and the sense of community that emanated from the center of this high-desert town did much to banish the tiredness from my bones and the dullness from my senses. There was an element of promise in the atmosphere, and I let it surround and embrace me without wondering much about the nature of its origin.

My reverie could not last. Night would soon fall, and my journey was incomplete. As per instructions, I proceeded to E. Palace St., the street bordering the plaza on the north side. It featured a long porch-like overhang which gave directly on to the street and served as a convenient gathering, loitering, selling or buying place for denizens of the plaza. Even at this hour on a Friday evening it was quite well populated, and I could feel numerous eyes on me as I passed along beneath the overhang. (I indulged in the poetic conceit of myself as Frontier Trail Guide, keen of eye, loose of limb, adorned in worn buckskin chaps and trail-scarred boots, my spurs jangling with decisive authority as I made my way. The fact that I stood 5'8" in my bare feet, weighed just 130 pounds, and was already an accomplished horsewoman was most helpful in picturing myself as a bold adventuress). As soon as I left the plaza behind, the street underwent a change of character, and became delightfully ancient and inviting, with wrought iron gates giving on to walled gardens and shadowy patios, a far cry from my secure realities and developed world of Salem, Oregon. I felt my pulse quickening involuntarily with a kind of anticipation as I searched in vain for a street number that would guide me to my destination. My father had specifically instructed that I would find the project office "in the very first block off the plaza," so even after failing in my first effort, I retraced my steps, and decided somewhat impulsively to go in the first gate that seemed to offer access. Having done this, I found myself at the end of a short cobblestone passageway facing a door with fading brown paint from which hung a small blue sign with red lettering:

U.S. ENG
RS

As my father Owen was a research engineer and was employed by an agency of the Federal Government, I suddenly was seized by the conviction that I had found the right place, and giving three quick raps on the door, I proceeded to turn the handle and push. This didn't seem like the kind of place where you waited for someone to open the door from within. The door yielded, and I stepped inside.

I had made the right choice.

Serendipity isn't always a welcome guest in our lives, as least not in the moment it actually appears. It wasn't until 8:30 AM the following morning that I was able to embark on the final stage of my journey. After registering with one of the secretaries at the Palace St. address the evening before, I had been directed to the nearby La Fonda Hotel, where I slept on a cot in a room shared with two other similarly inconvenienced voyagers. While being escorted through the vast, inviting lobby with its rugged Frontier West décor, I had noted the bar, with its happy and rather loud contingent of night-revelers, and I confess a longing to join them there and become a part of their impromptu celebration. Once my head hit the pillow, however, the longing for such celebration was immediately displaced by the fervent embrace of much-deserved sleep. The serendipity in question was the fact that, as a result of the night's lay-over, my final ascent to "The Hill" took place on a clear desert morning, rather than during the night hours, when the strange and occasionally terrible marvels of that 35 mile pilgrimage would have been hidden from my wondering gaze.

"Indian country," that was my first thought. As our well-worn truck left the environs of Santa Fe, it soon entered the kind of country to which we American youth had been introduced by a steady diet of Hollywood Westerns: a harsh and twisted landscape cut through with gulches and gullies, pockmarked with sudden outcroppings of smooth boulders and dotted with twisted trees and low-lying brush, stunted survivors of the endless seasons of dry winds and a harsh, unforgiving sun. There were four of us making the trip, and the old truck's gears ground agonizingly each time the driver downshifted. The narrow two-lane blacktop soon gave way to gravel and then entered a region of hairpin turns, scarcely more than a dusty track, barely capable of accommodating two vehicles abreast. Gradually we began to ascend. Beyond the rough shoulders of the old road the land would suddenly disappear, falling away for what seemed like hundreds of feet into deep, rock-strewn ravines and gulches. "If we were to roll off here, I imagine it would take a week for them just to find us," commented one of the other travelers, verbalizing a thought which I was trying at that moment to banish from my own mind. By the final half-hour of our transit, the road had achieved such a steep grade and the surface was so scattered with dislodged rock that the truck could barely manage to maintain headway. Not always able to bring myself to gaze out at the scarifying scene, I kept my eyes on our driver instead, reasoning that I could better judge exactly how dire our circumstances might be by his demeanor. He seemed inconvenienced only to a minor degree, however, and piloted us sure-handedly upward, perhaps mildly bemused by our growing anxiety and all but oblivious to the tortured agony of his truck. When at last we shuddered to a stop in front of a high gate patrolled by military guards, it seemed at least that we had once again entered the world of the twentieth century, the one in which most of us felt decidedly more comfortable.

Passing through those gates, we arrived on the high mesa at the place called Los Alamos where the Government's secret war project was being undertaken. My first thoughts as the truck made its way through the area was, how could my mom have let this happen? Always conscientious, meticulous, and thorough, how could she have set aside a lifetime of careful planning and preparation to allow her family to wind up in a place like this? It was like nothing I had ever seen. It was in a shambles, altogether an ugly, rambling, monstrosity. The top of the mesa had been taken over by a horde of bulldozers which had carved the earth into a series of terrible naked scars that, in the wake of recent rains, were now a sea of mud. There was unfinished construction everywhere, and I do not mean the kind of building that holds forth the promise of beauty and regularity when it is completed. It looked instead that they were going to enormous expense to throw up nothing more than a shanty town, a ramshackle agglomeration of plywood structures with power lines strung haphazardly here and there and barbed wire fencing (always a lovely touch) running randomly through it. Trucks both military and civilian crawled across the terrain, making their careful way around the large muddy puddles that had formed in low-lying areas. Almost without awareness of it, I found myself wiping tears from my eyes for my mother's sake. The site was an affront to everything she represented, and now she and her husband and son were going to be struck here "for the duration." I found myself clinging to the thought of our lovely little two-story home on a tree-lined street in Salem and almost wishing that the truck would turn around and make its way back down that torture trail into Santa Fe where I could retreat to the La Fonda and sit at the bar among civilized people and forget this entire episode.

Mom and Stephen were waiting at the depot where the truck finally ground to a halt. Otherwise, I might not have disembarked. I'm sure I looked shaken and dispirited, and mom took me in her arms and embraced me tenderly as though I were a five-year old again. "Oh sweetie, it's not as bad as all that. Just think of it as an adventure," she whispered in my ear. I drew back and quickly searched her face to see if her resolve was as steely as she pretended. She gave me a big smile without flinching and squeezed my hand. "We're pioneers, don't 'cha know?" she said jauntily. Stephen was holding my other hand, and there was no hiding the excitement in his face. "Claire, I've got to show you something really neat," he exclaimed. "C'mon, we've even got mud boots for you."

I simply suspended my disbelief then, and by degrees my apprehensions were quieted during the course of that Saturday afternoon. The family quarters were a cross between an apartment and a house, a modest set of rooms in a row of identical plywood structures, and my mother had worked her usual magic in converting the rooms to something resembling a home, with fresh flowers on the dining/living room table, artwork which she had procured from the Indian vendors back in Santa Fe adorning the walls, and the impeccable tidiness and order which were her hallmarks. Stephen had his own room, small but serviceable (at the age of 11, any space that you can call your own is acceptable, however humble). Mom and Dad had a bedroom as well. There was a bathroom (no tub, shower only), and finally the ample room that served as the dining and living area, with a small kitchen adjoining. "It keeps the rain off," my mom chirped as I surveyed our surroundings. When I shrugged, she took me briefly by the shoulders. "No, honey, I mean it really keeps the rain off. After some of the gully washers we've had, that's something you don't want to take for granted." She fixed the three of us a light meal of chicken sandwiches and produced a couple of nice cold Coca-Colas that went down most refreshingly. After that I donned my boots and Stephen took me on his Breathless Tour of the area, which included his hidden cache of empty nail kegs, a jaunty exchange with a bulldozer operator whom he had befriended (and who did something of a double take at the sight of the young beauty Stephen was squiring about), and a walk past an obviously important compound that was gated and surrounded by an ten-foot-tall barrier of something Stephen called razor wire. "That's where Dad works," he added in passing. "They call it the Tech Area."

"Can we go in and see him?"

"Nah. You gotta have a special badge to go in there."

"What goes on in there?"

"I dunno exactly, but I think they're building some kind of space-ship or something." He didn't seem particularly impressed by the idea.

"Right," I said. "We're certainly going to be needing something like that."

As the afternoon light began to fade, we made our way to the western rim of the mesa to visit another of the wonders of Stephen's expanding world, and this one was actually pretty special. We clambered to the top of a cluster of enormous smooth boulders and were rewarded with a hawk's-eye view clear to the distant horizon. The lengthening shadows softened the rugged terrain, and lent it an air of impenetrable mystery, so much so that I was overtaken with a peculiar keen yearning, almost like the awakening of some sexual desire. With the fading of the sunlight, the air was taking on a decidedly cool character, and I crossed my arms over my breasts against a chill that ran though me. "Say, buster, it's high time we were gettin' back to the ranch. Pop'll be ridin' in and Ma'll have some grub on," I said in my best Zane Grey.

"I wouldn't be too sure about Dad. He's been comin' home really late." We made our way back down the boulders and across the bulldozer scars back to our plywood mansion.

In fact my dad, Owen Waring, didn't show up until we were clearing away the dinner dishes. ("No point in waiting. This is just how it goes lately," Mom had said tersely when I suggested holding the meal so we could all eat together.) But when he did arrive, and dutifully kicked off his boots on the porch, he came straight in and swept me off my feet in a heartfelt embrace (at 6'4" it was something he could still easily manage.) He followed this up with a similar treatment for Mom, and for a grand finale, boosted Stephen up onto his shoulders. This was quickly curtailed when Stephen's head threatened to smack the roof rafters. "It's good to see you, Princess," Dad said, tugging me down on the couch beside him. Despite the hardships, life on the mesa seemed to agree with him, and I knew that made Mom happy.

"Stephen tells me you're working until all hours building a spaceship." We were holding hands and it felt like home.

Dad's eyes grew wide in mock seriousness. "He's not supposed to know anything about that. If he blabs the secret, we'll all be in Dutch."

"Maybe we'd better brainwash him," I countered, just as seriously.

"Not until he's had a shower, you don't," Mom said from the kitchen. "That's the first kind of washing that boy needs."

Dad snared Stephen by the belt and pulled him onto his lap. "Tell you what, boy-o. Mom and Dad and the princess here have been invited to a little soiree this evening, so we're going to tuck you in early and rely on you to keep the home fires burning. Think you can manage?"

"What's a swa-ray?" Stephen wanted to know. "Why can't I come?"

"Because the boring factor would overwhelm you, that's why. It's a time when grown-ups get together and become just as stupid and uninteresting as you've always imagined them to be."

"So? Claire's not so much of a grown-up."

"Huh?" said Dad, and his eyes caught mine. "You'd better take another look," he told Stephen.

While Mom and I were getting dressed in the bedroom, Dad was in the shower. From shower to out-the-door, the whole process took him about ten minutes. We ladies took a little more time. She was talking to me about the Project Director, the man who was responsible for the mesa and all of its inhabitants. He was a man, I gathered, of some mystery and allure. "Have you met him?" I asked her.

"Oh yes. He actually gets around the compound quite a lot, in spite of his schedule. And his Saturday night open houses are quite popular."

"And?" I was putting my long hair up and exposing my neck, which mom always said made me look older and more sophisticated.

"Well, he's not like anybody else I've ever met, I'll give him that. He provokes strong feelings in most people, one way or the other."

"How about in Dad?"

"Dad is quite fond of him I think you could say. He personally picked out this site for the project, is what I've heard tell."

"How old is he?"

"Our age, I should say." We had celebrated Dad's fortieth earlier in the year, and mom's was coming up.

"Where's he from?" I was working on my hair and making conversation.

"Not far from us, really. Down Berkeley way. Although I gather that he spent a fair amount of time overseas . . ."

My dad's voice broke in on us from the open bathroom door. "Martha, if you'll just pass me my skivvies, I'll get dressed in here, since you ladies have the bedroom tied up."

Mom complied with this request, and shortly returned to the bedroom. "It's funny, your father told me that the first time he met him, the Director looked at him in a way that convinced Dad that he could read people's minds."

"I'm sure that could come in handy in a place like this," I said lightly. My choice in lipstick ("Crimson Blush") might be a bit bold, I was thinking. Both mom and I had on "dress-up" dresses. "How's this?" I invited mom to review my look, something I probably wouldn't have done in Salem. She took me in, and in her eyes there was a fleeting look I can't describe, but I think it had to do with a mother seeing, as though for the first time, her little girl being replaced by a woman. She seemed on the verge of making a comment, but then she caught herself. "Bring your sweater, sweetie, nights it can get plenty cool up here, even in August."

It was after 9:00 when the three of us left the porch light on and pushed off to negotiate the mud. Some kind and thoughtful souls had actually laid boards across the more expansive puddles, and with Dad holding Mom by the elbow and me fending for myself, we picked our way carefully across the compound. The area was not well lit, and beyond the faint glare of the few lights strung on the poles that we passed along the way, I became aware of an expansive cupola of stars overhead. At night, with the scars of its ordeal hidden from view, the mesa had a remote, majestic quality to it, and I began to understand that it might hold a certain appeal for stargazers, poets, or wandering cowboys. I remembered my mom's comment about the Director having selected the site personally, and I wondered into which category he might fall. Maybe all of them.

Perhaps a quarter of a mile from our "plywood ghetto" we entered a more defined neighborhood, with rows of substantial ranch-style dwellings and cars drawn up on both sides of the muddy track as one might draw boats up on the bank of a river. A little further along and we found ourselves in front of a house that was set back from the road. In Salem it wouldn't have drawn a second glance, but here on the mesa it stood out as a dwelling of some importance. There were the makings of a small garden occupying the front yard, and steps with handrails leading up to an expansive front porch, complete with a porch swing. On the porch was a cluster of people talking, smoking and drinking, and they fell back to permit our passage. Dad said a few cordial hellos, opened the door and in we went.

The thing I had noticed about the high-school parties I had attended back in Salem (although my parents had generally kept me on a restricted party-attendance schedule, preferring to see me devote my free weekend time to caring for our horses) was that they were always really loud. I mean, having-a-conversation-is-impossible loud, with all that teenage energy buzzing around the room and too many people too eager to talk at the same time. Upon entering the Director's modestly sized front room, that was the very impression I got. Holy cow, these are scientists? They act just like teen-agers! In small groups they were jabbering away at one another excitedly, all the while smoking and drinking up a storm. Most of the men had coats on and a few wore ties. The women all had on what I guessed was their Saturday-night best. Above the din a record player was playing swing music. They might have come to the mesa with some serious business in mind, but there was nothing serious about Saturday night. They all seemed on the verge of, in the parlance of the day, "cutting loose." In no time at all Dad got separated from us, and I flashed Mom a glance, as in what-do-we-do-next? Taking me by the hand, she tugged me through the crowd toward the back of the house. The next room in which we found ourselves was smaller and not as densely populated, with most of the people standing or kneeling in one corner. "Stay right here, I'll see if I can't find us something to drink," Mom said, and off she went, leaving me momentarily by myself, probably the only actual teen-ager in a house full of teenagers.

Thanks to what my best friend Veronica liked to call my "lush looks," being observed or stared at, particularly by members of the opposite gender, was something I'd been accustomed to since probably the third or fourth grade. It can be tiresome in certain instances, but I'd learned to accept these silent tributes as something a girl just has to live with, unless she would rather have been born a wallflower. And it wasn't long in this instance before I began to feel the looks coming my way. Or at least, somebody's look. Surreptitiously I permitted myself a quick scan of the room but saw nobody who had broken out of their cocoon of conversation to pay any particular attention to this latecomer. Still, the sensation persisted that I was being intently observed. My attention was drawn to the group of six or eight people who seemed knotted in one corner of the room. When the knot loosened enough, the mystery was solved. Over the shoulders of two of the men I saw another man, seated, and realized that it was the presence of this person which held the attention of the others in the group. Though surrounded by acolytes, he was staring at me quite openly, and when my eyes met his, he locked them in and held them there. I struggled to be demure and look away, but quickly gave up the struggle. He flashed the briefest of smiles, and then was on his feet, making his way through the cluster, coming towards me. He stood before me, taking both my hands in his hands in a gesture of such comforting familiarity that I was immediately at ease. His eyes searched mine, not really posing a question, but I answered anyway. "I'm Claire Waring. Owen Waring's daughter."

"But of course you are," he smiled, still in possession of my hands, although I scarcely noticed. His eyes were the bluest I'd ever seen, his gaze both penetrating and confidential. Tilting his head, he held me there in suspension for a moment longer before returning to an earthly orbit. "And I see that you're momentarily bereft of one of our infamous libations. You can come with me, Claire."

Releasing one of my hands, he drew me lightly by the other through another door and into a kitchen, which was, for the moment, unoccupied. He moved to the far end of the countertop where he picked up a silver cocktail shaker and deftly began adding the necessarily ingredients to produce a cocktail. "We're drinking martinis, Claire. Of the very dry variety." Having been released from that captive look of his, I was able to observe him in more general detail. Half a head taller than me, his close-cropped hair framed a round face with prominently high and wide-set cheekbones. He was dressed in shirtsleeves without a tie, and had a somewhat rumpled appearance. Even though his shoulders were slight and his arms long and gangly, he emitted an air of considerable strength. As he manipulated the shaker, his long and agile fingers seemed to be those of a concert pianist. After a moment, I had sufficiently caught my breath to venture a bit of adult conversation.

"Am I correct in assuming then that you are the Director about whom I've heard so much?"

He didn't respond right away, but poured a fair measure of his concoction into two martini glasses which he had produced from the cupboard. Turning back in my direction with the glasses, he offered one to me. At this precise juncture, a couple of young men came sailing into the kitchen, apparently in search of the same libation. "Right there on the counter, lads," my host said, and without missing a beat, he steered me by the elbow back out of the kitchen. We were halfway across the room when our progress was halted by a casual cluster of fellows who seemed intent on engaging him. He lifted his glass, and all immediately followed suit, even though a couple of the glasses were empty, or nearly so. "Gents, I'd like to present the very lovely Miss Claire Waring. Miss Waring is first violinist with the San Francisco Symphony, very presently to embark on her third national tour. Quite an impressive resume for one so young." So saying, he shot me a sidelong glance that was pure controlled hilarity. I took the moment to lift the glass to my lips and drink rather freely, making an attempt to elevate my own spirits to match those of the other teen-agers in the room, most of whom apparently had made a good head start.

I was in for a bit of a revelation. The fellows in the group, given the opportunity to make the acquaintance of a lovely and apparently unattached young woman, and a national celebrity to boot, could have cared less. After the most desultory of huzzahs in my direction, they turned their attentions back to our host, and as I watched, I saw in their eyes the dedicated intent and the unwavering affections that would have caused any girl, similarly targeted, to blush radiantly. This round-headed, wide-eyed man was in possession of secrets, I realized. I'd always thought that those kinds of intimate, seductive secrets belonged to women and were almost part of their anatomy (or perhaps stemmed from their anatomy). But now I saw it differently. My secrets paled in comparison to those he harbored, which had nothing to do with anatomy.

After a couple of minutes, while I inhaled the better part of my very dry martini, and began to wonder about my parents, he managed to disengage himself, and taking me lightly by the elbow, he steered me to the back of the room and out through double glass doors that lead to a sizeable back porch. Though there were several party-goers taking in the night air, here we were undisturbed and stood at the porch railing with our drinks. The sudden introduction of the cool evening air, the stunning canopy of stars arching overhead, and the potent effects of my martini quickly combined to produce in me a feeling of boundless giddiness beyond anything I had ever experienced, and I struggled to keep myself anchored to an identifiable reality. "My little brother is pretty certain you're building a spaceship up here," I ventured.

He smiled indulgently and withdrew a pack of cigarettes. "Can you imagine a more appropriate place?" He took out one, lit it, and offered it to me. Had I not been reeling as I was, I might have accepted, but I declined with an upraised palm.

"So tell me, lovely Claire, about the dreams that stir in your breast."

"That's not the kind of question that I faced on my entrance application for the University of Oregon," I laughed. Through the open back door came the strains of "Perfida," one of the Glenn Miller hits of the day, and a song that would, as a result of this occasion, remain embedded in my waking thoughts for the remainder of my life. Momentarily I permitted my giddiness to sweep me away entirely, and I responded to the Director's poetic query by singing along with the words of the song's refrain: *"While the Gods of love look down and laugh on what romantic fools we mortals be."*

"My sentiments exactly," said the director, and leaning across, he planted a chaste kiss on my forehead at precisely the instant that my mother came though the double doors. Seeing her approach from over my shoulder, he was as smooth and welcoming as he could be. "Martha, I've just made your lovely daughter an offer which I hope she can't refuse, but which will no doubt will depend upon you and Owen for final ratification."

Huh? The two of us looked at him with equal measures of expectancy. "We're terribly short in the secretarial pool, and I've asked her if she wouldn't care to postpone her University plans for a year or so to pitch in and help us get this project off the ground." He was speaking to my mom and I was watching him, fascinated by the clever and thorough way his mind worked at sorting out the details of people's destinies. That's the kind of thing that can't be taught, and he was indeed gifted. Postpone for a year? At that moment I would've postponed my entire life just to be in his orbit. "That way your family could be together, and with the salary we could pay her, she'd have a decent nest egg to help her at University when she's ready to go," he added, no doubt to lay a more rational foundation for the spur-of-the-moment offer which had Mom quite dumbfounded. After another moment or so, the awkwardness of our situation was nicely resolved when another pack of roving teenager/scientists charged through the patio door in search of their mentor, and, shrugging with apology, he allowed himself to be shanghaied into their merry company.

"I see you've been introduced to our good Dr. Oppenheimer," Mom said dryly, leaning across to peer into my face. It didn't take a rocket scientist, although we were surrounded by them, to determine that I was high as a kite. "Sweetie, have you been drinking?" she asked somewhat redundantly.

"Only until recently," I said, and made no great effort to remove the self-satisfied grin from my face.

"It doesn't take much at this altitude," she counseled, and took me by the elbow. "Maybe it's about time we pushed off. Let's go find your father."

"For goodness sakes, mother, we just got here."

"Well, you're just a fast worker, young lady. Enough's enough."

Although slightly stung by her insinuation, I did not want to test my mother's resolve in this delicate situation, and I accompanied her without further complaint as we went in search of Dad, who, as I had hoped, was equally taken aback at her request to abandon the festivities after a scant half-hour. Face to face in the smoky midst of a rather large group of celebrants they debated the merits of her plan briefly while I lingered on the side, hoping for a glimpse of our host, whom I envisioned coming to my rescue and prolonging this night of unexpected revelations. With a start I realized that I had fallen into the passive role of a five-year old, and I stirred myself, barged forward, and took my mother firmly by the shoulder. "Look, Mother, let's you and me share one more drink while we hunt down the Director and say our farewells, and we can make our way back to camp while Dad stays here and takes advantage of the relaxation he's no doubt earned." It was an inspired move, and under the circumstances, it was an offer my mom could not very well refuse. We left my father with his group and headed for the kitchen.

As it turned out, we did procure another martini from a scientist armed with the silver cocktail shaker, and without further acrimony we shared it out on the porch watching the stars. I even got Mom to laughing when I recounted the saga of my recent experience in Los Angeles when, after much travail, I had seated myself comfortably on a train bound not for Kingman, Arizona, but for Placerville, California, owing to the fact that the track numbers had been changed at the last minute. She leaned forward and gave me a suddenly urgent hug. "You're such a big girl now, Claire, it scares me sometimes." When she pulled back, her eyes were welling up. And over her shoulder, who should appear but my knight with the shining countenance. "It seems you've found a spot that appeals to you, Claire," Dr. Oppenheimer said. I assumed he was talking about the back porch, but it was a statement that could have implied much more.

"Do you ladies need a refill?" he asked, spying the empty glass I was holding.

"We're actually about to push off," I replied, handling the social etiquette that might have been a little difficult for my mother at that moment. "We've really enjoyed your hospitality, Doctor Oppenheimer."

"That's Oppie to you, young lady. And I do hope, Martha, that you and Owen will give serious consideration to the offer I've made Claire." He reached down and pulled mom into a tight embrace, then worked past her and reached for me. Leaning in, he slid his cheek alongside mine and with those pianist's fingers positioned firmly on the back of my neck, he placed his lips at the base of my ear and let them linger there long enough to scorch my soul. Pulling back, he let his eyes linger on mine as he withdrew. Then he was gone, that angular, slightly-stooped figure that filled the house and the night and the mesa, and maybe even the world, with a certain sexual/intellectual magnetism which up until then I had never even imagined to exist.

As the two of us (Dad had indicated with a wave of his hand that we should proceed without him, that his evening was not quite ready to wrap up) made our way through the front room towards the door, another of my favorite songs was blaring out from the record player and, as earlier, mirroring sentiments that were running through me:

Poinciana, your branches sing to me of love, pale moon is casting shadows from above, Poinciana, somehow I feel the jungle heat, within me there grows a rhythmic, savage beat . . .

In the ensuing days, we, the Warings of Salem, Oregon, actually did give full and ample consideration to the unexpected offer tendered to me by the Director of the Manhattan Project on his back porch that night. Oh, you bet we did. At considerable length. And it wasn't always done in measured tones or with clear, unemotional logic. Dad had been pleasantly taken aback at the offer, but found it "frivolous, maybe even a trifle impetuous." Mother, of course, was dead set against it for reasons that she wasn't entirely candid in discussing (I had my theories, but out of respect for her, I'll not air them here.) Stephen thought the whole thing was pretty exciting, and would have been pleased to have his big sister with him to share in the bounty of this new and exciting world into which fate had cast him. And I'll candidly acknowledge here and now that my sudden desire to place my carefully-thought-out future indefinitely on hold to pursue this improbable whim was almost entirely irresponsible and adolescent in nature. Simply put, I had fallen head-over-heels in love with the Director ("your dangerous infatuation" my mother called it) and was, in my weakness, willing to make any sacrifice to remain close to him and give the situation time to run its course. But over the course of the next 48 hours my parents patiently buttressed and delineated their arguments, which came to include: the fact that nobody really knew how long the project would last, primarily because it was directly attached to the war itself, and that was the mystery of all mysteries; the fact that uprooting me, our family's last representative in Salem, might have long-lasting implications for everybody's future ("Our family is not going to abandon aunts, uncles, grandparents, just like that," my father pronounced); the fact that the Director's wife, Kitty, was known to be an extremely jealous women who could make life miserable for those females with whom the Director found favor, and mother was "not going to subject myself to that kind of humiliation"; and, perhaps most telling, the fact that that my parents had not nurtured, developed, and dreamed on my behalf so that I could "pursue a career in the damned secretarial sciences." Thus, by default, the decision was made for me to dutifully return to Salem as an incoming freshman at the University of Oregon. I of course remained unconvinced, as I do to this day, that it was necessarily the best decision.

My father did have one last card to play, and he did so two evenings later. It was about seven in the evening at the "Plywood Palace." Mom was in the kitchen preparing dinner, Stephen was in his room sorting through his growing accumulation of salvaged treasures, and Dad and I were on the couch in the living room sorting through the uncomfortable silence that had descended upon us since the rendering of The Decision when we heard the tread of footsteps on our porch, followed by a polite tap-tap on the front door. "Would you get that, sweetheart?" Dad asked me. Dutifully I made my way to the door, opened it, and found myself confronted by the object of my intemperate affections. He was wearing that slouch-brimmed fedora hat that the world would later see in so many photographs (I always thought it made him look like a DP, or Displaced Person), and had a pipe in his mouth, his demeanor as calm and neighborly as if we had run into each other at a local dry goods store. I hoped he could not see too clearly revealed the passions which surged in my breast at the mere sight of him, but it was a forlorn hope; I knew he could read my entire life right there on my face. "Miss Claire Waring, I do believe," he said, and then leaned in and over my shoulder, asked "Owen, might I borrow your darling daughter for a brief moment? There's something I'd like to show her." I didn't look back at Dad. I wasn't entirely dense, I knew a setup when I saw one.

Two days later, after returning down the torturous road from Los Alamos to Santa Fe, again in an ancient truck, and being dropped off in front of the courtyard with the beat-up blue door in E. Palace St., I made my way over to the Plaza to the bus stop to wait for the bus to the train depot. There followed over the next three days a reversal of my outward journey, as a succession of overcrowded, underperforming trains delivered me back to Eugene via Kingman, Los Angeles, and San Francisco. Those few days and those achingly long rides passed uneventfully for me. I traveled in a state of suspended animation, numb to my surroundings, suffering from the pangs of what I had diagnosed as a "broken heart." Or at least a heart suffering the distress of a compound fracture. I struggled not only with the pain of a prematurely truncated relationship with a man who had captured my deepest loyalties and affections, but with the distress of the separation of our family "for the duration." I keenly felt the emotional distance that had grown between my parents and me as a result of my headstrong behavior. On top of all that, there was the uneasy sensation that our English-speaking world might be on the verge of being overrun by the barbaric hordes who threatened both from the East and the West. In a spasm of conviction that was for me quite profound, I had in the space of just a few hours on the mesa found a place and a purpose that was perfectly suited to my talents, my disposition, and my heart's leanings, only to be rudely cast out, thrown back into a life that had, rather suddenly, lost most of its appeal. The trains that bore me westward during those days of August were bearing me, I was convinced, away from my future, and that is surely the most painful journey one can undertake.

The year nineteen forty-four came and went. I lived with my aunt and uncle, turned twenty, carried a 3.6 GPA, dated no one, and declined my parents' invitation to return to Los Alamos that summer, choosing instead to remain in Corvallis and work as an intern in the office of the Dean of Women, having determined that a career in academia would provide satisfaction enough.

During that summer we all followed the news from Europe, and by Christmas it seemed clear that the German Third Reich was experiencing its death throes. The news from Los Alamos was, as usual, scant and ambiguous. The work was "going along well" according to correspondence I received from my mom, and they all hoped that their efforts would "somehow contribute" to the Allies' eventual victory. As we passed our second Christmas apart, I tried to keep my mind and heart reasonably open to them, but a part of me felt rejected and overlooked by my parents, who had not only abandoned me to run off to the wilds of that mesa, but couldn't even tell me what in God's name they were doing there. Of course, the keenest edge of my resentment was saved for the Director, who had succeeded in wooing my father away from me and entrapping him there in the wilds. By May of '45, when I finished my second year at school, the fervent admiration and girlish passion I had unleashed upon "Oppie" had been largely replaced by a hardened outlook, a jaundiced viewpoint that regarded him largely as a "charlatan," a word I had recently come to learn and which I applied to him with the satisfied air of a skilled attorney making a good closing argument.

The war with Japan raged on. These people were fanatics, they wouldn't quit. We were going to have to send our boys into their cities on foot to dig them out of their holes one by one. The prospect was dreadful.

Then the news broke, and the whole thing came tumbling out. Around 10:00 AM on August 6, President Truman (a name and a title that still sounded unreal and fantastic in itself) came on the radio and talked about the *"largest bomb ever used in the history of warfare. It is an atomic bomb,"* he said. *"It is a harnessing of the basic power of the universe."* He went on to recount how an American bomber had dropped it on *"an important Japanese Army Base,"* and that if the Japanese did not accept the Allied terms of surrender they could expect a *"rain of ruin from the air the like of which has never been seen on this earth."* But the part of the broadcast which truly plunged me in to a maelstrom of emotions was his reference to *"the battle of the laboratories,"* and his explicit description of *"the many who had been working for two and a half years, few of whom knowing what they were producing."* I broke down in sobs and spent the better part of the next two days in that state, tears that were shed less in relief at the implications of this momentous event than as a measure of spontaneous, heartfelt atonement for the overwhelming sin of my disbelief.

Mother and Stephen were back in Salem just two weeks later. Dad accompanied them, but returned almost at once, and would not receive his final release from the mesa for another six months. Nonetheless, on that quick visit with him he bore an envelope, which he pressed into my hands during a quiet moment alone together. He looked briefly into my eyes and winked, and then left me by myself to digest the contents. Inside the envelope was a postcard of the campus of the University of California at Berkeley, and on the back, in an elegant scrawl made by a fountain pen in black ink, was the following:

Claire,

Thanks so much for the loan of your family!

I hope that all is forgiven.

Oppie

That was it. There were just the two sentences, but the curious thing was that they did not appear to be connected. The second sentence was a paragraph of its own, leaving little doubt in my mind, at least, that the forgiveness which he sought had nothing to do with the loan. The not-very-chaste kiss below the ear, then, and the torrent of potentially ruinous passion that it unleashed in a young woman's breast? Or, what came after? The results of his Manhattan Project, which, in the minds of many, including perhaps the mind of the Director himself, would be viewed ultimately as unforgiveable? I sobbed some more.

During the post-war years, as our lives resumed, all of us seeking a semblance of normalcy, I followed the arc of his career from a distance. Initially there were the awards and the accolades. Then came the public debate over the future of atomic weaponry itself, carried out against the backdrop of the government's testing programs. (Within five years they had developed and test-fired bombs that dwarfed the destructive capacity of the two used against Japan.) There arose a circus of political posturing as the Right and Left-wing elements clashed, each pontificating with crusading zeal against the diabolical motives of the other. The solidarity mandated by the urgency of war, which had been so strongly in evidence in the community founded by Director Oppenheimer in the New Mexican hinterland, dissolved quickly in an environment of unbridled patriotism and inevitable repression. In this battle, the Director did not fare well. I could have told you on that night back on the mesa that he would not—he was not a fighter, but an embracer of possibilities. Here was a man who had looked into the abyss, had seen the secrets heretofore known but to God; he had no desire to wield the cudgel against alleged miscreants, his mind burned too brightly for that. In due time he was stripped of his security clearance and drummed unceremoniously out of the Old Boys Club. He toured and lectured and went off to share his insights with the Europeans and the Japanese. I had heard that he spent much of his time on an isolated beachfront property in the Virgin Islands, and it seemed entirely fitting. During these years my own arc included a career in academic administration, marriage, and a family. In time I reluctantly released Oppie to the fates and to history. But it wasn't over yet. There was to be one more meeting, It came almost exactly twenty years after our first.

It was the first week of December, 1963. My husband Richard and I were in Washington, D.C. where we had traveled with our daughter Katherine the week after Thanksgiving to visit Richard's mother, who lived in nearby Fairfax, Virginia. The President had been assassinated less than two weeks earlier, and all of us were to one degree or another, numb and sleepwalking. The three of us had only just completed a tour of the Capitol, and were standing under the rotunda when an august group of dignitaries, half a dozen or so, was ushered into that great and resonating space. Surveying them casually, I thought I recognized the bushy-browed form of the noted physicist Edward Teller, who had gained considerable notoriety not only because of his work on the hydrogen bomb, but also because of his falling-out with Oppenheimer during those bitter witch-hunting years of the McCarthy era. I watched him from a distance, and slowly took in other members of the group; there was one who looked like a senator, and a couple of high-ranking military officers, what you might expect to see on any given day on Capitol Hill, I supposed. And then, even before I saw him, my pulse quickened. The sense of him actually preceded the sighting. There, on the fringe of the group, still tall but more stooped then I remembered, gone all silver and gray, his skin as translucent as ancient parchment, was Oppie himself. Touching my hand to Richard's arm briefly, I left his side and moved towards the group, drawn with a magnetic sense of sureness. From a distance, he looked my way and saw me coming; like that night on the mesa, he locked on to me with his eyes, and drew me into that private world where he lived alone in those splendid, empty rooms. I sailed right up to him and would have entered his arms had he opened them.

"Oppie? It's really you." Gushing, almost, at the age of forty.

"A chimera, actually, but it does the job." His face had over the years become almost immobilized in a mask of calculated withdrawal, but his eyes still danced with anticipation.

"It's Claire Waring. My dad Owen . . ."

"And your mother Martha," he finished for me. Several of the others in the group had turned to regard this intrusion. Having completed its stay at this station, the group was beginning to move away. He showed not the least inclination to be hurried along. Reaching out, he placed his hand on the sleeve of my winter coat. "Pray tell, how does this honor befall me?"

"Just in town on a visit with my husband and my daughter," I explained, indicating them, momentarily frozen and unmoving, watching us from a polite distance. "I had read in the papers about your award." He had recently been declared the recipient of the Enrico Fermi Award, to be presented by the President. It was, the Washington Post had editorialized, probably long overdue.

"That," he said with a dismissive roll of his eyes. "Yes, we've actually just come from the White House, where I have been washed in the blood." He switched gears smoothly. "You look positively marvelous, Claire. And your father is well?"

"He claims to be ready for retirement, but shows no indication of slowing down. Probably a bit like yourself . . ." Watching his eyes watching me, that long-ago summer night came back to me, and I again was seized with a sense of longing. Longing to be known as the knower of secrets would know me, both for the secrets, and for myself. I could see plainly before me, however, the damage that this knowledge could do. Suddenly wanting to leave him alone to himself, I reached out and grasped his hand. "Oppie, I just wanted to say hello, and to tell you . . ."

He watched and waited patiently. So many times I had heard and read the testimonies of friends and associates who spoke of his remarkable mental agility and the reach of his fertile imagination; how he so frequently anticipated your thoughts, completing your questions before the questions themselves had even been fully formulated. On this occasion, at least, he seemed devoid of such mental agility, oddly quiescent. But I needed, wanted, to express myself. "The last time we spoke, you said something that had quite an impact on my life, and I've always been grateful." I squeezed his hand and my eyes began to well up. "I just wanted to thank you for that, and for everything you've meant. To me. To all of us." I lurched forward and wrapping my arms around his neck, hugged him hard. There was the smell of his pipe tobacco, and behind that, the smell of suits hung in closets, of chalk dried on a board, of an ocean that reached a faraway shore. I released him but could not bring my eyes up again to meet his. With lowered head, I backed away, turned, and retreated to my family. When I was able to glance in that direction again, he had disappeared with his group.

I hardly needed a last look; I had those images of him, imbedded in the American conscious, that had lingered with me all those years: with his porkpie hat pulled over his eyes at a jaunty angle, his hands on his hips as, along with General Groves, he surveyed the sight of Ground Zero after the Trinity blast; his ghostly, masklike countenance during a later interview as he described the scene at the observation post in the wake of that blast (*"A few people laughed, a few people cried, most people were silent . . ."* Then reaching up quickly to flick a ghostly tear from his cheek); and my favorite, one I had actually clipped from LIFE magazine several years after the war and placed in a small silver frame, a news photo in which he is facing the camera, wearing a tie and a tweed coat, his porkpie straight and level upon his head, a cigarette dangling from his lips, his eyes peering unflinchingly and with an implied challenge directly at the viewer, giving the impression more of a civilized Western sheriff than a rogue Eastern intellectual. As if that weren't enough, there was always the memory of the trump card my dad had played on the mesa twenty years earlier. He had called in his charismatic boss to have the Director talk me down from the ledge where I had placed myself as a result of a night of very dry martinis and the seductive lure of the Unknown, not to mention those piercing blue eyes. Leaving the small house, we had walked together to the place I had come to regard as "Stephen's Point," the place atop the boulders where my brother taken me on the afternoon of my arrival. In his porkpie hat with his pipe and his coat thrown over his shoulder, the Director was a jaunty presence, almost collegiate himself, the twenty-year difference in our ages greatly diminished. As we looked west over the rumpled and saddle-stitched high country of

New Mexico, he had puffed his pipe and turned ruminative for my benefit. "You know, Claire, I admire your determination and your quest for knowledge. It's a precious asset. Almost too precious for us to apply here on the mesa."

I knew were this was going, I thought. "I don't see how that could be," I said glumly.

He turned to face me; his eyes had gotten serious. No stars in them. No invitation to dance. Earthly concerns instead. "Hostage-takers, Claire. The world's full of them. Promise me you'll do your best to keep that spirit of yours free. Out of their hands." He took my hands in his, but it was not the laughing, flirting touch of an earlier evening, and even in my naïve state, I could never mistake it as such. "As the poet says, *The night is spent, the day draws near: let us cast off the deeds of darkness and put on the armor of light* . . . what do you say?"

I met his gaze and probably blushed. It sounded oddly like a marriage proposal, and in a greater sense, maybe that's what it was. Despite the fact that he had been called out on this mission to repair the breach caused by his actions of two nights earlier, he had felt compelled to speak from the heart. Only much later did I come to surmise the identity of the "hostage takers" to whom he had darkly alluded. The phrase that had penetrated my post-adolescent brain and lodged itself there was "armor of light." Being translucent, composed of nothing heavier than particles and atoms, having neither weight nor substance, light is hardly the element we think of when we consider "armor." But he, having devoted his life to the acquisition and dispersal of knowledge, understood it differently. And he had tirelessly shared that understanding with all who sought him out for it.

He released my hands, and we walked back to the cabin without speaking further. He kissed me on the forehead, and I went inside to begin my new life.

Claire (Waring) Meyerson
Eugene, Oregon 1971

THE WINGMAN

"Gus had a feeling. More than a feeling, maybe. He'd been around it all his life, and he knew it was gaining on him." The old man took a pull at his drink, but it was down to the ice cubes now, and they rattled in his glass as he placed it back on the bar.

"I don't know," I said. "He went out and picked up that brand-new Corvette, didn't he? Doesn't sound like the thing a guy will do when he's thinking about death."

"Can you think of a better thing to do? Drive, baby, drive. And the faster the better."

"You mean like maybe you can outrun it?"

He looked over at me with that owl-eyed look of his, through the bottle-caps lenses of his glasses. His features alternated somewhere between a knowing smirk and honest bewilderment, but over the course of our ninety minutes together, he had spun a pretty convincing yarn. Or maybe I was just in a mood to be convinced. Being a journalist, that's not unusual for me.

"I'm not claimin' to be no psychologist. I just know how to do simple math. The numbers add up."

"Who told you about the lemon tree, by the way?"

"One of his son's friends. Guy he went to school with. Those boys, they got put through the wringer not once, but twice. They figured it out. And the lemon tree story, it's not something you make up, and it damn well ain't something you forget."

"I just don't get it, though. Knowing what he knew, and feeling the way he did, or the way you tell me he did, why would the guy stay with the program? Why would he go to work in the morning? And why, for the love of God, would he climb into the capsule and let 'em seal the hatch like they did? Kind of sign off on his own death sentence?"

"Like I told you, I never met the man." He stared straight ahead. Behind the bar, the windows opened onto the lake, where the afternoon was fading to twilight. "But I can tell you this about him. Once he saw his duty, he never backed down. Pure and simple. He had a duty. He stayed with it."

"So in effect, doing his duty was what did him in?"

"Does us all in one way or another, don't it?"

"What was once the furthest outpost on the old frontier of the West will be the furthest outpost on the new frontier of science and space."

With his usual flair for New Frontier hyperbole, that's what President Kennedy had told America in a speech at Rice University in April 1962 in describing the planned Manned Space Center, which would subsequently open its doors for business on 1,620 acres 25 miles southeast of Houston in September 1963. (Rice had donated the acreage.) The fact that Kennedy's term of office was abruptly truncated in another Texas metropolis just two months after that barely caused a hiccup in the start-up enterprise. After all, now you had a Texan in the Oval Office, and this was one coonskin which he would nail securely to the wall. It was, after all, LBJ's own legislation back in 1958 which had brought the Space Task Group into being. Texas and outer space were two enterprises that would grow together.

By the time the whole team moved from Langley, Virginia to the "furthest outpost" in Texas, America's space program had already been up and running for some time. In April 1959 newly-formed NASA had rolled out the nation's first astronaut corps with typical American cornball gusto, the so-called "Mercury Seven." From thousands of candidates NASA had culled the seven, these red-blooded, balls-to-the-wall test pilots, and then stood by happily as the press air-brushed them into heroic figures overnight, American Ideals, pure and perfect representatives of the very heart and soul of a nation on the verge of a New Frontier. Operating out of Langley, NASA launched six Mercury flights from Cape Canaveral, including four orbital and two sub-orbital, all within a span of just 24 months. The Rooskies had been first up, there was no getting around that fact, beating the U.S. by a mere three weeks and two days. (After having orbited Yuri Gagarin, the Russians were within their rights to refer derisively to the U.S. suborbital pilots as *"cloud-o-nauts."*). It was at this point that the old-timer in the bar in Seabrook picked up the story.

"You remember them Mercury flights at all?" he asked me. I'd been in high school, but sure I remembered. May of 1961. The normal class-time routine had been placed on hold as 18" black and white television sets were wheeled into a number of the classrooms so we could all watch Alan Shepard's flight. The whole episode, from lift-off to spashdown, lasted barely fifteen minutes. Cloud-o-nauts indeed.

"How about the second one? You remember who flew that?"

"Not 100% sure. Grissom, maybe."

"You bet it was. Two months later, July. Anything unusual about that flight?"

"Oh, hell yeah." In a painful episode fully documented by Hollywood some twenty years later, Grissom survived his sub-orbital flight intact, but nearly drowned when the explosive bolts on his escape hatch blew prematurely, causing the capsule to flood with seawater and sink in 16,000 feet of water. NASA was supremely embarrassed, and didn't hesitate to let the fault for the embarrassment be assigned to the astronaut himself. McDonnell Aircraft, the builders of the capsule, certainly weren't going to take the fall. The idea that the pilot had possibly "panicked" was floated, and nobody bothered to condemn it outright. In 1983, with the publication of his chatty, effervescent book on the early days of the enterprise of spaceflight, author Tom Wolfe more or less sealed Gus's fate by putting out there what a gullible American population was thinking: that, in test pilot parlance, Gus had "screwed the pooch." Although subsequent testing would confirm that the fault lay in the untried hatch itself (Shepard's flight had used a different version), the ride-along public generally bought the story. *Geez, what a fuckup. I mean, every workplace has its fuck-ups. Why should the astronaut corps be any different?* His employer and his fellow Mercury pilots let Gus dangle mightily in the wind. *There but for the grace of God* seemed to be their thinking. Besides, Gus fit the profile. Short, dour, without any telegenic appeal at all, and utterly at a loss for words at a time when the spinmeisters were taking over the airwaves, he was utterly unprepared for his 15 minutes of scrutiny. America shrugged and laughed it off. And Grissom became The Fuckup. The guy who panicked. The irony here was that, if NASA had determined that the fault for losing the *Liberty Bell* was in fact Gus's, he never would have flown for them again.

"You know anything about his career before he entered the program?"

"Test pilot, wasn't he?"

"They was all test pilots. This guy had a hundred combat missions in Korea under his belt. *A hundred.* This is not the kind of man that is gonna associate with panic. Not even gonna be in the *neighborhood* with panic. Ever."

"Well." I considered the merits of his absolute conviction. "He was still a human being. The possibility for panic is there."

The old man turned and cocked his head at me, a shiver of otherworldly light glancing off his lenses.

"You bet. And I can tell you when it happens, *if* it happens."

"When's that?"

"A guy like that will only panic after he dies. First he dies. Then, he might just decide to panic."

As Project Mercury wound down, NASA shifted gears. In September of 1962 they had qualified a second batch of hot pilots as astronauts, and competition to find a seat in the upcoming Gemini flights quickly heated up. But Gus Grissom was nothing if not a quick study and a fair-to-middling poker player. (It's not like he didn't have the face for it.) He figured out how to get ahead in the high stakes, winner-take-all astronaut game by volunteering as the astronaut office design rep. He spent months at McDonnell Aircraft in St. Louis where the Gemini spacecraft was being engineered and built for the upcoming two-man spaceflights. All during this developmental stage Gus kept showing up, providing input, and incrementally positioning himself at the heart of the program. His hard-earned degree in Mechanical Engineering from Purdue and his *bona fides* as a test pilot became his ticket. "Gus basically designed the fuckin' Gemini spacecraft," the old timer told me. "But he was clever, see? He took the trouble, while he was at it, to build in a little job security for him and the other pilots. The Gemini would not fly without a man at the controls. Strictly old school. Radar. Artificial horizon. Ejection seats. In all they flew ten manned missions in the Gemini, and there wasn't a single astronaut among those who flew in Gemini that didn't know who to thank for the ride of their lives. The three guys who flew the first lunar landing mission cut their teeth on Gemini."

The record will show that, like Project Mercury, Gemini proceeded at a breakneck pace: beginning in March 1965, after sending up two unmanned suborbital flights, they flew ten manned flights in just twenty months. There was no loss of life, no loss of spacecraft, no loss of public confidence whatsoever. The funding pipeline was untroubled, the Texan in the White House was swinging a Very Big Dick, all systems were go. When the first manned Gemini lifted off from the Cape that March, the Command Pilot was Gus Grissom. The flight was flawless, and the Fuckup was reborn as America's premier astronaut, the dean of the corps, and the first to escape Earth's confines twice.

At last the stars themselves seemed to be favorably aligned for Gus and his family. Nothing had ever come easily for this Indiana boy; his Depression-era childhood had seemed to mark him for a life of struggle and privation. Too small for high school sports, he became a Boy Scout instead. He scraped together nickels with a paper route, or picking peaches. Academically unmotivated, he eked out mediocre grades and graduated high school with neither plan nor purpose. Then, as it did for so many young men of that era, WWII took a hand in things. Gus enlisted as an aviation cadet during his senior year, and reported for duty in August 1944 following graduation. But then the Japs capitulated, and the show was over. Gus never did get his flight training, and he never earned his combat pay. He ended up flying those LSD's instead.

(For you civilians, that's military jargon for Large Steel Desks). Thwarted, he quit the Air Force and wound up back in his hometown installing doors on school buses. Maybe that's as far as life intended for him to travel.

But he didn't think so. Mitchell, Indiana was not going to write his epitaph. That's when Mr. Academic Nobody got it into his head to pack himself off to Purdue University and get a degree in Mechanical Engineering. With Betty working the long-distance lines, Gus flipping burgers, and a modest grant from the GI Bill, they pulled it off in three and a half years, during which time they holed up in a campus apartment that, in terms of living space, compared favorably with the Gemini capsule. (Well before feminism began to enforce political correctness, he unfailingly shared the credit for this accomplishment with his wife Betty, whose unstinting shifts as a long-distance operator provided a key portion of the couple's meager resources during this period.) After graduation, when nothing inviting presented itself, Gus submitted to that old pull of flying, and re-enlisted in the Air Force. This time he got his flight training, and then he got Korea. One hundred combat missions. (He wanted another twenty-five, but they nixed him on that, and made an instructor out of him instead.) As an instructor, he made an interesting discovery: "*At least you know what a MIG is going to do. Some of these kids were green and careless, and you had to think fast and act cool or they could kill both of you.*" Gus was a made man at last. During that century of sorties over Korea, or the daily training risks back Stateside, if ever the opportunity for panic presented itself (and you have to believe that for mere mortals, it was never far away), Gus Grissom had apparently ignored it entirely.

Now, having outlasted the doubters by sucking it up and keeping his nose to the grindstone (a posture that came naturally to him), Gus found that life began to turn less hostile. It even acquired a touch of sweetness. As one of the Original Seven, he had inherited a number of standing benefits that were never publicized: an extra $16,000 per year from LIFE magazine for exclusive rights to an astronaut's story and occasional peeks into his life, Corvettes on loan from dealers (the fellas used to play tag at 100 mph all the way up I-45 from the Manned Space Center to Houston), top seats at the Astrodome or the Houston Symphony if that was your choice, great deals on property, homes, clothing, and boats. Everything that citizenship in a robust free-market economy had to offer was yours for the plucking, because after all, you were a member of the sexiest, most elite club in the country, and everybody wanted a piece of you. (Even after the coming of The Nine boosted the astronaut corps to 16, the benefits were scarcely affected. Sixteen certified heroes simply amplified the press's insatiable appetite for stories. But the Originals were always first in line, it was understood that wouldn't change). Near the end of 1963, technicians, engineers, project managers and astronauts all decamped for the reclaimed coastal prairieland 25 miles south of Houston where sprawling residential developments with spacious, tidy brick homes and manicured lawns mushroomed along the shores of Clear Lake all the way out to the coast at Seabrook. Seemingly overnight it was all in place: strip malls, shopping centers, school districts, hospitals, playgrounds, marinas, lounges, golf courses. After years of utilitarian military housing in the bleak environs of far-flung Air Force or Navy bases, it was as if Gus and Betty had stepped into somebody else's lives, ready-made and waiting. There was boating and skiing on Clear Lake, trips to Colorado in the winter so Gus and the boys could hit the slopes, an annual family pilgrimage to Indiana for the Indy 500 (Gus was a knowledgeable motorsports enthusiast), and of course plenty of hunting and fishing. At Timber Cove the Grissoms had their own house custom-built, with a swimming pool in the backyard. (They would soon come to realize that, during South Texas summers, a swimming pool was more than an affectation, it was a survival tool). Genteel living was what it was, and it was about as far from Mitchell, Indiana as you could get. Gus's blond brick home did feature one detail that wasn't common to the area, but which very much reflected the astronaut's priorities: his home had no windows facing the street, not a single one. In the midst of all the hoopla of a space race, it was time for a little privacy. He had sure in hell earned it.

There was, however, no time for resting on one's laurels. After inaugurating Gemini with his triumphant three-orbit flight in the spring of '65, Gus stayed close to the program, helping shepherd the other nine flights. The Gemini, after all had his fingerprints all over it. When the last Gemini splashed down just before Thanksgiving of '66, suddenly it was time for him to switch gears, and immerse himself in a new assignment. Six months earlier NASA had announced that Gus would be commander for the first Apollo earth-orbit mission. (Which, not incidentally, put him in a choice position for the #1 flight assignment of all time, that being the first man to walk on the moon.)This in itself was a piece of serendipity. The ride had fallen to Gus because neither of the two men who might otherwise have snagged the plum assignment was on active flight status at the time. Shepard had been diagnosed with an inner ear disorder, and John Glenn, whose three-orbit flight in February 1962 had made him America's first true astronaut, had left the program to enter public life in his home state of Ohio six weeks after the assassination of JFK. Glenn had been everything that Gus was not: telegenic, articulate, and with broad, open features that radiated boyish heartland charm. His appeal to the public was so great that following Glenn's three-orbit flight, President Kennedy had shrewdly reached out and tapped the Glenns to become members of *his* circle. Even a president needs friends who are universally loved and beyond reproach. But it didn't matter now. They were gone and Gus was still in the game. If he hadn't outflown them, he had certainly outworked and outlasted them. Now, through the Apollo assignment, even NASA was acknowledging the fact that as the lunar missions loomed, Gus Grissom had become their go-to guy.

"Lemme tell ya straight, this was what you might call a shotgun wedding between NASA and Grissom. There was no love lost on either side. The *Molly*

Brown incident had pretty well spelled it out: as far as NASA was concerned, he was a System-Bucker, a guy who enjoyed sticking it to them every time he could. The way Gus saw it, they was a bunch of meddling cocksuckers, mainly concerned with keeping up appearances for the tax-paying public. It was called *protecting the funding*, and it was a way of life down there on the campus, you better believe it. Once he got out to Downey and got a load of what North American was up to, well, that pretty much tore it for both sides . . ."

"Back up a minute, if you don't mind. Maybe I don't quite remember about the *Molly Brown* business."

The old man snorted derisively. "The tradition was, every flight commander was entitled to name his spacecraft. So Shepard started it off with *Freedom 7*, right? Everybody's thrilled. Gus's first, the one that sank, was the *Liberty Bell*. Then there was *Friendship, Faith*, all that high-minded shit. Everybody's playin' nice in the sandbox. But Gus is still rankled about NASA hangin' him out to dry, and when it comes time for him to pick a monicker for his Gemini ride, he comes up with *Molly Brown*, as in *The Unsinkable Molly Brown*. Kind of a clever play on words, actually. But his bosses at NASA were not amused, shall we say. They rejected it: *that ain't gonna fly. We don't want any name that the public might associate with sinking. Think of a different name, Commander.* So Gus gives it some thought, and comes back at 'em with his second choice, which was not quite as clever, but certainly made his point." Here he paused for effect.

"What name was that?"

"Titanic." He takes a pull on his cigarette and looks straight ahead, out the window. "NASA saw what they had on their hands, and decided *Molly Brown* would fly after all. Which it did. All the boys got a kick out of that one. And it was a big monkey off Gus's back."

"Gotcha," I said. "So back to Downey. I assume you're talking about something other than a fabric softener?"

"Downey, California. That's where North American Aviation was headquartered at, and where they were putting together the Apollo command module. Both the Mercury and the Gemini ships had been built by McDonnell Douglas in St Louis, but by this time other large aviation contractors were beginning to lick their chops thinkin' that this lunar landing business was going to mean big bucks, and that it might be time for them to get their hand in. And when it came to aviation, North American had the track record to back up its bid. They had built Jimmy Doolittle's B-25's and Chuck Yeager's P-51's, not to mention the T-6 Potty Trainer, which was the airplane in which two generations of military pilots had first learned to fly. But what really put North American over the top was the F-86 Sabre, the ol' Korean War-Horse. They built somewhere north of 9,000 units of that particular model. But by the late Fifties fighter plane orders was way, way down, and North American had to go shopping for a new market. So they threw their hand in on aerospace contracting, and came up winners on the most expensive and sophisticated piece of flying equipment ever built."

"John Glenn flew the F-86."

"Flew the piss out of it, and he wasn't the only one. Gus loved that airplane, swore by it. So the fellows were not really upset to learn that North American would be building their next generation of spacecraft. That is, until they got out to Downey, where it didn't take long to realize that North American were in over their heads. There were serious technical problems, developmental blind-alleys, and generally substandard workmanship throughout the program. Gus had an engineer's sensibilities and an eye for detail, and he starts makin' a list of stuff that just ain't right. He makes a few lists. He shops his lists through the channels, and then he begins to realize the real battle is not gonna be with the technology, it's gonna be with the people."

"With NASA?"

"That's just part of it. You've also got the North American setup—the so-called "culture"—that's getting in the way. In the old days at McDonnell Douglas, the folks in St. Louis encouraged feedback from the astronauts, took their suggestions seriously, and incorporated their changes into the design. But North American didn't operate that way. No siree. They kinda viewed the astronauts as amateur hot-rodders who didn't have no business tellin' *them*, the professional engineers, how to do their job. They began to give 'em the cold shoulder, let it be known that their input was not really needed or appreciated. You can imagine how that went over with Gus, who at this point, given his Mercury training and his Gemini experience, probably knew as much about spacecraft design as any man alive. Even in the best of times, Gus was an intense kind of let's-get-down-to-business guy, and what little sense of humor or patience he had started to go South on him. He was in a war, you might say. And the friction he was generating was beginning to heat things up from Downey all the way back to the Cape."

"With so much at stake, why didn't everybody step back and take a deep breath, kind of reassess things?"

The old man gave me one of his uncomprehending stares. "You're going to the moon, remember? Before the end of the decade. Your President told you so way back in 1961. Now it's 1967. You're runnin' out of time. Everybody's pressing. The time has long since passed when you can question the goal, or mess with the timeline. You're gonna have to make do with the team you have, and the spacecraft they've put together. The schedule has taken over and is driving the whole project. Reassess? *What 'chew talkin' bout, Willis?"* He snorted dismissively and raised a finger at the barman, who glanced in our direction. Another round was on the way. We weren't wrapping up just yet.

Shuttling between Downey, Houston, and the Cape, battling the intransigence of the contractors and the obdurateness of his employer, Gus had placed himself under enormous strain. Not that he minded. It came with the territory; he had accepted that ever since the selection process had culled him (somewhat to his surprise) out of a pool of 110 supremely qualified candidates to become one of the Chosen back in 1959. So many design changes were being instituted at this point that the ship in Downey in which the astronauts trained wasn't even configured the same as the simulator on the pad at the Cape. Still the glitches persisted: malfunctions in the environmental control system, coolant leaks, faulty wiring. Photographs of that era display the stress factor quite clearly in Gus Grissom's pinched features, the lunar craters under his eyes and the thousand-yard stare in his gaze as he does his level best to deliver the undeliverable. In his brief stops in Houston, Betty notices that her husband, who has always made a point of not bringing his work or his worries home with him, can no longer afford himself that respite, and she and the boys begin to feel a measure of the strain. In a moment of darkness, he says to her, *"If there's ever a serious accident in the program, it's probably going to be me."* Not exactly dinner-table conversation. But nobody could stop The Schedule. As 1967 dawned, the focus shifted to the Cape, where Grissom and his Apollo 1 team of Ed White and Roger Chaffee were scheduled to begin pre-flighting their ship. According to backup astronaut Walt Cunningham, "We knew the spacecraft was, you know, in poor shape relative to what it ought to be. We felt like we could fly it, but let's face it, it just wasn't as good as it should have been for the job of flying the first manned Apollo mission." Gus, candid as always, and a realist and engineer to boot, had spelled it out for them some years earlier during the ramp-up to the Gemini flights: "Sooner or later, inevitably, we're going to run head-on into the law of averages, and lose somebody."

While the overall schedule could not be derailed, it could be slowed, and it was. There were innumerable holds during training exercises, and delays while engineers worked on reconfigurations or modifications. They all added up. Of course every delay simply ramped up the overall pressure to get the job done and move on to the next stage. The first Apollo launch was scheduled for February 21, just a month away. When asked by a reporter what the chances were that Apollo would meet its mission requirements, Gus didn't bother to sugar-coat the pill: "Pretty slim," was all he said. On the weekend of January 21, he stopped briefly at home in Houston on his way back to the Cape for the "plugs-out" test. Wound up tighter than a drum, he wasn't much functioning as either a husband or a father at that point, but his concern for his family's safety and well-being never wavered. It's just that at this point Betty and the kids knew to let well-enough alone. On that Sunday, not long before he pushed off, Betty saw her husband out in the backyard near the swimming pool. They had a lemon tree growing there (south Texas is an ideal environment for certain citrus trees), with lemons the size of small grapefruits. Gus found the biggest one he could, and twisted it off the tree. He came in through the kitchen door. "What're you gonna do with that, hon?" she asked him. Maybe she hoped he would slice it up and put it in the blender for fresh lemonade or even a tangy margarita mix. But that was not likely in January, nor given the mood he was in. "I'm gonna take it down to the Cape and hang it on that sumbitch," Gus told her, and they both knew which sumbitch he was talking about. He left home later that afternoon, a man in a hurry being held back by forces that were just slightly beyond his control.

A Mercury Redstone Rocket like the one that had lifted *Liberty Bell* into its sub-orbital apogee back in the summer of 1961 stands today on the grounds of NASA's Clear Lake facility south of Houston. Robert Goddard, the original Rocket Man, and the father of modern rocket science, would be impressed. Over eighty feet tall and practically six feet in diameter, it's lean and mean, a classic ballistic missile, with a payload capacity of 4,000 pounds (gasp!). If it looks uncannily similar to the V-2 rockets launched by the Nazi's against the civilian population of Great Britain (only half as tall, the V-2 nonetheless had the same girth, and reached a height of 50 miles at speeds of over 3,000 MPH), this is understandable and also explains why the Allied forces went to such great lengths to acquire the Nazi team which had designed and built it. (Escaping the fate of other men condemned as war criminals, Germany's rocket scientists, headed by Werner von Braun, were among those who subsequently headed up America's rocket program.) The Mercury Redstone was the impressive result of that purloining of German talent. For a man to lie on his back some sixty-five feet in the air on top of the booster's combustible brew of ethyl alcohol was, in 1961, about the most scarifying proposition imaginable. Once the candle was lit (in astronaut parlance), it would burn unabated for precisely 143 seconds by which time the rocket's passenger would be 100 miles high and moving at over 6,000 MPH. This was not high enough or fast enough to actually go into orbit, but it was so far beyond the established performance envelope of human flight that it is easy to understand why Chevrolet dealerships all over the county vied for the right to outfit the Mercury astronauts in tricked-out Corvettes just for the privilege of being associated with the special kind of bravery they exhibited in the practice of their craft. Of course, even though it deeply stung the astronauts themselves, an idolatrous public conveniently overlooked the fact that the first living being to ride a Mercury Redstone aloft was actually a chimpanzee named Ham. Ham returned grinning and clapping his hands, but he never got himself a Corvette deal.

Now, almost six years to the day since Ham's great accomplishment, the three Apollo 1 astronauts made their way over to Pad 34 and began the long ride up to their workplace after again sharing their dismay about the module's poor state of readiness with NASA's Apollo Program Manager Joe Shea. ("If you don't believe it, you ought to get in there with us," Grissom told him bluntly). The three-stage Saturn V rocket on which the module was perched was (and is) the largest launch vehicle ever built: with four and a half times the height, five times the diameter, seventy times the payload capacity and one hundred times the initial thrust, it literally dwarfed the Mercury Redstone. The engineering complexity and scope of the Saturn V rendered the Mercury launch vehicle of just six years earlier a primitive tool belonging to an entirely different era. If you board a slow-moving elevator and take it up to about the 32nd floor, you will have made the same ride they made that Friday midday, just over three weeks into the new year. Into the White Room they stepped, and from there, aided by launch technicians, they were shoehorned into the close confines of their trouble-plagued command module. (When it had arrived from Downey the previous August, the module had been accompanied by 113 significant incomplete planned engineering changes. It would generate another 623 engineering change orders after the delivery). After some initial futzing around, the ninety-pound two-piece hatch was sealed at 2:45 PM and the capsule was pressurized with pure oxygen. A long and trying afternoon followed, during which the astronauts, reclining on their couches, worked with technicians to troubleshoot the many nagging glitches that arose. A countdown was begun (this was to be a launch-simulation test), was stopped, was started again. As dusk began to fall, the command module was switched to its own electrical power supply ("plugs out"). At T minus 10 the test director called another hold in the count. It was nearly 6:30 by now. Communications between the command module and the Saturn blockhouse just one hundred yards away were sketchy. "I can't hear a thing you're saying," Grissom snapped. "Jesus Christ, how are we going to get to the moon if we can't talk between two or three buildings?" He would never receive an answer to his question.

"You ever heard of Shepard's Prayer?" the old man asked me. He was looking out at the lake as dusk gave way to darkness. We could see the lights of the marina glittering on the water.

"Shepherd's Pie, maybe, but not Shepard's Prayer." As the day wound down, and the grim climax to his tale approached, I suppose I was trying to lighten things up.

"When he was sittin' on the pad in *Freedom 7* waitin' for launch, Alan Shepard got to thinkin' about what was at stake. The Cold War was runnin' hot, the Rooskies had just orbited Gagarin, the whole damn country was fixated on this launch, we'd already poured a shitload of money and prestige into the program, and it seemed like everybody from the President on down was lookin' over his shoulder. Considerin' the position he's in, he sends up a little silent prayer: *"Dear God, please don't let me fuck this up."* He takes a pull at his Camel, and laughs without mirth. "I figure Gus might of had a similar moment, but with a new twist on the prayer: "Dear God, please don't let *them* fuck this up." He is silent, looking out the window.

"But evidently they did."

"Oh, not to hear them talk about it. It was the same old deal. Neither North American or NASA was lookin' to bite the bullet on this one any more than McDonnell had wanted to step up back when the *Liberty Bell* went down."

"So what was the official verdict?"

"*Voltage transient*, they called it. They even tried at one point to lay it off as the result of Astronaut Grissom repeatedly shifting on his couch which might of chafed a bundle of wire and caused an arc etc. etc. That kinda bullshit. Nobody bought it. Especially not after the fellows died the way they did, strapped in and depending on other people, people from the Cape all the way back to Downey, contractors all over the country, depending on these people to do their jobs. At that point there were nearly half a million people directly involved in the Apollo Program nationwide."

"I guess, at any rate, once that arc got into the oxygen, the result was inevitable."

"It sure didn't need to be, but then again the guys are in a pressurized pure oxygen environment surrounded by 34 square feet of Velcro. They're wearin' nylon, and their so-called escape hatch is over their heads and behind 'em and has to be unbolted manually. And they can't even do that until they've vented the cabin pressure. Given them circumstances, I'd say, yeah, they probably had more on their plate than they could ever handle in the allotted time . . ."

"Which was what, exactly?"

"Say again?"

"The allotted time. What was it?"

At this point, the old man turned his head and peered at me. "How long would you say it takes you to back your car out of the garage once you start the motor and put it in gear?"

"No chance, in other words."

"No chance is about right. Especially once the oxygen was all used up. At 2,400 degrees Fahrenheit, you'd be amazed at how fast that stuff goes. They didn't burn to death; they was asphyxiated." He looked back at the lake. The bartender glanced in our direction, but the old man was done buying. "I've thought about this, and to me, here's where the real irony comes in." I waited in silence for him to bring it in. "You know anything about Gus's flyin' time in Korea?"

"Only what you've told me. A hundred missions, wasn't it?"

"That's right. Ask me how many kills he had. You know, with five kills, you was rated an ace. Glenn got himself three."

"And Gus?"

Here the old man joined his thumb and forefinger to make a perfect circle and held it up in my direction. "Zero. Not a fuckin' one. You wanna know why? *Because he never flew lead.* He was assigned as a wingman, and he flew every one of his missions as a wingman. You know what the wingman's job is, right?"

"Cover his flight leader, isn't it?"

"That's right. 'Cause when his flight leader goes after a bogie, he has to be able to concentrate totally on that job. He can't be concerned about anything else that's goin' on in the sky around him. When he's on the six of a bogie an' tryin' to hose 'im, he's completely exposed. Except for one thing."

"His wingman."

"You damn betcha. Wingman's job is to stay glued to his leader and at the same time make sure that there's no opening for any other bogie to get at them while they're busy takin' down the bad guy. A good wingman has to have split vision and a knack for knowin' what multiple other pilots will do even before they do it. He's got almost a kind of ESP thing goin' on. Plus he has to be able to fly circles around anybody else in the squadron. This kind of flyin' ain't what all the movies are about, but it definitely requires a whole different set of skills. The kind of skills most pilots never master. They never have to."

"That kind of a pilot wouldn't know what panic was."

"He *tapdances* on the panic button, for shit's sake. Now ask me, in a hundred missions, how many times a bogie was able to draw a bead on Gus's flight leader. Just draw a bead, to say nothing of actually getting off a burst in his direction." I didn't need to ask. The old man had the perfect circle up in my face for the second time. "You see where I'm going with this, right?"

In fact I didn't quite. But I didn't want to upset his rhythm. It was his story, and he was going to wind it up the way he was going to wind it up. Now he sat up straight on his stool, eyed his empty glass for a moment, then looked back at me. "When he climbed into the command module that day, Gus had everything he needed to move that mission along except for the most important thing of all. He didn't have no goddamn wingman. He didn't have no Gus Grissom to follow him into the fight. He was completely exposed—easy pickin's for a bogey. And the bogey took 'im down.

"And there's your fuckin' irony."

Placed in the context of our history, the fatal fire on pad 34 took place in the same month that Jim Morrison and The Doors launched their first album.

The same month that Lester Maddox was sworn in as the Governor of Georgia, that Albert DeSalvo, the Boston Strangler, was convicted and sent to prison. The Human Be-In took place in Golden Gate Park, setting the stage for San Francisco's Summer of Love, all in that same rather epochal month of January 1967. And it was the month which marked the largest U.S. ground operation ever in Vietnam, *Operation Cedar Falls*, an operation which sent two U.S. Army divisions, including infantry, paratroopers and armored cavalry, on a "search and destroy" mission intended to break the stranglehold of the Vietcong in the Iron Triangle. Rather than choosing to engage the enemy on such a large scale, the Vietcong faded into the forest and the operation stood down on January 26, one day before the Apollo I astronauts became the country's first space casualties.

Reminiscent of another catastrophic Friday just over three years earlier in Dallas, the country recoiled in horror as people cancelled weekend plans and fastened themselves to their televisions to grasp every detail of this unimaginable event. Shock waves of high anxiety and modest degrees of soul-searching rippled through NASA and North American Aviation. What would the price be for this blunder, and who would pay it? If they wanted to salve their consciences, Gus Grissom had already written them the perfect prescription. In a passage from a ghost-written book that would be posthumously published, there it was:

"Sooner or later, inevitably, we're going to run head-on into the law of averages and lose somebody," he

wrote. If nobody else could quite comprehend this kind of thinking, a test-pilot certainly could.

The program was nothing if not resilient. The three men were accorded textbook heroes' burials and there was no flagging of enthusiasm from the White House, nor any significant glitch in the funding. The back-up crew of Walter Schirra, Donn Eisele and Walter Cunningham lifted off 21 months later on a successful 11-day earth-orbit mission. They flew in a command module that had been completely reworked, including the correction of 1,407 wire problems and the installation of an outward opening hatch that could be removed in three seconds. By July 1969, just two and a half years after The Fire, Neil Armstrong took his "one step for a man" onto the lunar surface. Old wounds heal more quickly when there is so much to celebrate.

But the old wounds didn't heal. In stark contrast to the officially orchestrated grief for the Challenger and Columbia families in later similarly haste-driven blunders, after Gus's burial at Arlington, NASA severed all ties with the Grissom family. (There's a candid photograph of Betty that was taken at the gravesite on that day. An attractive, composed woman, her features are set in a line of grim understanding and unmistakable condemnation; one can virtually hear Gus's words ringing in her brain: *"It's probably going to be me."*) There were no phone calls, no embraces from the President, no trust funds for the boys' college or any other offer of material support. And Betty received no official explanation whatsoever of the cause of her husband's death. Four years after Gus died, Al

Shepard passed the word to Betty that they were going to drop her from the LIFE magazine's annuity funding so that the money could be redirected to, you know, a family who actually has an astronaut in the program. Deeply affronted and with a widow's angry reluctance, Betty found herself a couple of enterprising young lawyers and they went after North American Aviation. It took four years, during which time Betty was viewed by many as an ingrate, you would've thought she was suing the *country*, for God's sake, and when they finally settled for a paltry $340,000, Betty wound up with less than half. In 2002 she remarked to an interviewer "I've waited 35 years for somebody to come to my home and explain to me about the Apollo 1 fire. I'm still waiting."

In 1972, the Apollo program concluded its last lunar mission when Apollo 17 splashed down a week before Christmas bearing Eugene Cernan, Ron Evans, and Harrison Schmitt. (After the country's tough seven-year slog through the deltas of Vietnam, there were an increasing number of voices which argued that the last two, perhaps three lunar landings had been redundant. The country had other priorities going begging for funding, it was high time to move on.) Back in '61, when JFK had seized upon the idea of putting the nation on a lunar quest, the preliminary estimate for the cost of such an endeavor had been pegged giddily at about $7 billion. Once they brought Jim Webb aboard, he crunched the numbers with a more knowledgeable eye, and told Vice-President Johnson that the real figure would be in the neighborhood of $20 Billion, undoubtedly causing even the large-living Texan to draw a deep breath. How prescient was Webb? In 1973, when NASA presented its Apollo closeout figures to the GAO, the actual figure was $25.4 billion. It's only a number, after all. But when you travel down to NASA, dear American citizen, and stand in the hall where the 361-foot Saturn V rocket lies in her transport cradle flanked by the Apollo mission banners, don't be surprised if you find yourself coming to terms with all those billions, and thinking to yourself that it was, in all likelihood, worth every penny.

The old man and I parted company in the paved parking lot in front of the bar. It seemed that he was done talking, but lingered for a moment as though he hadn't quite said everything that was on his mind.

"I appreciate your meeting with me, kind of helping me to get a better picture of Gus," I offered.

Not one for niceties, he grunted in return, and stood looking up at the night sky, which on this particular night was not graced with the maidenly presence of the moon. "It's just as well. Gus likely wouldn't a met with you himself. He was his own least favorite subject."

"Well, his work kind of speaks for itself."

"It's beginning to."

"How do you think Gus would feel if somebody used the term *hero* to describe him?"

"Plenty people did, after the fact. But if you'd 'a suggested it to him while he was alive, he would'a written you off as another one of those NASA flacks and avoided you entirely. He wasn't the sentimental type, if you get my drift."

"Right," I said, and thought briefly of Gus's flat, unrevealing countenance.

"But let's just leave it this way. If he had written his own epitaph, it would be something like: *Gave his life for his country in the line of duty.* Regarding the business with NASA and the other hard-knocks, well, Gus was the kind to let bygones be bygones. But one thing I know for certain, and maybe you can use something like this in your story: in all, we had six lunar landings, which means we put 12 men on the moon. Of all the astronauts, from the original 7 to the last 19, Gus was the shortest one. Five-six, or something like that. In fact, when they were putting together Gemini, they designed the couches to fit Gus because he was so compact. But every single one of those 12 guys got to the moon for one very good reason: because he stood on Gus's shoulders to get there. So maybe he stood a little taller than most people realized."

Now he was done talking, and he turned and abruptly walked off into the night. I lingered because I hoped maybe he'd turn and give me a parting glance or even a comradely wave, but he didn't. Like Gus, he was gone without giving you a chance to say a proper goodbye.

Joseph Stiborik
Naples, Florida, 1976

∞

No Need to Push It

I was with Jayne Mansfield the night she died.
Well, don't let me misstate myself. Not with her
in the Biblical sense. Although that wouldn't
have been too bad either. But I was at Gus Stevens'
Supper Club in Biloxi, Mississippi, where she was
appearing. I think she was scheduled to be there
most of the week, taking the place of Martha Raye,
who had called in sick, resulting in Gus's calling
Jayne and asking her to step in as a favor.

In later years, on hearing this, people thought,
*Jeez, why's a Hollywood star doing a summer night gig
in Biloxi, Mississippi, for Christ's sake? She must've
been a real bottom feeder by then.* Well, to people that
say that, I can only say two things: you never knew
Gus's. And you never knew Jayne.

Surprising as it may be to hear it, I can tell you
that she had quite an act. She sang a few songs to
piano accompaniment: *Funny Valentine. He's Funny
That Way. Sunny Side of the Street.* And there was
All Of Me, which she sang as a double entendre of
course, while displaying her ample cleavage, as

she pretty much did throughout the show. And why not? But let me say this about that: tits are tits. They'll only get you so far. Sooner or later, if you don't have a sense of humor, or some charisma, or some guts, you're stuck with tits and that's that. But Jayne had all of the above. Even if you had never seen her before you saw her show at Gus's, you would know that about her: she had all of the above.

Her show lasted about an hour, a good hour I would say. It was a supper club. You had your table, you had a nice dinner, couple of highballs, and you had your entertainment, of which Gus had the pick of the litter: Tony Bennett played Gus's. Louis Prima and Keeley Smith. Rosemary Clooney. The Ink Spots. You've got to remember, this was the Sixties, and clubs featuring real classy adult entertainment had practically gone into the crapper. You had the Beatles, the Rolling Stones, all the druggies, the long hairs, the heavy metal acts taking over, and outside of Vegas and the coasts, there were damn few places where people of good sense and refined sensibilities could get together. Gus's was one of those places. You came with a date, usually, or you probably went home alone. No swingers at Gus's. Not that I ever condemned swingers. They just weren't my crowd, and they really weren't Gus's crowd, either. And I'm pretty certain they were not Jayne's.

She was doing two shows nightly, as I recall. Nine and eleven, something like that. Naturally I'm at the second show. And I don't have a date, in fact, I didn't even expect to be there, it was kind of a last minute thing. I was driving from Tampa/St. Pete to Dallas, and I pitched camp for the night in Biloxi, which was roughly about the halfway point. This was in the days before the interstate, naturally, so it was a pretty good haul, two long days at the wheel. After one of those days, there was nothing like a hot shower, a fresh shirt, a stroll along the beach, and a good dinner. I was expensing everything in those days anyway, so when I saw Gus's, and the showboard out in front featuring Jayne Mansfield, I made a beeline. No coat and no tie, but I'm a respectable-looking guy who blends in real well with a nice crowd, so I was received without any difficulty whatsoever. I'd already wolfed down a couple of burgers earlier, so I take a seat at the bar and order up a double scotch. At the time, I remember thinking, better go easy on the booze there pal if you want to get your early start, but then I'm also thinking, Jayne fucking Mansfield, how great is this. So I order the double and settle in for the show.

You've got to remember, there were a lot of people who thought that Jayne was going to be the next Marilyn Monroe. Well, that worked as long as Marilyn was alive. But when the Kennedy boys snuffed her in '62, all of a sudden it all fell on Jayne, and to my way of thinking, it put a lot of pressure on her to be, or to become, someone who simply could not be replaced. A no-win situation. She couldn't buy a decent script, her management was plainly inferior, and Hollywood just wasn't ready to anoint a new Marilyn. People made comparisons anyway. But Marilyn's whole sad story, that was part of the beauty of her, the fact that she was a foster child who ended up marrying the most popular guy in America and couldn't make it work, couldn't have children, couldn't find happiness, and in the end gets murdered by the President and his cronies, who could possibly top that? Who would want to try, for Christ's sake? This much I can tell you for sure. When Jayne hit the stage at Gus's on that night in June of 1967, there was no ghost of Marilyn in the room. It was all Jayne, and you had to take her for who she was and what she was. If you were willing to do that, trust me, you couldn't help but love her to death. She had absolutely nothing to apologize for, and she knew it.

As I've said, the show lasted about an hour. Her only accompaniment was a pianist. She may have told a joke or two, but mostly it was just singing and flirting. She had one costume change, and I can't remember much about that either, except, as I've said, the lady knew how to put herself together, and she was pretty fabulous looking. I never cared much for the busty blonde type myself, but with Jayne, there was more to her, you could sense it. I think, to be honest with you, that she was a pretty brainy gal. Sharp, you know. Didn't miss much. Aware. And knew how to work a room. Did she ever.

I only drank the one double. After that I backed off a little. After all, I was by myself on a long road trip. I think I may have had one more scotch, but nothing else. At one point, before the show is over, there's a discussion going on at the end of the bar, the end where I'm at. A discussion between Gus, who is clearly recognizable from his picture on the marquee, and another gentleman, who is speaking on Jayne's behalf, and who, as I subsequently come to find out, is her divorce attorney and current boyfriend, Sam Brody. They're talking about transportation. A car. I hear New Orleans mentioned. Jayne is still on the stage, but I can overhear their conversation clearly because I'm maybe four feet away. So I gather that after the show, Jayne wants to go to New Orleans, and she needs a ride. I nurse my scotch and think about this. When the two gentlemen finish their conversation, I catch Mr. Brody by the sleeve of his coat as he's moving away.

"I couldn't help but overhear. I'd be happy to drive Miss Mansfield. To New Orleans. Or wherever she needs to go."

He takes me in, kind of sizes me up and down. I don't mind. He doesn't know me from Adam, and I'm butting into his personal affairs. "Who asked you, if you don't mind my asking?" A charming guy he isn't.

"Nobody asked me, and I don't blame you for asking. It's just that you've got a situation, and I'd be happy to help. I'm a big fan."

"You're a fan. Do you know who I am?" He's being a little testy, but as I've said, who could blame him? Guys have been hitting on his girlfriend since she started wearing a bra. Or maybe sooner.

"I'm guessing that you're the man who takes care of Miss Mansfield."

"I take care of her all right. And thanks for your offer. I'll get back to you." And he pushes off.

He's not what I would call rude. Just preoccupied. I would imagine that taking care of a woman like Jayne Mansfield could make you that way.

Not long after that, the show's over. I've finished my drink. I'm ready to settle up. I get the bartender's attention. He brings me my tab, puts it on the bar in front of me. I'm reaching for my wallet when a hand comes over my shoulder and plucks the tab right off the bar. I turn around and it's my new friend, Mr. Brody.

"Come with me a minute, would you, pal? Somebody wants to meet you."

Well, I'm not slow. I know who Somebody is. I follow him. It's the first time I've been up since I first sat down at the bar, and the scotch has me light on my feet and completely at ease. This is turning into quite a night.

We go along the bar, past a curtain, through a door, then another door, and wind up in a very small, what I guess you could call a dressing room, where Jayne sits in front of a well lit mirror. She watches us in the mirror as we enter, and she turns to face us once we're inside. My first impression is that she appears smaller in person than she does on the stage. Smaller, softer, quieter. A little tiredness around her eyes I'm thinking. I manage to keep my eyes above her cleavage, which isn't that easy. Oddly enough, I do notice what great legs she's got. Dancer's legs.

"Sammy tells me you're going to New Orleans," she says to me.

"If that's where you need to go, that's where I'm going."

She smiles sweetly but kind of automatically. "Well, I've got my kids with me, you know."

"I've got a big backseat. They could stretch out and sleep."

"Jayne and me would ride in front with you." Sammy has become quite agreeable. But he also wants me to clearly understand the scenario.

"What is it that you do?" Jayne asks me. She has turned back to the mirror, still watching my face.

"I drive for a living."

They consider this. Jayne smiles at me again.

"How long it take us to get to New Orleans?" Sammy wants to know.

"At this hour, not long. Maybe two and a half hours without pushing it."

"No need to push it," Sammy says. He now has his hand on my elbow, indicating that the interview is over.

"Jayne," I say. I'm old enough to call her Jayne.

She glances at me in the mirror, then turns around to face me again.

"I just wanted to say I think you're not only a beautiful woman, but also one hell of an entertainer. I've always thought so, anyway." I hold out my hand.

She does not take my hand in a traditional handshake, but with her palm down offers hers instead.

"That's very kind of you. And thank you for coming to the show." On impulse I lift her hand and very smoothly touch the back of her fingers to my lips.

"Thank you." Then Sammy and I are on our way out of the room and the last thing I see is Jayne's face in the mirror. Her eyes are following me.

Well, you probably know the rest of the story. I was not the one driving the Buick Electra that night. In fact, the car I was driving at the time was a Pontiac Bonneville. Midnight black. Four-fifty-four four-barrel, dual overhead cams. Next to the Bonneville, the Electra was an old lady's church car. But it didn't bother me that they took the Electra. Gus fixed them up. It was a kid from the bar, a cousin or something, who worked for Gus. About 21 years old. Jayne's kids were in the back, with a dog or two. Sammy and Jayne were in the front, just like Sammy wanted. It was the responsible thing to do, I'm sure. On the other hand, if the kids had been asleep in the front seat, everybody would have survived. Well, everybody except the cousin.

The kid was probably not a bad driver. You could argue that it could've happened to anyone. The road is damn narrow at the Rigolets. I've been over it many a time, both before and after that night. There was no indication that the kid was alcohol-impaired, as they like to say. The mosquito truck was just a bit of bad luck. That, combined with the eighteen wheeler, double indemnity. But let me just say this about that: you put me behind the wheel with Jayne Mansfield in my car, and I'll guarantee to deliver her safely to any spot on the face of the earth, any day of the week, any month of the year. Over and over again. Double the indemnity, triple it if you want. I'll still get the lady there safe and sound. I knew it that night, I've known it ever since. She'll always be safe with me.

And wherever she is, I think she knows it too.

Terry R. Devany
Mobile, Al. 1974

❧

A DIFFERENT TIME

Winter leaves the high passes of northern Switzerland reluctantly. When spring has already gained a foothold further south, on the Mediterranean side of the Alps, in the fastness of fortress Europe, up north near medieval Basel, the biting air, the grey skies, the fields white with snow show no sign of imminent departure.

After six months in the close confines of correct Swiss society, my wife and I were yearning for southern climes, and not only because of the oppressive hand of winter. It was the pagan gusto of Mediterranean cultures that we craved. We had arrived in Switzerland after months spent roaming the open country of the Far and Middle East, exulting in the embrace of the vibrant, earthy people of these cultures and the ancient places they inhabited. By contrast, Switzerland was cloistered by the Alps, closed in upon itself, obtuse, methodical, and damnably correct in all things. Put up your hand when you cough. Package your household waste properly before setting it on the curb. Respect your elders, obey the traffic laws, be on time and mind your manners. (So unlike the unbridled give and take of the market sellers in Istanbul, the rude tide of humanity coursing along the Chandri Chowk in Delhi, the rough good humor of the Druse lads of the Galilee.) We had been stripped of all those treasures when we crossed the Alps, and as the winter grudgingly held on in Sissach, we had but one treasure remaining to us. As Americans, it was uniquely ours and we held it close.

We had our Ali.

Muhammad Ali, former heavyweight champion and tireless messenger for the Nation of Islam, was all the things that were despised by Swiss society: a relentless self-promoter; a bold braggadocio; loud, insistent, outspoken, impolite, and unashamed. On top of all that, he was regarded as something of a traitor to his country. During WWII the Swiss had avoided the fray as a neutral country. In the aftermath they had welcomed the Allies as liberators, and had unabashedly come to regard the Americans as saviors of Europe. They had no use for a man who declined to bear arms in defense of his country. As I fell into that category myself, I treaded very lightly around the subject (and few of them, true to their culture of polite disinterest, ever seemed to question why, as an apparently able-bodied young American I would be cleaning machines in a Swiss watch factory during the height of the Vietnam war.) Thus, in the run-up to the most highly anticipated heavyweight match of the post-war era, my co-workers in the factory and the other riders in our car-pool had made their sentiments well known: they had no use for the former champion. Neither his politics nor his persona held any appeal for them. They were actively cheering for his defeat.

My wife and I felt defeated already. Not only did we find ourselves dead-ended in a tiny, snow-bound Swiss hamlet, but our first-born child had been diagnosed with a hiatal hernia within weeks of his birth, and was scheduled for abdominal surgery as soon as his body weight reached a point sufficient to bear the procedure. There is a snapshot which I took of his mother during this time of waiting. Dressed in dark corduroy, head down and hands clasped behind her back, she is walking near the house in which we are renting a room. Behind her the somber hills loom, and a ragged line of snowmelt skirts the distant tree-line. The sky is a uniform gray. She is walking uphill, leaning into the incline, as we were leaning under the oppressive weight of our circumstances at that time. As the title fight approached, we looked to Muhammad Ali to strike once more his magnificent lightning and release his potent magic in an unbelieving world, liberating us from the limbo of our surroundings.

Not many of us had felt that way seven years earlier. Seven years almost to the day. It was February 1964. On the 22nd of the month, three days before Heavyweight Champion Sonny Liston was to take to the ring in what would be only his second title defense, The Beatles had flown home to the UK after unleashing two weeks of sheer pandemonium (otherwise known as "Beatlemania") on American shores. Columbia records had released Bob Dylan's portentous ballad "The Times They Are A' Changin'" just the previous month. Our American cultural interstices had apparently reached a flashpoint, and the country was dry as a tinderbox. But nobody, absolutely nobody, had the temerity to assume that the skinny loudmouth kid from Louisville was going to factor in the changes sweeping the nation. Sonny Liston (rhymes with piston) was a certified lead-pipe cinch to keep the fight game in the place where it had been mired for most of the 20th century, with one foot in the inner city and the other in organized crime. Sonny had done hard time, Sonny had done hard drugs, and now Sonny was at the top of the only game that would have him. (The Floyd Patterson camp had done their best to keep him from even contending for the title, so murky was his background and so well-known his ties to organized crime. Their instincts of self-preservation had been correct: in two fights with Liston, Patterson never escaped the first round.) As a young reporter, with my own weekly sports-radio show, I had gotten on the bus with all the other purblind prognosticators, and confidently predicted that Cassius Clay would prove to be short work for the Champ. Death, taxes, and Sonny Liston. Some things you just didn't go against.

But the skinny kid, a 1960 Olympic Gold Medalist after all, surprised from the first bell. Sticking his jab with a long reach and circling giddily on his toes, he kept well out of harm's way and actually made the champ appear ponderous and clumsy by comparison. After a hapless third round, Sonny was losing on points, and displayed no clear strategy for a victory. As it developed, however, Sonny actually found a way to prevail. He directed his corners to apply salve to his gloves, a stinging salve which he subsequently transferred to Clay's forehead during their sweaty clinches. Once the salve reached the challenger's eyes, he was effectively left blind, and spent the fourth round spinning, weaving, weeping and desperately hoping to escape a thunderous volley that would put him down for the count. When the round was over, he returned to his corner with an urgent demand: "Cut 'em off!" He wanted his gloves removed, thus signaling his capitulation, taking himself out of the ring, and possibly out of any future at the heavyweight level. By hook or by crook, The Big Ugly Bear had gotten his way. The Fates were going to send Cassius back the Louisville in defeat. That's what he got for running his mouth after all.

Cooler heads prevailed. Understanding that his man had been fouled, Clay's trainer, the redoubtable Angelo Dundee, also understood that the sweat which had transported the offending substance into his fighter's eyes would, in time, just as surely remove it. Through the early stages of the fifth round Clay handily survived. Once his vision cleared, he spent the last half of the round fully in command of the fight, his fluid bicycle motion and the speed of his hands reducing the once-proud champion to the status of a weary and confused old workhorse, yearning for the pasture. (Though his birth date was unknown, Liston was reckoned to be some ten years older than the challenger.) As the bell tolled for the sixth round, Liston revealed another side to his character by spitting his mouthpiece onto the canvas at his feet, branding himself as a quitter. (This was a judgment that would be amply reinforced in their rematch 15 months later when, barely two minutes into the fight and before many ringside patrons had even gotten settled in, Liston toppled to the canvas determined to stay there, felled by a "phantom punch." Plainly, Sonny had no stomach for the fight.) Thus, not much more than a month after his 22nd birthday, Cassius Clay, the Louisville phenom, had become boxing's Heavyweight Champion. In so doing, he moved himself to the center of a storm of sociopolitical change which was transforming American society. As few had foreseen his ascendance, few would envision the span of years he would occupy at the center of that society, and the influence he would shed while there.

I had graduated from high school the spring before Clay's victory. The school was located in a small town in the piney woods of the deep south, a town divided by a set of railroad tracks and by a century of strict racial segregation. One of the favored pastimes of the upperclassmen of our school was to load into a couple of automobiles on a Saturday night and cruise over the tracks to unload epithets, tomatoes, eggs, or other missiles of convenience upon the wooly heads of the unfortunate inhabitants whose paths they chanced to cross. That this particular pastime was considered completely benign and beyond reproach, and that the fear of retaliation was non-existent, very much describes the status of the two races in the Deep South the early 1960's. Just outside the city limits of our bucolic little southern town was a tavern which had a small service window on one side. Still underage to consume alcohol, we children of white privilege would drive around to that side where we could be seen through the window, and wait until the boy in the white jacket came out and approached the car. Slipping him a ten dollar bill, we would wait expectantly while he went back inside. He would return minutes later with a "short dog" of Early Times whiskey, accepting with a servile display of the whites of his eyes our jocular banter and the dollar tip in the bargain. My classmates laughed at the system and how it worked for them: they could pelt the dumb niggers with rotten fruit and still the nappyheads would Uncle-Tom all over themselves when the whites solicited their services. Clay's becoming world champion couldn't and wouldn't change any of that. At least, not right away. Since the days of Rocky Marciano, except for the brief interlude of Ingemar Johanssen, there hadn't even *been* a white champion anyway. Like basketball would come to be, boxing was a black man's province, and he could have it. The popular dictum of the day was that "In the North, they don't care how big the Nigras get, as long as they don't get too close, whereas in the South, we don't care how close they get, as long as they don't get too big." *How about that bottle, boy? You take care of that for us?*

The Nation of Islam? What the hell was that? Background noise. Buncha bowtie-wearing nigras passin' out papers on streetcorners. Under the shadow of a presidential assassination, with the business of Vietnam looming, the country was already in a clamor. When Cassius Clay announced after his victory that he had joined the NOI, it scarcely moved the needle on the dial. Almost a year to the day after Clay's triumph, one of the Nation's most prominent members, Malcolm X, was gunned down in the Audubon Ballroom in Manhattan. The event was viewed by the white population of America largely as a matter of good ol' NYC gang housecleaning, and good riddance. As the most outspoken proponent of the NOI's precept of a separate Nation for black people, Malcolm X had generally been considered a menace, it was true, but an articulate and informed menace at least. (*The Autobiography of Malcom X*, co-authored with Alex Haley and published in the months following Malcolm's death, would sweep through the counterculture and add immeasurably to the sense of solidarity and anti-establishment sentiment which bonded young people—people of Cassius Clay's generation—together in their implacable stand against the ways and the means of their parents' generation.) By the time the Heavyweight Champion Muhammad Ali defended his title against Liston three months after Malcolm's assassination, it is no stretch of hyperbole to point out that certain features of the country's social structure, certain understandings and accommodations hammered out in the previous decades of the Twentieth century, were now null and void, and that in just 15 months a new negotiation was underway. When mob-connected, Uncle-Tommin,' alcohol and drug-addled Sonny Liston lay spread-eagled on the canvas in Lewiston, Maine, Ali stood above him with prideful scorn and contempt written large on his features. By the end of the summer of 1965, Americans would awake to see on their televisions flickering images of U.S. troops in combat gear highlighted by the lurid flames of war. The troops were not overseas in Vietnam (yet). They were in South Central Los Angeles. After Watts, nobody could ignore what it all meant, and if there was any single individual who embodied what it all meant, or might mean for the future, Muhammad Ali was that individual.

If you were under thirty years of age, there seemed to be no immunity from the general uncertainty and the hunger for experimentation that were by now running though America like a low-grade fever. I spent the following summer serving aboard the *S.S. Coeur D'Alene Victory*, the decks of which were piled high with crated canisters of jellied gasoline (also known as napalm) on an eight week run from San Francisco to Saigon and back. By the time the ship had docked at Pier 33 on the Embarcadero in late August, I had developed a new plan for my life. Having exhausted my passion for study and feeling uneasy with the militant direction being taken by my peers both for and against U.S. involvement in Southeast Asia, my sister and I set out to fulfill a long-time dream of hers. On the night of September 23, 1966, we caught a Pan-Am flight from JFK to Lisbon. Two evenings later we boarded the overnight train *Lusitania Express* and disembarked the following morning in Madrid. Within another week we were enrolled in fall semester classes at the University of Salamanca. Founded in 1134, it was said to be the second-oldest university in Europe.

We had traded the New World for the Old. Six months later, I wrote a lengthy letter to my draft board which would change forever the direction of my life.

In that same month of April, 1967, in Houston, Texas, Muhammad Ali made a similar decision, unleashing consequences in his own life. By failing three times to step forward at the induction center when the name "Cassius Marcellus Clay" was called, he announced his complete rupture with the system of his youth. The price he would pay for this decision was arguably far higher than mine, but we were both in essentially the same boat in the years immediately following. He was prosecuted, stripped of this title, and denied the opportunity to practice his profession, while I was indicted by a Grand Jury and a warrant of arrest was issued in the event that I should ever return to my country of origin. For the Heavyweight Champion to have freely offered himself up in this way as a lightning rod for our highly polarized society revealed either an immense degree of naiveté, or a measure of inborn courage that had been heretofore hidden from view. His logic, however, was compelling: *"Why should they ask me to put on a uniform and go ten thousand miles from home and drop bombs and bullets on brown people in Vietnam while so-called Negro people in Louisville are treated like dogs and denied simple human rights?"*

He had another way of phrasing his argument that had an even greater popular impact: "I ain't got no quarrel with the Vietcong. No Vietcong ever called me Nigger." While some unaware souls may have attributed this kind of talk to the intemperate ramblings of Just Another Mouthy Nigger, it had a disquieting directness and an inescapable racial dialectic that stung America to its core by announcing a repeal, for once and for all, of the Jim Crow slave system that had been in place throughout the century. Like Martin Luther before him, Muhammad Ali had left the Church for good.

Across the next three years, like restless pilgrims, Ali and I peregrinated on separate continents. By 1970, with his case being appealed before the Supreme Court, the dethroned champ managed to secure licenses to box in several states. He held his coming-out party in Atlanta in October of that year. The entire social register turned out for the event, which saw him stop Jerry Quarry in three rounds. Two months later he followed it up with a hard-fought win against Oscar Bonavena in Madison Square Garden, thus clearing the way for the Fight of the Century: a match between two undefeated heavyweights. One was the current champion, Joe Frazier, and the other was the "People's Champion," Muhammad Ali. The only heavyweight match that could be compared with Frazier-Ali for marquee power and international interest would be the title bout between Joe Louis and Germany's Max Schmeling at Yankee Stadium in June of 1938. Two years earlier Schmeling had handed Joe his first professional defeat in the 12th round of a non-title bout; with war looming and the claims of "Aryan Supremacy" filling the airwaves, the pride and prejudices of two nations were on the line in the rematch, which is to this day considered one of the most momentous heavyweight title matches in history. Since his defeat at the hands of the German, Louis had become the first black Heavyweight Champion in over twenty years, setting off explosive celebrations among black Americans nationwide. In the rematch, a symbolic battle against the forces of Nazi darkness, Joe attacked relentlessly, pounded the German into submission in just 2 minutes and 4 seconds, setting off celebrations of Americans of both races nationwide. (This feat of Joe's was remarkably similar to Sonny Liston's ascendance to the Heavyweight title, when he defeated Floyd Patterson in Chicago in 1962 in 2 minutes and 6 seconds. To add one further historical footnote, just six weeks before Frazier and Ali were scheduled to meet in Madison Square Garden, Sonny was found dead in the master bedroom of his Las Vegas home by his wife Geraldine. A murky character to the end, the reasons for his death at the approximate age of 38 were never clearly determined.) Frazier at 26-0 and Ali and 31-0: two heavyweights with unblemished records were about to fight in their primes for the biggest purse and the greatest viewership in history. Scheduled for March 8, 1971 at New York's Madison Square Garden, it held the promise of an epic match. And it would not disappoint.

Boxing, or "prizefighting" as it has been more aptly described, is unique among all other athletic contests. There is no other type of competition so gladiatorial in nature. In a boxing match the combatants are enclosed in a ring which both defines the boundaries of their contest and contains them forcibly within those boundaries. Like so many other competitions, points are awarded for certain performance characteristics, but in a boxing ring those points are calculated by the measure of physical punishment inflicted. Whereas in wrestling, rugby, even basketball a certain amount of physical abuse may be corollary to one's participation, in boxing, the *goal* is physical abuse, and the combatant who proves to be able and willing to administer that abuse in greater measure will usually prevail. Hence a fighter training for a bout must direct his efforts both towards inflicting the maximum hurt on his opponent, and withstanding the hurt which his opponent will be directing at him. In a world of pain and hurt (and for all the poet's celebration of the mystery and romance of life, in the end, pain and hurt are everyman's inescapable lot), this equation is eloquent in its savagery and perfect in its simplicity. This is especially true at the heavyweight level, where most fighters have the wherewithal to dispatch of their opponents with a single blow, or flurry of blows. Each fighter goes into the ring alone, with no team or confidants, or mentors to shield him, rescue him from danger, or save him from disgrace. He likewise prepares for his ordeal alone. Running long miles in the predawn darkness, spending hours cocooned in a gym with the tools of his trade, pushing himself daily past the point where his body wants to go, he reaches inside himself and discovers (or develops) the kernel of his faith. He nurtures that mustard seed of which the Bible speaks, that alliance with the forces of the universe which he must call upon to sustain him in his moment of weakness, his hour of doubt, his instant of wanting-to-quit. The corollary to this spiritual alchemy is his dedication to developing the wisdom that will enable him to seek out and penetrate his opponent's sanctuary before his own can be similarly breached. To call a fighter at this stage a spiritual warrior is thoroughly accurate. To have any hope of prevailing, of reaching the pinnacle of supremacy, a prizefighter will spend a lifetime fearlessly seeking out and engaging in this type of warfare. Those physical skills which he (or she) brings into the ring are useless unless they are firmly buttressed by an understanding of the true nature of human struggle, and a willingness to pursue it to its most common denominator. A fighter's performance in the ring is essentially a passion play, and as the witnesses, we live again the painful, triumphant story of that passion. There are few stories to match it.

Bound in our snowy Swiss hamlet, *sans* TV, *sans* newspapers, *sans* even a word-of-mouth community environment, my wife and I awaited the outcome with confidence but also trepidation. When, many hours after the contest was concluded, word finally reached us, we experienced shock, incredulity, and then, reluctant acceptance. "Must be the season of the witch," my wife reflected—Ali's loss by a unanimous decision was a piece of the puzzle of our own discordant existence that somehow fit. Not until much later, years later in fact, would we ever learn about the match in detail. Over the course of 15 rounds the two superbly conditioned fighters had inflicted upon one another an almost unbelievable level of punishment, punishment which, in the closing rounds, lent Joe Frazier the swollen and distorted features of a frightening alien presence and sent him directly to the hospital for a nine-day stay that prompted rumors of his demise. In the last round, after a perfectly landed left hook sent him to his back for the first time in his career, Ali's jaw ballooned grotesquely. All the fight in him spent, he endured the final half of the round only by clinching with the champion, cradling Joe in his arms like a lover. It befell us to accept the smug self-righteousness which our Swiss acquaintances exhibited over the outcome. But it also reinforced our conviction that Switzerland, despite its dramatic mountain landscapes and the charm of its Alpine villages, was simply not the place in which we could linger for an extended period.

In time we extricated ourselves from this well-ordered society and moved on to other lands. Eventually we returned one again to our place of origin, where, slightly more than three years after Ali's shocking loss to Frazier in Madison Square Garden, due process ran its course and through the artful and diligent court-appointed representation of one Herbert Garon (may his seed live forever) we found ourselves acquitted of all charges. (Ali's conviction had been overturned by the U.S. Supreme Court two years earlier.) We walked two blocks down Royal Street in New Orleans' French Quarter and ate lunch with friends at the Court of Two Sisters where we drank mimosas and tried to adjust to the idea that we were free to get on with our lives.

Fast forward twenty years. After a 12-year back-to-the-land sojourn in the hills of the Ozarks, we have returned to New Orleans to be near my wife's family. (With three sons of our own, it is deemed prudent that the boys have an opportunity to grow up alongside their cousins, aunts, and uncles). I have rented a small office near the lakefront out of which I market goal-setting programs. Across Causeway Boulevard from my office sprawls Lakeside Mall, said to be one of the very first true shopping centers opened in the United States. There comes a day when I read in the local paper that Dillard's department store, one of the high-end anchors of the mall, is going to feature an in-store visit from the former World Heavyweight Champion, Muhammad Ali. Ali will be hawking a new men's fragrance, and for the price of a bottle of said fragrance, the buyer can meet the Champ and receive an autographed 8 X 10. Though these kinds of corporate-driven meet 'n greets have no appeal for me, it doesn't take me long to make up my mind: I have stood in line for the *S.S. Queen Elizabeth*, for the Taj Mahal, for the New York Yankees. I will stand in line for the Champ.

And there is a line, a surprisingly long one, which forms up near the back of the store on the main floor and makes its way between perfume and lingerie counters towards a large display window near the store's main entrance. The display has been removed from the window and replaced with a small dais where the champ has been seated. An attentive and rather serious-looking Nation of Islam lad sits at his side. All those in line have duly made their purchase, and we make small talk as we approach. Most of the folks (while there are a few women in line, the event has attracted a preponderance of men) are knowledgeable fight fans, or at least knowledgeable regarding Ali's fights. We all remember the Thrilla in Manila, and the Rumble in the Jungle, in which Ali again suffered a terrible beating but employed his "rope-a-dope" strategy to fell World Champion George Foreman in the eighth round, this marking the second time he would lay claim to the Heavyweight title. Foreman, one of the most durable and personable of the world champions, eventually ended his career with 76 wins, 68 by knockouts, thus winning more fights by knockout than Ali (with 56) won in his entire career. As with so many once-dominant athletes, however, neither man was able to quit the ring cleanly. Ali especially lingered too long and absorbed too many painful defeats at the hands of fighters who were clearly lacking in the skills and the heart of the man they were punching into submission. Though most of us undoubtedly also remember the stripping of his title, his stand against the war, and his travels throughout the world to spread a gospel which is so feared and misrepresented by his white American brethren, these thoughts are not shared. There are perhaps still some wounds festering there. Boxing, on the other hand, is ground that all may safely share.

We finally clear the last of the perfume counters and up ahead of me I catch my first glimpse of the Champ, who is momentarily standing while the NOI brother repositions his chair. The massive rounded-ness of his shoulders, the ponderous deliberation of his movements, his broad face and his almost-cherubic features: it is as though I have come to meet the Buddah himself. Like Ali on his prime, I have not come without a strategy for the encounter.

The line bumps along, and suddenly I am in front of the Champ. The old baggage from across the years threatens to come tumbling out of the overhead compartments and I stand there, momentarily overwhelmed and speechless. Ali diligently works at affixing his signature to my souvenir photo. (Later, on closer inspection, I will discover that his signature was already stamped on the photo, and that with his Sharpie he merely added a little curlicue at the end. The ravages of his Parkinson's, though not as apparent as they would later become, have already ruled out the tedious and repetitive task of reproducing innumerable signatures in a timely fashion). When I realize that he is merely going through the motions, I drop to one knee in front of the dais, bringing the two of us together at eye level. "Champ," I begin. (It seems a natural means of address; I don't feel I have achieved the right to address him intimately by his first name, or casually by his last). "There's something I want to ask you." From the corner of my eye I see that the young NOI stalwart is watching attentively; he's not at all sure where this is going, and is ready to intervene if my aim is not true. Both he and Ali are wearing bow-ties and suits. Seeing that Ali has completed his exercise with the Sharpie, I extend my hand across the table, looking for that bond of brotherhood that can only be transmitted by physical contact. Ali rolls rather than extends his mighty paw in my direction and I slip my hand into his, which is massive, warm, and inert. "Champ, I honor the stand you took on

Vietnam. I took the same stand." My face is warm, my voice is thick with suppressed emotion. "But what I want to ask you is this." Looking up, directly at him, I am rewarded as he perceives that I am attempting to make a personal connection with him. The NOI soldier too is momentarily rapt, detecting in my voice only honest entreaty, and nothing of a disrespectful or hurtful nature which, even after all these years, is still likely to be launched occasionally against a man who in his prime so polarized a nation.

"When you became champion, you used to say you were The Greatest. *I am The Greatest.* Now your message has changed. You talk only about being humble, staying humble. These seem to be two different messages. Or are they somehow the same message, only for a different time?" As I deliver the question, I am watching his eyes, looking for recognition, engagement. He beholds me evenly but seemingly from a distance. His features are untroubled, his skin still wonderfully clear and smooth. I shoot a glance at the Brother, who has taken his eyes off me and is also watching the Champ. Leaning forward ever so slightly on his elbows Ali speaks his piece. Stay humble, he says. *Any man want to be great first need to understand, he got to stay humble.* Stay *humble.* He delivers these words in that sibilant, silky baritone so aptly mimicked by Will Smith years later in the biopic *Ali.* I wait a moment longer to see if there is a coda to his comment, but he has lapsed back into his silence, regarding me quietly from some distant mountaintop, the one it has taken a lifetime to ascend.

My window has closed. Behind me the line stirs restively. I squeeze Ali's unresponsive hand and return to a standing position, collecting my 8x10. At this point the tears of remembrance that are coursing through me have made their way to my eyes, and through slightly blurred vision, I extend my hand to the Nation of Islam brother who has been privy to my moment with the Champ. Though his demeanor remains cool and correct, the warmth and welcome of his grasp indeed echo the sentiment of a universal brotherhood.

This is a different time.

Peter Devine
Houston, TX. 2012

TONY COMES TO EARTH

He was a big, beautiful man. He had a high, open forehead, expressive brown eyes, and a flashing smile. And he was tall: six feet four, or thereabouts. When he walked in a room, he took it over by the sheer force of his presence. But what people frequently noticed, besides all of the above, were his arms and hands. He had wide shoulders, powerful forearms, and broad, soft hands. What topped off the whole rugged picture was the ruddy complexion and the deep outdoorsman's tan that he always sported. Believe me, Tony stood out. If you didn't know who he was and you were trying to figure him out (and who could resist?), once you crossed out big-game hunter, rumrunner or movie star, you had to figure him for some kind of an athlete. But then you'd see him belting those highballs and smoking those Marlboros, and that didn't quite add up either. A white guy who loved flashy clothes and good times that much either ran a string of ponies, or a string of women, that's what you figured. He was just a big, beautiful man having a hell of a good time doing whatever he was doing. That much you could tell for sure.

Of course, once you learned that he was a professional golfer, it all kind of fell into place. The snazzy clothes. The hail-fellow personality. The drinking and smoking. And of course, that also explained the hands, the forearms and the shoulders. In those days, a professional golfer wasn't really thought of as an *athlete*, for cryin' out loud. On the social scale he was about two steps above a pimp or a Mafia hustler. I mean, he didn't really *work* for a living, did he? The cashmere sweaters, the pastel leisure slacks, oh c'mon now. He was obviously a swinger. Of course, Frank Sinatra was a swinger, and nobody had anything unkind to say about Frank. (Well, if they did, they said it once, and you never heard from them again, let's be honest . . .) So, since when was swinging against the law? Like I said, if Tony rubbed anybody the wrong way, it was simply because he was usually having more fun than anybody else in the neighborhood, and this was back in the late Fifties, before The Pill arrived on the scene, before cannabis went mainstream, before Hugh Hefner began taking girls' clothes off. In the minds of most people, Fun with a capital "*F*" was still a little suspicious, unless it was drug or alcohol-induced. And with Tony, it was neither. He loved his work, and he was good at it. That was the source of his fun.

He hadn't always been good at it, of course. Professional golf, for those of you who are not aware, is an unkind mistress. She is stingy with her largesse, and more than generous in doling out heartache. A tolerance for pain, indifference towards failing in public, and stoicism in the face of shattering disappointment are standard equipment for the individual who chooses the profession. Which goes a long way towards explaining the late-night carousing, the loose-living hijinks, the he-man tactics for blowing off steam that go with the territory (or used too). When I first got to know Tony after meeting him down the peninsula in Burlingame, I frankly doubted that he was ever going to let something as serious as golf get in the way of his drinking and playing around. He probably wasn't even making enough to pay his bills, but he was always the last one to leave the bar and I never saw him buy a drink for himself. People just enjoyed his company. It sounds like a cliché, I guess, but in those Fifties barnstorming days, when Tony and Dow and Al G. and others were on the road, he was a man's man and a ladies' man at the same time. Again, the comparison with Sinatra comes to mind, except that Tony didn't run with goons, and genuinely loved people. Those were two important distinctions, in my book. Even when he was a lovable loser, Tony had a winning way about him.

I would be lying if I didn't say he was a skirt-chaser in those days. I said he was always the last one to leave the bar. That didn't meant he left alone. But the difference was, his relationship with women was kind of like his golf swing—it appeared effortless. Where Tony was concerned, more often than not it was the skirts who did the chasing, and that's the truth. He was always respectful, always cordial, he never put on a front or talked down to the girls, and by the end of the night Tony would be at the bar just shooting the breeze with a couple of fellows while the two or three good-looking women went to the powder room and drew lots to see which one would be accompanying the big guy back to his room. The PGA tour's stops back in those days—Greensboro, Tulsa, Flint, Baton Rouge, Port Arthur, Champaign-Urbana—weren't nearly as exciting as today's, but they still provided plenty of opportunities for a fellow to meet eager fans and have some mighty good times. The lovable loser—that was the story of Tony's life in those days, and I didn't see it changing.

Then, of course, after five years of hacking it, he won the Imperial Valley Open. This was not one of your marquee events, by any means. But it was a professional golf tournament, and in spite of his penchant for late nights, the big guy had managed not to shoot himself out of contention by Sunday. Tied for the lead, on the last hole he hooked his approach into the gallery. It looked like he was in jail, but the ball inexplicably caromed back into play, he parred the hole, and won with another par on the first playoff hole. Dumb luck? A simple twist of fate? A payoff for all the dues he'd paid? Who knew? Who cared? The big guy's number had come up, and he'd won himself a slice of golf heaven. That evening the boys caroused at the bar a little more wildly than usual, then everybody loaded up and headed for the next stop. Nobody, including Tony, suspected then that stumbling into this tournament win was going to change his life the way did.

He didn't win again right away. He kept hammering away, getting deeper in debt, living the high life. If he had a breakthrough moment, it didn't occur until October of '62 at the Orange County Invitational in Costa Mesa. On Saturday he was hovering around the top of the leaderboard, and that night in the hotel bar, after he'd polished off a six-pack of Miller High Lifes, he impulsively announced to a dozen press scribes that if he sewed up the win on Sunday, he'd buy champagne for each of them. (I guess he figured it didn't hurt to have the writers rooting for you, at least.) Well, he won the thing, the champagne flowed, and just like that his legend was born. "Champagne Tony" they anointed him, and both the name and the winning habit stuck. In fact, in the four years remaining to him as a golf professional, he won ten more times, and finished second 11 times. He never missed a cut in a tournament from 1963 on, and finished top-ten in more than half of the majors in which he played. He won at Pebble, he won at Westchester, he won at Warwick. He won the Cleveland Open at Highland Park where he beat Arnold Palmer in a playoff. In 1964 he won five times in all, including his most prestigious win, the venerable British Open. No longer the lovable loser, he had become the toast of the town by then. In the pantheon of American Sports Personalities, journeymen golfers remain goofy fringe characters while the golfers who win consistently and who win the big tournaments, well, they become Household Names. They are embraced by people who don't even play the game, have no interest in the game. Golf is like that—in the mind of the public, it is considered not quite a sport but more than a pastime, kind of silly but at the same time worthy of the greatest honor. Once the big guy went on his tear, the sporting press embraced him and lionized him, stripping from him any vestiges of goofiness, sanitizing his history, and proclaiming the greatness in him. But that's really not what made him the man he became. What made him the man he became, and at the same time affirmed the truth of the man he had been all along, was—and this should come as no great surprise—a woman.

Her name was Elizabeth, but she had been a "Betty" since grade school. She originally hailed from Oklahoma, and Tony met her in early 1963, about six months after his Orange County triumph. By then he was slowly pulling away from the bar crowd, saving himself for the golf course, and saving his money at the same time. Betty was a stewardess back in the day when more often than not, that meant a lithe and toned beauty. As I heard it, she had pitched in to help out a girlfriend who was working as a volunteer at one of the tournaments in which Tony played in the fall of that year. To call her simply a looker (and she was all of that) is not to give Betty her due. She had a head on her shoulders, and an abundance of what we would later come to call the nurturing gene. She was not petite by any means, standing maybe 5'10" in her stockings, and well-endowed by her creator with certain womanly physical attributes. But I think it was her personality that reeled Tony in. She was kind of quiet, almost analytical—she sized up people pretty well, and didn't reveal all she was thinking either. Tony was practically afraid of her at the beginning. He spent two weeks doing his homework before he even dared to call a friend and asked the friend to intercede on his behalf and solicit a date with the raven-haired 26-year-old. Their first date was, by the accounts I heard, unspectacular except for the follow-up. Two weeks later, Tony asked her to marry him.

They were on the telephone—he simply hadn't the nerve to face her with the question. With his touring schedule, he would've had to put off a face-to-face for another month anyway, and he didn't want to take the chance. "I had a feeling this might be coming," was what she told him when he popped the question.

"Is that a good thing?" he wanted to know.

"Well, it's not bad, at any rate."

"You know damn well I'm crazy about you, Bets."

"Well, I knew you were interested," she laughed. Always running just out of his reach, and gently mocking him in the process. He had to have this woman.

"I'll beg and plead if you want me to." He tried to be mocking as well, but it came out sounding more like the gospel truth.

"That might be nice. But I wouldn't want you to make a habit of it."

The nuptials took place in California wine country just six weeks later. Betty became Mrs. Champagne Tony. The wife of a tour winner. They honeymooned in Hawaii, and of course, true to his nature, Tony played golf every day they were there. Betty rode with him every hole he played. Of course, during tour events, such an arrangement is not permitted, but it set the tone for their married life together. They became inseparable. There are plenty of couples that "can't get enough of each other" during the honeymoon, but in their case, that closeness, physical and otherwise, never abated.

She straddled him and swayed above him after midnight. She made menu selections for him, she sent out the laundry. She rubbed his neck and shoulders (or arranged, in some cases, for a masseuse to perform the task). She managed his personal correspondence, scheduled his dental appointments, watched his alcohol intake, and even cut his fingernails and toenails. She was old-fashioned that way—or maybe they both were. "To have and to hold" was something they took at face value. It turns out that what Tony had wanted all along was to be taken care of, and he had found the perfect girl to do it. Neither her parents nor his parents, nor his business manager, nor the hangers-on who trailed after the couple as his star steadily rose were permitted to penetrate the bubble of intimacy in which the happy couple lived and loved for all the days that were allotted to them.

As it developed, nobody could have guessed or imagined how few of those days there would be.

After he won the British Open in '64, just over a year after they were married, they entered into a new, more rarefied air. Tony had become an intimidating presence on the golf course. (The man who finished second to him in that tournament, by five strokes, was the heavyset crew-cut kid from Ohio, who, already having won a U.S. Open, was quite an up-and-comer himself—Jack Nicklaus). The other players found themselves scanning the leaderboard for the sight of his name, or cutting sidelong glances at Tony as he worked on the driving range. Catching him after hours in the bar was history, of course—if you didn't see him in the press tent or the locker room, you had missed him until the next tournament. Betty was not exactly a clothes horse the way Tony was, but she cut a fine figure standing at his side, or slipping along the ropes with his gallery during tournaments., Even though I had grown distant from Tony by then, I did chance to walk a few holes with Betty at Firestone in 1965, a tournament which he won. She favored pantsuits on the course, and she had on a flattering lime-green outfit. Her hair was cut close, like Audrey Hepburn. Her voice was low and carefully modulated, but she always let others do most of the talking. In our brief conversation, she made it clear that Tony had become the center of her world.

"These are some pretty exciting times for the two of you, I would guess," I ventured.

"Oh, Tony's just doing great. I mean, I just try to keep to with him."

"You travel with him pretty frequently, Betty?"

"He wants me there," she smiled. "You know."

As we parted company and she moved on ahead, I'll confess that I let my eyes linger on her departing figure for just a moment, and came away marveling that the man had gotten himself a handful of woman. I would want her there too, I told myself.

On to that fateful day. At the Firestone County Club near Akron, play at the 1966 PGA

Championship had concluded. (Tony finished in a respectable tie for seventh). Tony's manager, Bill Hoyt, had arranged a corporate outing on Monday near Chicago which would feature a handsome appearance fee for his golfer. In fact, to play 18 holes and schmooze over drinks and a buffet luncheon, he was going to be paid more than the prize money he'd received for grinding through the 72 holes at Akron. The tour stop that week was going to be at Cog Hill, outside Chicago, and would include the traditional Monday Pro-Am. PGA pros, particularly those with Tony's star quality, were strongly encouraged by the PGA of America to show up at these events and "give something back" to the game. Tony took a somewhat jaundiced view of the arrangement. "All those years I was giving everything I had to the game and going broke in the process, where was the PGA then?" Tony was said to have scoffed. "I gave at the fucking office." He was adamant in exercising his right to pull down cash when the opportunity presented itself. His decision to forego the pro-am for the corporate outing had been made, and it would stand.

Hoyt had scrambled to charter a small plane for the 750 mile trip. Tony had made it clear that he and Betty wanted to be relaxing in the hotel by Sunday night. His days of humping it in automobiles, even luxury automobiles, were over. He had no use for the scenic rigors of the road, and as more than one of the couple's acquaintances noted, he took an active pride in taking good care of Betty. "Hell, she works harder than I do," he told his pals. "Anything I can do to take the strain off my girl, I'm doing it." Did

Betty appreciate this kind of devotion? You didn't need to ask. If it pleased Tony, it pleased Betty. It was a perfect circle: the pleasure of one was the pleasure of the other, no questions asked, no reasonable expense spared. The $1,500 for the airplane was chump change and a tax write-off besides.

When they got to the small county airport outside Akron, however, witnesses say Tony was taken aback to learn that the pilot was a woman. At heart, I guess he was always a chauvinist. (Back then, who wasn't?) Women were put on earth to take care of men, no doubt about that, but operating heavy equipment, particularly when human lives were at stake, didn't quite fall within the parameters of that contract. "Christ, I wasn't counting on this," he remarked to Hoyt.

"Jesus, Tony, she's licensed," Hoyt countered. "Let the FAA do its job, why don'cha?"

Tony eyed his pilot, who was in her late thirties. She had a weak chin, overly-large eyes, and wore a nondescript grey-green uniform that made her look like she worked for a parcel delivery service, which, in effect, she did. In all, she did not leave a strong positive first impression. Tony and Betty stood briefly on the tarmac, holding hands while she did her walk around. Finally, Tony turned resignedly to Hoyt. "Well, wish me luck then."

"I always wish you luck, Tony."

"No, I mean, wish me luck on this flight."

Tony and Betty boarded and sat in the back of the twin-engine Beechcraft Bonanza so they could be together. The pilot, Doris Gibbs, was 38 years old, had been licensed for six years, and had over two hundred hours aloft in twins. Like Betty, she had close-cropped hair, but there the similarities ended. She did not have a fashion-model figure or a face that could stop men dead in their tracks at fifty paces. Once seated up front in the left-hand seat where she began flipping switches and tapping gauges, however, she readily assumed the role of pilot, and Tony put his apprehensions out of his mind. As was her custom, his wife slipped her arm through his as they taxied, and squeezed his hand during the takeoff roll. Tony shot a glance at his watch. Ten past six. By 8:30 he'd be soaking in the tub while Betty soaped his back and shoulders. They'd order room service, watch some TV, play around a little bit, and intertwined with Betty's lovely leg draped across her husband's midsection, they'd drift off into an untroubled slumber. Married life. What a gas, Tony thought. As the plane climbed out, he reached his free hand over and gave Betty's thigh a squeeze. She nuzzled him behind his ear. God, he loved his wife.

There wasn't much small talk. Those Bonanzas weren't the best insulated aircraft in the world, and you had to strain to make yourself heard above the slipstream and the engines. The front right-hand seat was occupied by the owner of the charter service, one M.B., who had wolfishly taken the opportunity to spend the afternoon with the planet's most celebrated golfer. He leaned back from his seat and asked Tony about the tournament.

"Tie for seventh," Tony shouted at him. "Pretty strong field."

"Love to see you take the Masters next year," the owner said.

"You and me both, pal," Tony grinned, and then the owner turned back to watch the hazy sky ahead. Underneath them the rolling farmland of Southern Illinois unfolded. From their assigned altitude of 8,500 feet it was a different view than when you flew commercial. You could see the occasional tractor ploughing the late summer field, and the regular outlines of the parking lots, most of which were empty on a Sunday afternoon. It being July, the air was thick and humid, and the Beechcraft bucked and rolled gently, like a small boat on a great sea. Betty dozed briefly with her head on Tony's shoulder. In his mind Tony replayed a couple of shots from the tournament. There are always those shots, the ones that cost you most dearly. The way he figured it, three shots had cost him a chance at the winner's circle. Geiberger had done his part, but let's face it, the guy had come out of nowhere and outlasted the competition in the wilting heat. If Tony had played those three shots differently, and brought some real pressure to bear, the guy might have folded like a cheap tent.

After that, Tony drifted off briefly, but he was snapped back to wakefulness by the muffled voices in front raising and falling in some kind of a heated discussion regarding the airplane. The pilot was tapping her gauges, and the owner was leaning over trying to get a better look-see. It was then that Tony realized that the craft had changed its attitude, and was flying nose-down at a shallow angle. He glanced out the window and saw the ground considerably closer than it had been earlier. He glanced at this watch. They still had 30 minutes to go. It seemed unusual that they would be flying an approach already. Betty still dozed, and he was just wondering if he should wake her when her eyes opened and she looked straight into his. "What is it?" she asked him. She could always read him like a book.

"We're coming down," he told her. It was the truth. That was all he knew. He didn't know what it might mean.

"You mean, as in landing?'

"I'm sure that's the plan," he told her, trying to be flippant, but not really feeling it.

At this point, aware that his passengers were awake and alert, and probably wondering, M.B. bit the bullet, and turned to face Tony. Tony leaned forward to catch his words. "Something not quite right with a fuel gauge. As a precaution, we're going to bleed off a little altitude here." He said it as conversationally as he could, but it was by no means a casual remark. He kept his eyes on Tony's face, and avoided Betty's probing gaze.

One of them had to ask, and Tony got the words out first. "Do we have enough fuel to make a landing?"

"Oh God, yes," M.B. said, his face tight. "Not to worry," and then he pointedly turned his attention back towards the front of the aircraft.

Tony had plenty of the kind of people-knowledge that only years of carousing after hours can bestow, and he studied the pair occupying the front seats. The pilot had her shoulders canted to one side and seemed as stiff as a board. She frequently twisted her neck to peer down at the ground below in a move that was certainly not calculated to instill confidence in her passengers. The owner, who was not a pilot, alternated between peering out his side of the aircraft and looking over at the suspect gauges, studiously ignoring Tony and Betty. More than the anxiety he was feeling, and certainly more any trace elements of fear which might have been present, Tony was experiencing strong waves of aggravation. His hunch had been right, the damn female pilot had evidently fucked things up. Their early arrival at the hotel was now a disappearing hope. He was having visions of a hundred mile taxi ride, or maybe even a night stranded in a farmer's field.

"Honey, do you think it's serious?" Betty wanted to know. She trusted Tony so much that she was going to take her read entirely from him. Knowing this only added to Tony's burden. He might have to stretch the truth a bit.

"Well, the good thing about these babies is that you can put them down practically anywhere—on a highway, in a field, even a large parking lot. The worst is that we might end up hitch-hiking to Chicago from fucking Peoria." And he turned to grin manfully at her. Impulsively, she thrust her face forward and kissed him briefly on the lips.

"We've never done that before, have we?"

The owner turned back to face Tony again. "We're going to rock the boat a bit and see if we can free up the lines," he said over the noise. "Tell the missus not to worry." And moments later, the

Bonanza began rolling side to side on her axis. It was disconcerting, but even more disconcerting was the changing view out of the window. Tony's eyes shot over the pilot's shoulder to the altimeter. Less than 3,000 feet remained between them and terra firma.

Betty was quiet, but increased the pressure on her husband's forearm.

Tony didn't need to ask to know that the rocking maneuver had not had the desired effect. When the plane's nose suddenly dropped another five degrees or so, he felt a coldness settling into the pit of his stomach, followed almost immediately by the sensation of prickly heat flooding his armpits and the back of his neck. "Hey, let's not forget to fly the goddamn airplane, shall we!" he heard himself blurt out forcefully to the occupants of the front seat in general. The rocking stopped almost at once, but otherwise his comment was not acknowledged. Tony craned his neck—now they were barely at 2,000 feet. It wasn't much, but it was plenty to pick out a landing spot, and the engines were still performing. He felt no sense of panic, but resented the fact that they'd forced him, a paying passenger, to step in and take charge of a situation which they should have handled.

His wife tugged him closer, and placed her lips next to his ear. "Tony, sweetheart, I'm not worried as long as we're together," Betty said.

"We'll be fine," he said tersely, without looking at her. He wanted to vault over the seat, wrestle the controls away from the troll, and set the plane safely on the ground. He was a man in command of his destiny, and he had worked hard every step of the way. He was not going to let himself be sidetracked now. And he was not going to let harm of any form come to his lovely Betty. In spite of himself, his shoulders were hunched, and his powerful forearms, the forearms of a golfer, were knotted with tension.

The pilot had just set the Bonanza in a shallow, easy turn when the starboard engine coughed, sputtered, and died. Even before the plane's motion changed, Tony knew what would happen. Being pulled now by just one engine was going to violently alter the aircraft's equilibrium. She would have to control it immediately with her rudder and the other engine. The owner knew it as well, and one, or maybe both of them impulsively shouted to warn her. There was no need to look at the altimeter now. The ground had become an all-consuming presence. It was going to meet them, one way or another. And soon.

Then Tony saw it. He had seen them many times from the air, but seldom from such close range. It was a golf course. The fairways were soft and verdant, and the sun at twilight had turned the water hazards into metallic sculptures. It was friendly and inviting. In spite of the plane's increasingly corkscrewed motion, Tony felt a sudden surge of confidence. All this just so he could get back to the place where he had started. Betty saw it too. "Sweetheart, we're landing on a golf course!" she exclaimed, with surprised wonderment in her voice. They were together, and because of it, she was not worried. She had told him she would not worry, and now she didn't.

You can bet that Tony did his best to get them down safely from the back seat. He was, as are most successful golfers, a man of supreme confidence and considerable psychic power. Golfers are accustomed to directing the flight of airborne objects. It was certainly not his fault that as the Bonanza swept low over the twilight fairway of the seventh hole, the pilot failed to keep her wingtips level, and when one of them caught the turf, it was a surprise more than anything. Of course, it meant that the craft immediately catapulted out of control, bounced once, and came down hard—hard enough to ignite the fuel that remained trapped on one wing, setting off a small boom that sent dread through the hearts of the few golfers still on the course at this late hour on a July afternoon. Still moving, the flaming craft caromed to the edge of the pond fronting the sixteenth green, finally coming to rest with the forward half of the fuselage submerged in the tepid water. Steam and the sharp sounds of overheated metal contracting rose from the spot. Otherwise there was silence.

Word of Tony and Betty's tragic demise raced through the airwaves and around the world in just hours, setting off a period of mourning in the close-knit world of the professional golf community. All four bodies had been hurled forward at impact and were found unpleasantly mangled, partially burned, and fully submerged. None of this bothered Tony and Betty, of course. Their last moments had been spent together, on a golf course, holding hands. All who knew them agreed it was "the way they would have wanted to go." Just not so soon, to be sure.

Just over thirty years later, another champion golfer would die in an aviation accident. Like Champagne Tony, he was flamboyant, much-loved, and at the peak of his considerable powers. But, in a sign of the times, his death lacked the romance and poignancy of Tony and Betty's. His plane was a jet and it fell from the sky like a bullet, boring a big hole in a farmer's field in far-off North Dakota. He had been flying strictly with business associates, and his death had neither the grace nor the poetry of Tony's. Tony had virtually floated to earth, and landed on a broad fairway not much harder than a well-struck three-wood. At his side had been the woman he loved, who believed until the end that everything would turn out all right because her husband had told her it would.

And who's to say it didn't?

Franklin P. Chalona
Baton Rouge, Louisiana 2003